KING CHARLES' MINE

King Charles' Mine

Titus Thornber

The Pentland Press Limited
Edinburgh · Cambridge · Durham · USA

© Titus Thornber 2000

First published in 2000 by
The Pentland Press Ltd.
1 Hutton Close
South Church
Bishop Auckland
Durham

British Library Cataloguing in Publication Data.
A catalogue record for this book is available
from the British Library.

ISBN 1 85821 764 4

Typeset by George Wishart & Associates, Whitley Bay.
Printed and bound by Bookcraft (Bath) Ltd.

Contents

Foreword

The action narrated in this book is based upon true happenings in the years 1627-1635, and 90 per cent of the characters were real people with their real names, living in the places named, during that period. The villages, towns, farms, and halls are real places, and can still be found on the Ordnance Survey maps, or even visited today.

Regrettably Thieveley Farm itself was demolished in 1974 because of the Public Liability Laws, and Nicholas Townley's house, Royle, which could not find a tenant because of its proximity to the Burnley Sewerage Works, fell into disrepair, and was demolished immediately after the Second World War. Happily, Towneley and Gawthorpe Halls are magnificently preserved as museums; the Abbots Residence at Whalley is a diocesan centre; and the other halls are lovingly cared for, with their Tudor beauty enhanced by the passage of time – possibly none more so than Saville Radcliffe's Todmorden Hall.

The site of King Charles' Mine can be freely explored today on public footpaths. Nicholas Birch's watergroove is particularly evident, as is the entrance to Gervase Gascoigne's drainage adit, and the 'wondrous steep hill' on which John Talbot's horse fell may still be climbed. Possibly this fall led to the construction of the Packhorse Ginnel along the bridlepath from the Whitakers' Hall to their farm at Thieveley. There is little doubt that the packhorses, heavily ladened with lead ore, would have used this facility. This ginnel and the water goit from the furnace dam to the smelt mill are the only remains from the Townleys' smelt mill which can be enjoyed today.

With the elimination of pollution from the East Lancashire cotton towns, this story is set today in an area of outstanding scenic beauty, of which particular reference must be made to the village of Holme Chapel, its 'hostel', now the Ram Inn, and the Whitakers' 'Holme', nestling beneath the towering Thieveley Scout. These rival any popular beauty spot in the British Isles.

The 'romantic' episodes are included to accentuate the licentious and bawdy customs of the times, which explains why the people loved Charles II for having sixteen children by his mistresses, though failing to produce an heir to the throne from his wife. I can even substantiate the 'orgy in the inn' from an antique copper plaque in my possession showing the three revellers being attended by a servant-maid whose nakedness is covered only by a single loose garment.

As for the miners' wives' obsession with witchcraft, it must be remembered that Cliviger was included in the purge of seventeen witches as late as 1633, with four being sent down to London to be examined by Charles I himself. Luckily, he proved to be more enlightened than his father and they were freed, but not before some had died in Lancaster Castle.

It now only remains to say that the elucidation of this quite remarkable story was only made possible by the existence of Duchy of Lancaster papers held in the Public

Record Office, and deciphered into a folder of typewritten sheets by R. Sharpe-France, the Lancashire and Cheshire Society's Archivist.

For me, the revelation was that little changes. Even in Stuart times planning permission, licences, reports, detailed accounts, the all-important questions of taxation and central government interference, were the handicaps which, even as today, industry had to contend with.

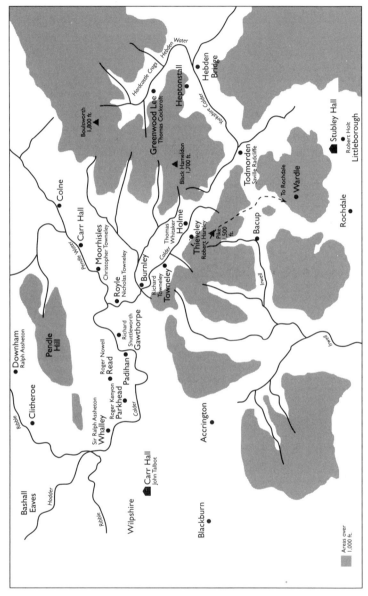

The Roadless Wilderness.

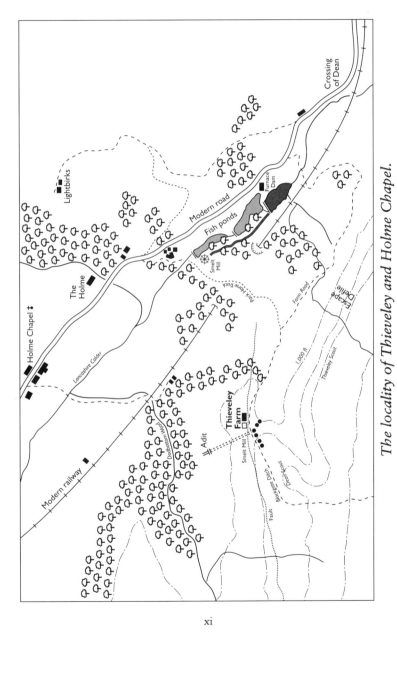

The locality of Thieveley and Holme Chapel.

CHAPTER I

The Farm on the Hill

Robert Hartley was impatiently waiting for his wife to finish her work about the house. She had long since put the children to bed, in the attic at the top of the ladder, but she was still fussing around in the dairy. There was cream to be separated for the butter-making, curds to be wrapped in muslin for the cheese press, and the ale to be seen to. Would she ever finish? He was comfortable enough in the basket chair draped with sheepskins, seated by a glowing peat fire in the single large room of his wood and wattle farmhouse, cosy and snug beneath its low thatched roof. But his hands played impatiently with pieces of grey crystalline earth which seemed to dominate all his thoughts. He was a man of action and could not rest if his mind or his body were disturbed.

That is why he had spent all day digging a long ditch on the wasteland which adjoined the enclosed fields of his farm. He had no intention of being caught out at a disadvantage this year, as he had last. Water was vital on a farm, and when the spring ran dry, after an inordinately dry winter followed by a drought in the spring, he had had to spend infuriating hours carrying water, hours and energy which were needed for the sheep shearing, the hay time, and the harvesting of his few acres of oats and barley. Alice had done more than her share but the handling of sheep and cattle and the mowing of grass and corn, with the long-handled scythe, was man's work. True, the enclosed pastures had a bottleneck which ran down to the Calder; which, thank God, never ran dry, and the beasts had soon found their way to the water. But at the farmstead water was required for everything, for his young family, for washing, for the poultry and the calves, for the butter and cheese making, yes and for the brewing of ale. But the unkindest cut of all was that the river was down in the valley 600 feet below and the drop was amazingly steep, with the only track zig-zagging down the hillside. To have to carry water was bad enough, but to jockey so awkward a load as living water in jars and jugs up that cruel climb was almost beyond human endeavour.

Robert had discussed the difficulty with his landlord old Thomas Whitaker of the Holme, but had been told that this was a visitation of God, to be endured, it had always been so at Thieveley, perhaps if he were lucky only every seventh year, and that was why the rent was so low. But, being as he was, Robert came back to the Holme to explain that there was a good supply of water on the Common which could be led in a ditch or goit to the farm and that he would gladly dig the ditch if the laws of the manor did not forbid it.

Old Thomas whose grandfather had risen from the rank of yeoman to that of gentleman, and married Elizabeth Nowell of Read, now considered himself the equal of the Nowells, the Townleys and the Barcrofts. Had not his uncle William been made Master of St John's

College, Cambridge by Queen Elizabeth I, and his cousin Alexander sailed to the Virginias with Sir Thomas Dale, where he was reputed to have tutored and baptized the Princess Pocahontas? With these proud connections he felt he had little to fear from the petty freeholders of Cliviger, so he bade Hartley go ahead and divert the stream across the Cliviger Common, but make sure to turn it back to its natural course when he had done with it.

This was the task which had occupied Robert Hartley all that day, and, as he was digging, he was planning the wooden spout which would run the water into the half of a wooden barrel into which he and his wife could dip a bucket or a jug. But he had something else on his mind which his natural impatience could brook no longer.

'Alice, lass, come thee in and sit down; what's not done can wait till tomorrow.'

His wife came in and sat down on the second chair. Robert's brother James was a basket-maker. He had made the two chairs for them at the setting up of their home, and had helped Robert to make the table and dresser which were the only other articles of furniture in the room.

'Now what's worrying thee? Tha's got summat on thy mind.'

'It's these that I found whilst digging t'ditch. They're neither rock nor muck. What's make on 'em, lass?'

He handed her the pieces of grey material, which she took over to the window, turning them over to what light was remaining.

'I don't know, I've never seen owt like it afore.'

'Nor I, but tha knows what I'm thinking; it's some kind of metal, like what thy brother Godfrey was telling us

3

about, what he went digging for i' Derbyshire when he and that other lad ran away from home.'

'Aye but he didn't do so bad for hissen; good wages they paid; he'd a done weel to a stop't theer.'

'Well, I think this here's lead. As ta felt weight on it? It's heavy enough for lead, and everyone's after lead for all the fancy new houses they's buildin'. If there's ony amount on it we could happen mek usens some real money – enough perhaps to get us a farm of our own. I were talking to a fellow fri' Haslingden at last Burnley Fair and they're trucking and trading wi' farms o'er yon, someat to do wi' King James having confirmed their copyrights, given 'em a title to t'land for payment of three years rent, and after that they're as good as freeholders and can sell t'farm to anyone wi'out interference from t'Duchy. We could buy usens a farm as easy as that if only we had the brass.'

'Aye, but it's not our lead; if it is lead, it don't look like lead to me.'

'Oh, it's not lead yet. Godfrey were telling me all about it. It's ore – they melt it in a furnace, like t'blacksmith's forge at Mereclough, t'lead runs out like watter when its hot. They runs it into stone troughs where it cools down and sets into solid bars. It's a bit like thee mekin' beast custard in a dish.'

'Well, let's try this stuff in t'fire and see if owt happens.'

They put wood on the fire and when it was burning at its hottest balanced the grey pieces on top. They both watched it carefully for several minutes but apart from slowly changing colour it remained in solid separate pieces with no sign of melting.

Robert picked up a piece of board and fanned the fire

to an even greater heat, but there was no sign of any shining molten metal.

'It's nowt but stone, some kind of rock tha's found. It'll never melt. Tha couldna get a fire hotter than yon.'

'Aye, happen tha's right, but its middlin' heavy for rock. Happen if I 'its 'it wit t'hammer like t'blacksmith, metal'll run out.'

He went outside for a hammer, and a flat stone. Manipulating the pieces onto the stone with the hammer and the poker, he began to hammer them as he had watched the smith with his anvil.

'Careful, tha'll have 'em flying all o'er and setting t'house afire.'

'Nay A wiant, A knows what A'm about. Sithee, t'pieces is sticking together. It's metal I tell thee; if it were stone it 'ud fly i' pieces.'

He put some more wood on the fire, and then reheated the lump which he had beaten together. But all he succeeded in doing was to knock it into a different shape. Refusing to be beaten, he repeated the whole process again and again, until Alice could stand it no longer.

'Have done,' she said. 'Tha'll be waking t'childer. Leave it be for tonight. It'll still be there in t'morning.'

He hammered the lump into a ball, and placed it back in the fire.

'Ah tell thee, leave it be.'

'Aye, lass, aye, I'm leaving it be, in t'fire.'

In the morning Alice, before beating the fire, raked the ball out onto the stone hearth and left it to cool. When Robert came in from looking to the stock he picked it up and rubbed it all over in the palm of his hands.

'Sithee, sithee here, it's metal I tell thee.'

He took it over to the window and examined it carefully and then placed it down on the window sill.

'I'm tekin' it o'er to show Godfrey, come Sunday.'

On the following Sunday, after doing the bare necessities of his farm work, Robert set off on his walk to Rochdale. Although Thieveley farmhouse was set on the end of a knoll 600 feet above the valley floor, he started off uphill over the ridge of the knoll, called Dean Scout, looking down its almost precipitous face to his few acres of ploughland, the only piece of level land in sight. It had been formed by a brast, or burst, of near liquid peat bog, which after weeks of heavy rainfall had roared down from the high moorland and had spread out into a level morass across the floor of the little valley which divided Dean Scout from Thieveley Scout. Once the little stream, which dried up in summer, had cut itself a groove, encouraged by man, through the morass, the peat had dried out and made a useful 5-acre field sheltered on three sides from the wind. Being free from rock it was easy to plough and the one acre which had been limed and manured grew useful crops of beans, oats and barley, which was the mainstay of the farm and family.

Where the knoll of Dean Scout joined onto the main mass of Thieveley Hill, Robert continued upwards, following a trackway which had been beaten into the moor by the hooves of sheep and packhorse ponies. This track ran straight upwards over the high moorland to the highest point – Pike Law. Here he was at 1,579 feet above sea level on the summit of the ridge, between the Parish of

Cliviger, in the Duchy of Lancaster, and the Forest of Rossendale. Below to the north-east he could see almost the full length of the Cliviger Gorge, which ran from Todmorden in the south to Burnley in the north. It had been formed by a cataclysmic rending of the earth's crust forming a down throw of some 1,200 feet of the Cliviger Fault, creating the gorge which was later deepened and swept bare by the melting of the last Ice Age. When the first Anglo-Saxon pioneers entered the valley they named it Clivvig-Shire, the rocky district. From the watershed of the gorge, at Crossing-of-Dean, the Yorkshire Calder rises and runs eastward to the North Sea and the Lancashire Calder runs westward into the Irish Sea, so Crossing-of-Dean is truly a watershed of England.

The view to the north was almost completely dominated by the length of Pendle Hill resting on the horizon like a sleeping lion, but on a clear day Ingleboro', Penyghent, and Whernside could be clearly delineated with the near hills of Cumberland playing hide and seek with the distant haze. Beneath his feet to the south were the upper reaches of the Irwell as it started off on its journey thro' Lancashire to its junction with the Mersey beyond Manchester; and beyond were all the rugged hills of Rossendale.

Pike Law was a Beacon Post at which materials for a huge bonfire were kept in constant readiness by the Lord Lieutenant of the Duchy. Once the warning fires were seen, on the hills to the south, it was lit, and sent its warning northwards to Pendle, and Bleasdale, thence to Lancaster, and northward again to Carlisle. And so the nation could be summoned to arms in a matter of hours.

Robert had been told by his grandfather of its lighting at the time of the Armada when he had mustered at Towneley Hall with all the other young men. They had been drilled, and then sent into the woods to cut staves, straight and true, over ten feet long, while every smithy in the district was beating out pike-heads so that each man could be trained to withstand the Spanish horsemen who rode with the Devil in their midst.

Ever since he had left his farmstead Robert had been tramping upwards over the Cliviger Common, on which all the freeholders and their tenants had rights of usage. It was one of these rights, to graze a certain number of cattle and sheep on the common which made the twenty-odd acres of enclosed land at Thieveley a viable proposition. Nevertheless it was only a bare living, and should any disaster of weather or disease occur there was no escape from starvation, and even death for himself and his family. And if he did not look to his farm in a diligent and sober manner he could be given his notice at Ladyday, to find a house and a living elsewhere. His thoughts were occupied on these grim responsibilities, rendered more urgent as his family increased, as he hurried along feeling the weight of the ball of ore, on which his hopes rested, banging against his thigh.

Pike Law was the highest point on the watershed between the Cliviger Gorge and the Irwell Valley. This watershed was the natural boundary between the Parish of Cliviger and the Forest of Rossendale. Indeed in forgotten times a wide ditch, now called the Old Dyke, had been dug as a dividing line between the two. Robert continued his journey from the Pike, following the route of the packhorse trail which ran aslant the moor downwards on the Rossendale side, on firmer ground than the peatland of the higher moor. This ground was only a thin covering over an outcrop of rock which near the surface nature had weathered into striations, which could be split off easily to make flagstones, and roofing slates. In the time of Henry VIII Sir John Townley had laid a line of mearestones along this outcrop edge before witnesses from the Duchy Court, claiming this line as the lawful Cliviger boundary. This led to a series of disputes, laid before the Court, which dragged on for almost the whole of Elizabeth's reign. The men of Bacupbooth claimed that they had been deprived of 240 acres of good common, and that the Cliviger freeholders had impounded and ill-treated their stock. Robert could remember the excitement, in his boyhood in 1601, when the Court, seeking to be rid of the dispute, had decreed that the Bacup men should drive a heifer to within twenty yards of Thieveley Pike and leave it there for the Cliviger men to impound and then take their case to the Lancaster Assizes. The King's Justices would then be saddled with a problem which had baffled the Duchy Court for half a century.

Robert and other boys had been set to watch for the arrival of the Bacup heifer but it never came, and he guessed that by now – over twenty years later – it would never come. The Bacup men must have decided that the costs of their suit were too great a risk to take, and abandoned a case in which ancient custom was clearly on their side.

The packhorse route which Robert followed was called

the Hacgate, later Haggate, the road over the peat bog, and has remained the Cliviger boundary to modern times. The Hacgate took him to the heights above Bacup, where a mearestone denoted the meeting point of the three commons of Cliviger, Bacup and Rochdale. The pack-horse trail crossed the top of the heights into the Wardle valley where Nicholas Mercer had his farm and wool-weaving establishment.

CHAPTER II

The Search

Mercer and his wife were pleased to see their son-in-law, Robert Hartley. They approved of this serious young man who had come a-courting their youngest daughter, and they hoped that he would have a steadying influence on their own son Godfrey. He, like many sons, had not taken kindly to the disciplines of his father's business, and after a drinking bout in Rochdale, had gone off, with some companions, attracted by the talk of the high wages being earned in the Derbyshire lead mines. But he wasn't a bad lad, at heart, and he had sent messages home by the packhorse drivers and itinerant traders who plied a regular trade from Derbyshire in lime and lead to Manchester and Rochdale, with return loads of hard-wearing woollen cloth.

Then, after two years, pale and thin, he had returned home to his mother's table and slipped back into the routine of the farmwork, and the weaving, as though he had never been away.

'Is Godfrey still at home?' Robert asked anxiously.

'Aye,' replied Nicholas. 'He's just looking to t'beasts on t'Common, but he'll be back shortly.'

And as they were drawing their chairs up to the table

for the Sunday dinner, Godfrey came in, with the appetite of a young man who has just tramped miles over the open moor.

After the meal the men settled down for a Sunday rest around the fireside, and to exchange news. Robert could hardly wait to broach the subject of his visit. Taking the ball of ore out of his pocket he passed it over to Godfrey.

'What does ta mek o' that?'

Godfrey weighed the ball in his hand and replied without hesitation.

'It's brouse.'

'What?'

'Brouse. That's ore that's bin in t'furnace but not properly smelted.'

'Does ta mean lead ore?'

'Oh, aye, it's lead alreet. Nowt else 'ud be as heavy, besides tha can see t'lead in it.'

He pointed with his finger to the texture of the ball.

'Wheer's ta getten it frae?'

'On t'moor at back o't' farm, it were in t'ground wheer a'm digging a ditch to bring watter from top o't' Scout.'

'But it must a' bin in t'smelt mill, and what mill is theer up yon?'

'Now howd on a minute till I tell thee t'proper story. I were diggin t'ditch and tekin it through a bit of a ridge. I had to go a yard or so deawn, when I comes to blue shale and these bits o' grey stuff mixed in wi' it as though they'd growed theer like roots or summat, so I rakes 'em all eyout and I could feel bi't'weight as they were more likely metal than rock so I puts 'em in mi pocket to tek whoam, and arter supper I shows 'em to Alice, and I were tellin what tha'd tellt me about smeltin t'ore i' Derbyshire and she says well chuck 'em in t'fire and see what 'appens. Well we med best fire we could but they wouldna melt, nought ran out on 'em like tha said t'lead ran into a big iron pot, but when I lifted 'em eyout they were sticky like, so I fetches t'hammer and a hammers 'em on t'hearthstone like blacksmith does wit t'iron and I ends up wi' 'em all in a solid ball, but A couldna mek 'eads nor tails on it.'

'It's lead ore alright, what they calls "galena", but tha wouldna 'ave enough heat i't' kitchen fire to smelt it proper, but tha's half done t'job.'

'Does ta think there'll be more o't'stuff up theer?'

'Oh aye, if there's ony at all there mun be more – it comes up out o't'bowels o't'earth in what they calls a spout and spreads eyout like branches of a tree, and sometimes tha' finds a branch and sometimes it's ony t'leaves, but if tha finds main spout tha's a rich man in no time.'

'That's what I were thinkin, but t'trouble is it's eyout on t'Common. Does ta think there'd be any on t'farm like, on our land?'

'But it's not thy land, it's Thomas Whitaker's,' Nicholas interposed.

'Aye, I knows, but I could see old Thomas and mek some arrangement wi' him, if only I could find it on t'farm.'

'Aye, that's what they do i' Derbyshire. It's sometimes every fifth dish for t'mine owner and every thirteenth for t'King. But tha couldna start a mine on thi own – only t'Lord o't'Manor could afford to do that; ther's cost o' sinking a shaft, and laying out a dressing floor, and i'

Derbyshire they carries t'ore to t'nearest mill – 'appen two or three miles away; but tha couldna be tekin t'ore all t'way to Derbyshire. Tha'd 'ave to build thi own smelt mill.'

'Aye, A've thought of all that, but appen summat could be done in a small way, A was sort o' wondering.'

He turned to Nicholas.

'If me and Godfrey found t'ore, could tha back us up to build a smelt house? Thee'd be t'boss o't'partnership like, and keep us at it. Tha could 'ave t'selling o't'lead i' Rochdale.'

Nicholas smiled.

'Thee find t'lead first, and see what tha can fix up wi' Master Whitaker. He'll be thi biggest stumbling block. More than likely he'll want it for hissen, and there's nowt much tha could do to stop him.'

'In Derbyshire,' Godfrey put in, ''t'irst discoverer of a vein gets first choice o' two meares to work for hissen.'

'What's meares?'

'Thirty-two yards o' land along't vein wi' eight yards on either side, but Lord o't'Manor has to set up t'mine, keep it free o'watter and build t'smelthouse.'

'But this isn't Derbyshire,' Nicholas interposed.

'It's Duchy o' Lancaster, and t'Duchy's laws of its own. Tha'd 'ave t'Duchy to deal wi' as well as old Thomas.'

They continued to discuss the matter until it was time for Robert to leave.

'I'll come o'er next Sunday and see what a thinks,' said Godfrey as Robert set off on his long walk home.

And, when sitting by his own fireside, he had told Alice of the day's talk and of his plans, she did not respond to his mood.

'A've been thinking on it all day, and the more I thought the more I had a feeling that we'd best leave it a' be. Let's stick to t'farm, to t'cattle and sheep as the Lord intended. No good'll come fro' interfering wi' His work and delving into t'ground. Best leave it there, wheer He put it.'

'Nay, lass, don't tek on like that. It's noan different fro' takin stone to build t'walls and t'barn. Tha needs lead to turn t'watter.'

'It doan't seem same to me riving it out o't'earth and burning it. This furnace sounds like the Devil's work, not what God intended.'

'Eh dear. A've never heered thi go on like this afore. Don't thee worry lass. This fire in t'hearth is God's work, we couldn't live wi'out it i' winter, and this furnace is nowt different.'

'But I doan't like it, I've bin afeart all day as nowt good'll come on it.'

On the following Sunday Godfrey walked over to Thieveley and after the Sunday dinner, he and Robert sat for a brief rest by the fireside.

'T'thing is,' said Robert, 'if we could only find t'ore on my side on't fence, we'd 'av a free hand at diggin for a while, but on t'Common we mun only be diggin t'ditch; and a've finished yon.'

'Well, t'best thing is for thee to show me wheer ta found t'ore and a'll see if a can find t'run o't'rake. You see thee only finds ore in cracks in t'rock where there's bin a fault . . .'

'What's ta mean, a fault?'

'It's wheer t'earth's slipped downwards, like, and

15

broken t'rock and tha can follow t'break down into t'ground, and tha can generally follow it on t'surface if tha knows it's theer.'

They picked up their sticks and prepared to go out.

'We're just gooin to 'ave a walk on t'Common.'

'Now, doan't they be adiggin on t'Lord's day. Tha never knows who's up on t'Commons on a Sunday.'

'No, lass, now doan't thee be aworrying.'

Robert took Godfrey thro' the gate out onto the open moorland to where the newly dug ditch ran down the shoulder of Dean Scout. The peat had all been eroded off this bleak ridge which was covered with white bent, a thin-bladed grass with gossamer-like flowering, which gleamed white in the sunlight. Robert had dug his ditch through a bare three inches of soil and into the boulder clay beneath. At one point he had had to go deeper and the clay had given way to blue shale. It was here that he had found the ore.

He showed Godfrey the exact spot and they bent down and picked at the shale with their fingers, and dug into it with their sticks.

'Aye, it's here,' Robert cried in excitement as he turned up a piece with his stick.

Godfrey examined the piece.

'It's galena alright, what they had us searching for i' Derbyshire. We 'ad to break it off t'rock wi' our picks; it were like glued to t'limestone but here it's loose i't'shale. It'll be different when we get's down to t'rock but there'll be more on it.'

'But we can't do that out here on t'Common. It's what I said – we'll 'ave to find it on t'farm.'

'Well, as I said, if we can find t'rake we can trace it
back to t'farm, but it's a funny bit o' land here wi' that
knoll stuck up in t'air, and t'farmhouse on t'end on it,
wi't'land falling away down in to t'valley. A've never seen
owt like it i' Derbyshire. Tha knows what tha's agate on
theer.'

After haytime Godfrey came over to Thieveley and stayed
for a few days, while he and Robert, ostensibly com-
pleting the water supply, tried to discover the vein or rake
of ore. It was not easy for they found that they were
digging in a blue shale of indeterminate depth.

'T'main rake's allus in a fault i' Derbyshire and tha can
follow t'fault in both directions once tha's found it, but
there's nowt o't'sort here. It's a mystery bag to me.'

But they carried on digging, not daring to go too deep
or departing from the line of the water channel for fear of
inquisitive commoners. It was virtually impossible to do
anything unusual, even on that lonely moor, without,
sooner or later, it becoming a topic of conversation in the
whole neighbourhood. The only encouragement was that
they continually found the pieces of galena, and soon had
several pounds of it hidden in the farmhouse.

By a strange coincidence and great luck, it appeared
that the ore ran almost along the line of the ditch, so they
concentrated on finding how far it reached and soon had
some fifty yards of blue shale uncovered, all showing ore.

They decided that the vein must run on this line and
then covered the shale with puddled clay to form a
watercourse. Robert fixed his barrel and wooden spout,
and turned the moor water into the ditch. At least he had

gained a second water supply. Curious commoners made a surreptitious examination, but as the water was run back onto the Common, decided that they had no real cause to complain.

Throughout the summer of 1627 Godfrey paid regular visits to Thieveley and did several test diggings on the farm's acres along what he considered to be the possible line of the vein of ore but the topography of the farm was so strangely laid down in mountainous slopes, knolls and corries, where the great Cliviger fault had rent the valley, and subsequent landslips and brasts had piled rock, shale and peat in indiscriminate confusion, that there was no correlation between the land on the Common where they had found the ore and the enclosed land of the farm.

As winter approached they had to admit defeat and decided that the only way in which they could – in some measure – recompense their effort was to sell the lead ore.

'If we could only get it o'er to Rochdale,' Godfrey said, 'I could get a chapman to take it down to Wirksworth where they 'as a market for ore.'

But Robert did not own a horse; he ploughed his small field by ox plough as had been done from Saxon time, however Godfrey solved the problem and maintained an element of secrecy by borrowing a packhorse pony from Wardle. It was child's play for the pony – used to carrying over 200 lb – to carry the hundredweight of ore over Pike Law and down the familiar track to the Mercer's farm.

Several weeks later Godfrey walked over to Thieveley and arrived in considerable excitement.

'Isaac Clegg, who teks all Dad's cloth, took t'ore down

to Derbyshire and he were back at t'farm t'other day after more. He gie me three shillings for it and A've browt thi thy share, but thing is he wants more, he ses as it's high quality ore and they're going mad for it i' Derbyshire, wi' all this building work going on, end what's more he ses that if we can start a mine he'll find t'brass for a partnership. So what do we do now?'

'Well, we canna go diggin on t'Common wi'out all t'district finding out,' said Robert.

'Aye and tha'd like as not end up in t'dungeons at Towneley Hall. They clapped Sam Whatmough in there and he were nobbut diggin coal. They said as it all belonged to t'Lord of Clitheroe,' Alice put in.

'Aye and it ended up wi' Thomas Whitaker paying £20 a year for all t'coal i' Cliviger and he sold it to Sir John Townley who let Sam carry on digging for five shillings a year. 'Appen we can do summat same wi't'lead,' Robert replied.

'I dunno,' said Alice. 'There's a lot o' difference atween coal and lead.'

'Weel a tell thi what'll do. There's nowt else for it. I'll have a word wi' old Thomas deawn at t'Holme.'

CHAPTER III

The Power of the Duchy

By the year 1627, when Robert Hartley discovered the traces of lead ore, due to over a hundred years of strong Tudor monarchy, England had taken the first step towards the transition from an agricultural to an industrial nation. But to the people, agriculture was so much the mainstay of the nation's wealth that any change would seem inconceivable. The very prosperity of agriculture, and particularly of the wool trade, had brought about a new composition of society which was far removed from the simple lord, tenant and serf relationship of mediaeval times. The tenant had become the yeoman, be he either freeholder, copyholder or tenant farmer; and from this yeoman stock a new class, of what today would be termed businessmen, had arisen. These were such as the clothiers who financed and super-intended the making of cloth from the sheep's back to the finished bolt. Others were the promoters of mines, quarries, and ironworks. Seeing the prosperity of these men, the so-called gentry or larger landowners were not averse to joining their ranks.

The nation had not yet developed a class distinction based on speech, and even the members of the peerage spoke the broad dialect of their countryside. Consequently, within broad bounds of behaviour, a man was a gentleman if he could afford to be, the only yardstick being success. He could even rise by ability and royal grant, whether paid for or earned, to the peerage; or equally he could disappear into the oblivion of the working class, or even of the despised poor.

Destitution was a sin, and the destitute were whipped from parish to parish until they arrived back at their birthplace where beneath the law they could claim some modicum of relief.

The working class had also altered beyond all recognition, from the serf or cottar attached to a farm, who laboured on the land from dawn till dusk. Large numbers had become minor capitalists owning their own manufacturing equipment, such as hand looms, woodworking tools, forges, or other simple implements of craft and industry. Others could sell their labour by virtue of their ability, and membership of an increasing population of artisans only depended upon their skill. But the bedrock of the nation was still agriculture, and the vast majority of gentry, businessmen, artisans and labourers were associated with an agricultural establishment upon which they could fall back in times of need, and so avoid the dreadful fate of destitution, or from which they could draw their resources in times of expansion.

At the head of this increasingly thrusting and wealthy society was an autocratic king, Charles Stuart, fed on the doctrine of Divine Right by an Anglican Archbishop – Archbishop Laud. The King chose his ministers of government from a hereditary peerage of less than two hundred, and to approve of his measures and vote him money there was an elected Parliament with somewhat dubious powers.

The King and his ministers believed that Parliament could be summoned and dismissed at will merely to confirm the King's and Archbishop's laws, and also to raise money for their expenses, whereas Parliament believed that the King, although supreme, was the head of the executive to uphold the laws and wishes of Parliament, as representing the will of the people. This, they protested, was according to the ancient rights and customs of the Anglo-Saxon regime, accepted by William the Conqueror, re-enforced from King John by Magna Carta, and shrewdly but firmly handled by the great Tudors.

In this year of 1627 relations between King and Parliament were only two years away from breaking point.

Robert Hartley, and Godfrey Mercer, were the children of this dynamic but unstable society, admittedly well down at its lower end but by no means at the bottom of the ladder. The opportunity, and the means to rise up the social scale were both there if the obstacles could be overcome. The problem which now exercised Robert's mind was the tantalizing prospect of great wealth not many yards from his domestic hearth, but buried beneath soil which he did not own, land which was of the most desolate, a wasteland for which no man paid rent, but on which all the freeholders of Cliviger had certain rights to use in relation to the number of farm animals which their farms could support in the winter time. Cliviger was a township administered by the steward of the Lord of Clitheroe Castle. This steward presided over the Halmot Court, where all disputes in respect of the use of the Commons were settled, and all fines and punishments dispensed with unwavering severity, for the Lord of Clitheroe was also the Duke of Lancaster and he, since 1399, had been the King of England. That had been the tradition, but in recent years the steward had become an absentee. The Halmot Court was now held in the vestry of the Parish Church of St Peter's at Burnley, and these courts were supervised by Justices appointed from the local gentry who presumed to themselves the powers of the ancient Lords of the Manor. They became, in effect, minor Lords of the Manor.

Through two centuries of family prosperity Thomas Whitaker of the Holme was such a man. His ancestors had built a fine wooden-framed, wattle and daub, hall in a sheltered alcove at the bottom of Green's Clough, facing the wide water meadows of the Lancashire Calder. These flat, low-lying meadows, often flooded, had given the hall its name from the Scandinavian word 'holm', meaning flat ground by a river, submerged in times of flood.

By acquiring more and more freehold land and by inter-marriage with nearby landowning families such as the Townleys, Nowells and Barcrofts, the Whitakers had become of sufficient influence to be given permission by the Abbot of Whalley Abbey, to build their own chantry chapel provided they attended at St Peter's on all feast days. By dividing their land into small farms, by leasing quarries and coal mines, and by building rude cottages for labourers and artisans, they established a tenantry to whom they became known as the Lords of Holme. The small hamlet which sprang up around the chantry chapel became known as Holme Chapel, and has been so called ever since. But the Whitakers were only Lords of the Manor to their own tenantry, and were not real Lords of the Manor in the constitutional sense of the great Lords who had held the honours and manors by grant from the Norman Kings. As far as Holme-in-Cliviger was concerned the real Lord of the Manor at the time of Robert Hartley, tenant, and Thos. Whitaker Esquire, was King Charles I, Duke of Lancaster.

But King Charles was an unapproachable figure, many days' journey away in London, whereas Thomas Whitaker, to whom Robert paid his rent twice yearly, at Lady's Day and Michaelmas, sat in the Hall down in the valley below his farm, and with luck could be seen almost any day. So Robert decided to gamble upon giving his confidence to Thomas, and asking for his advice as he had already done upon the question of the water supply. But he was to find that in Thomas's mind there was a great distinction between water, which came freely from the skies, and lead which he was finding to be a most expensive item in the rebuilding, in stone, of his wooden hall.

After he had made known the purpose of his visit, Robert received a severe lecture on the duties of a tenant farmer, to be diligent in every aspect of the care of his farm, and should he be found negligent in this he could quite easily be given his notice to quit. Up to now Thomas had been well pleased with the manner in which his tenant had applied himself to his responsibilities, but should he go gallivanting off on some wild goose chase, associating with nebulous characters in the alehouses of Rochdale, he could find himself in serious trouble. As it was he had a good farm for which he should be thankful. But even a good farm required a man's full attention for twenty-four hours a day, with perhaps the odd day off to attend Burnley Fair. Now if he was thinking of setting up a hand-loom in the attic, or spinning wheel, to keep his wife and children occupied, that was a different matter, for nothing could disrupt a farming life more than idleness. And so it went on until Robert was glad to escape.

'I could tell by thi face that summat 'ad gone wrong,' said Alice after he had unburdened his mind. 'But it's 'appen for t'best. Old Thomas is 'appen right – tha'd best leave it a'be, and attend to t'farm.'

'Aye, but I do'ant know what Godfrey'll think – a've leet cat out o't'bag awreet neaw. Old Thomas knows as there's lead on t'Common, and he knows wheer it is, an all.'

Meanwhile down at the Holme, Thomas was indeed giving the matter a great deal of thought. In 1556, in the reign of Queen Mary, his grandfather, also called Thomas, had received a grant 'for ever' of all his coal mines in Cliviger, but he had sold this right to John Townley for £20, believing there to be little future use for coal. And as wood and peat were still the most sought-after fuel, Thomas was not much worried about the loss of the coal mines. But lead was an infinitely more valuable commodity; with demand, in all the civilized countries, far exceeding supply. If he could obtain the sole right to all lead mines in the Cliviger wastes the family fortunes could be established on an even wider base – perhaps exceeding those of the Townleys, Ormerods and Barcrofts.

He knew, beyond all doubt, that the ownership of all mineral beneath the wastelands belonged to the King, and that these rights were jealously guarded by the Chancellor of the Duchy of Lancaster. Unfortunately the Chancellor sat in the Duchy House at Holborn in London, and Thomas felt that he was too old to undertake the arduous journey to London on horseback.

The nearest official was Ralph Assheton of Downham Hall who was Receiver for the Honour of Clitheroe of all monies, such as the Lord's rent which all freeholders paid on every acre of their holdings. Thomas mused that he could stay overnight with his cousin Roger Nowell at Read Hall, and then wait upon Ralph at Downham. Yes, he would offer a rent of £5 a year, and there would be a sum of £20 available to assist his application past the officials in London. But he would have to play the whole matter down as only a vague possibility, lest Ralph wanted the licence for himself. Perhaps it would be better to wait until Ladyday, and just mention the matter casually. Yes, that was the best plan, there was little fear of anyone forestalling him for he had ascertained that the discovery was a secret well guarded by Robert Hartley and his brother-in-law Godfrey Mercer.

However, old Thomas, Robert and Godfrey would have been most disturbed had they known of a conversation which was going on in the tap room of the Black Boar at Middleton. A chapman called Ralph Highley was buying tankard after tankard of strong ale for James Shaw, a packhorse driver in the employment of the clothier Isaac Clegg.

'And you say this hundredweight of lead ore came from Nicholas Mercer's farm at Wardle?' he was saying to keep the conversation going.

'Aye, that it did and good ore it was so the Barmaster said at Wirksworth, he'd seen none better,' replied James.

'Now I wonder where old Nicholas would get a hundredweight, of lead ore from, I've never heard of lead ore in these parts afore.'

'I dunno, but it were there awright, we humped it on old Jinny who leads the pack, and she took it all t'way to Derbyshire. It wiant as heavy as two bales o'cloth but it were middlin' hard and rattled her old ribs a bit.'

'And where was it at Nick's Place? Was it near where they'd bin diggin' or owt like that?'

'Nay, it were just in t'weaving shed wi't'cloth, like, just waiting for us to pick up. But oud on a minute. Godfrey – that's Nick's son – borrowed one of our ponies afore this for a day, said he had to fetch summat o'er fra his sister's i' Cliviger.'

'By gum, A think tha's getten it, that's weer t'lead'll come frey, frey Cliviger, it's just reet sort o' place, yon, for a lead mine, they're allus in t'hills. Here 'ave another pint to help thee on thy way.'

Now although Ralph Highley and his partner William Butler were already in a prosperous line of business – William ran the fulling mill for finishing the raw woollen cloth, and Ralph had just added a dyehouse – Ralph was such a man who could not resist any new venture. It was his belief that fate offered him opportunities intending him to take them up, and if a man was either too dim to recognize the fact or too lazy to act upon it, he deserved nothing better.

He made it his business to make discreet enquiries in the Rochdale area, and he had soon learned the story of Godfrey Mercer leaving home to work in the Derbyshire lead mines, and more interesting still, that Godfrey had been back there recently and returned with another miner called Humphrey Greave, and that the two of them had gone off to Godfrey's sister's in Cliviger. That was it, Ralph was certain, they had gone to get some more of that high-quality ore.

Now it so happened that Ralph was setting off on a journey to London where he was due to tender at Westminster for the supply of blue cloth, woven in the Rochdale area, and dyed and finished at his own works, for the new Navy which King Charles was building to protect England's infant colonies and new overseas trade, which the King saw as his least troublesome source of income. But, Ralph pondered, the problem with the cloth trade was that it was either up or down, boom or slump, prosperous in wartime, followed by depression in peacetime. Now lead was different, all the old wooden-framed houses in the country were being replaced by fine new stone houses, and even the new farmhouses were of stone, and thatch was giving way to slates with lead flashing, water spouts and gutters. The demand for lead was insatiable, and would last a hundred years. He would attend to the paperwork, the business and the finance, and his partner William Butler, the practical man, would look after the mine, the treatment, and smelting of the ore. This was not original thinking, for many others of the wealthy clothiers were seeking interests in mines, in the Lake District, in Swaledale, Wensleydale and Bowland. What a triumph if he could control an entirely new area in Calderdale.

He had been in business long enough to realize the power of paper, or rather of the pen; and he had had sufficient land dealings to have fathomed the complexities of land tenure in the Duchy of Lancaster. He knew that the minerals beneath the land were the property of the King, and he did not intend to come away from his visit to Westminster until he had received the Duchy orders confirming his title to all the lead mines in the township of Cliviger.

CHAPTER IV

The Sturdy Rogue

When Godfrey Mercer had rebelled against the tedium of his father's handlooms, he had joined the lead miners in Derbyshire for the adventure of a man's calling and the rough humanity of male comradeship. He was set to work with an older man called Humphrey Greaves. It was not long before Godfrey became captivated by the spell of this man's personality, for Humphrey had been through the mill of human hardship, and had survived with cheerful resilience and a fund of stories which whiled away the candlelit hours of toil within the catacombs of Derbyshire's limestone hills.

Humphrey's ancestors had been greaves of a manor in Shropshire; and as, under the feudal system, greaves were very important officials roughly equivalent to the modern chief executive, inheritance had bequeathed upon him an authentic stamp of authority which despite his present humble circumstances made him – in any emergency – a natural leader of men.

When the manorial system decayed and was replaced by the parish rule of justices appointed by the King, the Greaves family had fallen into complete destitution. The only hope for a young man lay in continental wars, and the enterprises or privateers. Humphrey had been both soldier and sailor, and had stories to tell of European wars, and of adventures in the West Indies. Discharged from the Army by James' peace and too independent to endure the slave-like conditions of the plantations, he had fought with the privateers against the Spanish treasure fleets and had finally taken part in Raleigh's last disastrous expeditions to the Guianas in search of the gold of El Dorado. Put ashore at Plymouth from Raleigh's discredited fleet, dockside pimps had stolen his money and his papers so that he had had to make the journey home to Shropshire categorized in every parish as a 'sturdy rogue'. He told Godfrey, in detail, of his ordeal, the stealth, the starvation, and the whippings when he was caught. The greatest danger, and the one he feared most, was from the mastiffs and wolfhounds guarding the homesteads at night. He owed his very survival to two factors – servant women and pigs. The women, approached by stealth, had provided him with food, clothing and footwear. He had repaid them in any way he could, by chopping wood or carrying water, and on many occasions in the concealment of the shrubbery, or at night-time in their warm beds. To Godfrey, listening avidly to these adventures, it appeared that no woman, young or old, could resist Humphrey, and there is little doubt that this was true. Caught, one night, in the bed of a comely servant girl, he had been surprised by the houseowner, a Justice of the Peace, having the same idea. He had only escaped from the pursuit of dogs and menservants, by swimming and drifting down a river. Overcome by cold, he had been fortunate enough to find a herd of pigs deep in a wood, and he had managed to creep in amongst them without arousing their resentment. The wonderful warmth of their bodies had saved his life. And they saved his life a second time in the days which followed. By closely observing which roots they dug up he was able to provide himself with sufficient food to maintain life, and to continue on his way.

Taking a liking for the younger man Humphrey warned him against the dangers of falling into the unpropertied lower class, which had no status other than to labour and be ruled, to be whipped, and to starve. The only hope for any man was the acquisition of money and property. He himself had failed because whatever money he had earned had run through his fingers. The wages in the lead mines were an illusion – barely covering the necessities of life – and the only hope was to become a free miner, renting a meare of ground from the owner of the mine, and being paid for the ore he produced. But this required capital to sink a shaft, to employ labourers, to buy rope and timber, to live and to endure should the shaft be a failure. And Humphrey had never accumulated this amount of money, so he had remained a labourer in a market overflowing with eager hands and hungry mouths.

When the initial glamour of the mines and the riotous company had worn off; and after enduring one winter of misery, and a summer in which both wages and demand for labour fell, Godfrey, seeing the wisdom of Humphrey's advice, returned home to his father's establishment and his mother's table. Again, because of this advice, he settled down to the daily routine of the farm and the weaving loft, but in the long hours of work he went over Humphrey's stories again and again.

Should he take ship for the colonies, should he press his father for help so that he would not have to go as a wage-slave, or should he just carry on in the security and shelter of the farm?

And when Robert came with the discovery of the lead ore, all Godfrey's restlessness was reawakened. He remembered Humphrey's words: the only hope in the mines was to become an independent free miner with a meare of ground and a shaft of one's own. Then came Isaac Clegg's offer to finance the venture, coinciding with a disastrous slump in the cloth trade, in which the clothiers could take no further stocks of woven cloth, or pay the weavers.

With his father's tacit approval he made a journey down to Derbyshire, accompanying on foot the many packhorse trains and cattle drovers who used the upland tracks of the Pennines for good footing, and free pasture on the wastelands for their animals. He helped out during the day, securing loose packs, lifting fallen animals, and herding cattle for the drovers, and in exchange he shared the security, warmth and food of their overnight camps. Nor was he suspected of being a 'sturdy rogue' so long as he worked his passage, and hung on to the small amount of money which he had saved.

In Derbyshire he had little difficulty in finding Humphrey for such a man was known to all in the miner's coes, the camps of turf dwellings, thatched with reeds and rushes, in which they lived. He told him of the discovery and of Isaac's offer of money and was greatly relieved by Humphrey's immediate interest.

'Now are you sure that you and your brother-in-law were the first to discover the ore?'

'Yes, certain, no-one ever suspected it afore i' Cliviger. Why?'

'Well it's law o't'land, and written in t'Barmaster's office as t'first discoverer has t'first choice of a meare in t'new mine, so tha can demand a meare, and no-one can stop thi.'

'Well, will ta come wi' me up to Cliviger and wi' Isaac's help, and Robert, we'll tek a meare and sink a shaft? It canna' fail. A've sin t'ore wi' mi own eyes, and the deeper we dug the more there was on it.'

'Aye, that'll suit me fine – I'll come wi' thi. A've getten fed up o' this place.'

Godfrey was elated, whatever doubts he had had of sinking a shaft had vanished, for with Humphrey's experience and resourcefulness he felt that they could not fail. During the many hours that he had worked with Humphrey underground he had developed an unlimited confidence in the man's resourcefulness and natural ability to take every obstacle in his stride. Indeed on one occasion – when water had burst into the mine – Humphrey had saved both their lives, by instantly kicking down a ventilation screen, grabbing the candles, and leading Godfrey to safety along a labyrinth of shafts to the eye pit, where at last blessed daylight winked down upon them from high above.

After being provided with money by Isaac Clegg in Rochdale, they bought an old but sturdy packhorse pony, complete with its harness and panniers. It would be able to do all they required with long rests in between jobs on the Mercers' farm or at Thieveley. They bought a pick, a shovel, a saw, and a wheelbarrow, and after a night at Wardle, set off for Thieveley with all their gear stored on the pony's pack and the wheelbarrow lashed across the top and secured with bits of old rope begged from the farm.

There was a short period of awkwardness upon their arrival, for although Robert and Alice were glad to see them they scarcely knew what to say.

Thinking that they were worried about accommodating two extra men, Godfrey endeavoured to relieve the tension.

'Tha's no need to worry about boarding us – we'll mek our own turf house, and look after our sens just as we do i' Derbyshire.'

'Nay, lad, tha'rt welcome, come thee in both of you, and get summat to eat. It'll not tek me a minnit to put summat on t'table,' Alice replied.

After the meal Godfrey explained his ideas, and sensing some atmosphere of doubt, he at last played his trump card.

'And it's law o't'land that first discoverer of a mine as t'first choice of working on it and sinking a shaft, so we want you to join with us i' getting t'ore, and we'll tek it o'er to Rochdale for Isaac to tek down to Wirksworth i' Derbyshire.'

'Well, I dunno what to say,' Robert replied. 'I've had a word wi' old Thomas down at t'Holme, and he says that if I start meddling wi' a lead mine, he'll tek t'farm off us and put us on t'parish and we daren't risk that.'

'The miserable old devil.'

'Aye, but he's every right to, he says a've enough to do attending to t'farm wi'out goin' diggin' on t'Common for lead, and t'worrit of it is he knows there's lead theer now, and wi' him actin' like lord o't'manor, and his relations all justices he'll 'appen start diggin' for it hissel'. Ey dear, a've made a proper mess on it, a should ne'er a told him, but a didna know what else to do, 'cos everyone knows as t'minerals on t'Common belong to t'Duchy. One mon were clapped i't'dungeons at Towneley Hall just for diggin' up a few coals.'

'But i' Derbyshire,' Humphrey explained, 'if a man finds a vein on the wastelands he becomes what is called a free miner, and he has every right to what's called a meare of ground to work for hissel', and it's not just t'law i' Derbyshire, it's law i' London for all t'country. Tha has to register t'mine wi' t'Barmaster, and pay every thirteenth dish to t'King and t'Barmaster, and t'parson is after his share, but after that it's all for thissen.'

'Trouble is this is t'Duchy, and t'Duchy belongs to t'King, and seems different from t'rest o't'country.'

'Nay – I don't see how that can be – there's only one law o't'land, London law fro' Westminster. A've never heard o' any other.'

'Well, I'll tell thi' what we'll do,' said Godfrey. 'Me and Humphrey'll build a turf house on t'Common and start diggin' t'ore, and if anyone ses owt we'll tell 'em it's nowt to do wi' thee, but tha' can still join in wi' us on t'quiet. We've nowt to lose, only Isaac's bit o' money, and we can soon pay him that back in ore.'

'Now thee do what's best for thissen,' Alice said, 'and tha's welcome to stay, but we mun a' nowt to do wi' it.'

She looked at Robert, and noticed the misery in his face. But he looked straight back at her and then turned to the two men.

'Aye, Alice is reet, thee do what tha' thinks best, and good luck to thee, but we must ha' nowt to do wi' it.'

CHAPTER V

The Duchy Chamber

The administrative fact that, in the year 1627, the Cliviger Commons came under the Chancellor of the Duchy and were administered from the Duchy Chamber in the Palace of Westminster, was only vaguely understood by such men as Robert Hartley and Godfrey Mercer, and even less so by the stranger Humphrey Greaves.

Ralph Highley, however – who was determined to survive, despite the disastrous slump of 1625 in the cloth trade, by setting up his dyeing and finishing works in co-operation with the practical William Butler – had fathomed the mysteries of the establishment, and the all-important necessity of holding a written title to his possessions. He had paid dearly to James I for the confirmation of his copyhold lands in Lancashire, and he had begun the process of buying up smaller copyholds as the holders fell into distress.

Consequently we find him standing in a corridor in the Duchy Chamber in King Charles' Palace of Westminster awaiting an audience with Edward Barret, Lord Newburgh, Chancellor of the Duchy.

He had been waiting for many hours, pressed back against the wall by palace guards, as supercilious gentlemen strolled by, or subservient clerks and messengers hurried along as though their lives – which may well have been true – depended upon their speed. And he had seen one gentleman escorted out of the Chancellor's chamber by four guards, buffeted along the corridor, and thrust into a room whose heavy oaken door clanged ominously shut to the banging and rattling of locks and bars.

At last he was almost thrust into the Chancellor's presence, with a guardsman standing on either side of him, two more by the door, and four behind the Chancellor as the great man lolled in a chair behind a huge oaken table.

He took a long insolent look at Ralph, who looked back directly, but respectfully, into the hard, calculating eyes.

'Now, for what favour have you come wasting my time?'

'My Lord, I wish to apply for an order to search and dig for lead ore in the Duchy Parish of Cliviger.'

'Cliviger – the recusant Richard Townley owns land there, does he not?'

'I know him not, my Lord, my information is that the most faithful of his Majesty's subjects – Thomas Whitaker – is the first gentleman thereabouts.'

'That's as may be, but if I find that you have come from this Richard Townley, that insolent head won't stay long on those shoulders. My guards will make short work of you.'

'It is as your Lordship pleases, I wish merely to apply for an order which may enable me to increase the riches of your estate. I act for no-one other than myself and my lord the King.'

'What is your following?'

'I attend the Parish Church of Rochdale to which I offer my dues for standing in the nave.'

'And what lands do you hold as security for this favour which you ask of us?'

'My Lord, I am a merchant, a clothier. I hold copyhold lands of some eighty-six acres on which – in line with the wishes of the late and great majesty, King James – I have at great cost and labour developed a cloth dyeing and finishing trade.'

'So, why come to me upon this matter of a lead mine?'

'My Lord, as you know better than I, there is great distress in the cloth industry, and I am hard put to to keep my weavers – of whom there are nearly a thousand – from death by starvation.'

'You must be a very wealthy man to keep a thousand souls – I have scarce that number of retainers myself.'

'My Lord, they are not my retainers, they are cottars who supply me with unfinished cloth, but who rely on me for their sustenance, and if I can aid myself with a lead mine, it would be to the Duchy's advantage, and these poor may not be thrown upon the relief of the justices.'

'You are a clever rogue in your talk, but think not that I believe a word of it.'

The Chancellor turned to a clerk who was almost invisible at one end of the table, obscured by a mountain of paper.

'Have you taken down what this man claims? I would have him verified.'

'My Lord, you may enquire my substance from the

Clerk to the King's Navy, with whom I have the honour of treating in the supply of cloth.'

'Don't think that will save you if I find that you lie. Now tell me about this lead mine in Cliviger.'

'My Lord, there is no lead mine – I have requested this audience only to obtain permission to search for lead on the Duchy wastelands in that most wild and savage country.'

'Now, man, take me for a fool at your peril, and if there is no mine – how do you dare to waste my time? Guards, take this man away and teach him such that he will never dare waste my time again.'

Two guards seized Highley in what may have been a well-practised charade.

'My Lord, if you will only let me explain. Indeed there is no mine, nor dare any man sink one without your permission, but traces of lead ore have been found by a simple husbandman amidst the pebbles of a stream, on those wild and uncharitable wastes over a thousand feet above sea level, land only fit to carry a few sheep of a very poor and skinny sort. But I have a mind to set two men, two experienced and skilled Derbyshire miners – who are at present experiencing a mean time in that area – to search and find the rake, if rake there be, from which this ore has been washed, and for permission to do this I humbly offer the yearly sum of £5 until such time that the mine be proved, and I place £20 down on this table as earnest of my honest intentions.'

Ralph shook himself free of the guards and placed a pigskin purse of gold coins upon the table.

'You are an insolent rogue, but I admire your standing,

and may find it possible to grant your request. Wait upon my clerk of the council, Edmund Brewster, in one month's time, but do not think that a paltry £20 will influence my decision.'

'My Lord, I had meant the £20 as a yearly token for as long as the mine succeeds – if there should be a mine at all.'

When Highley had left the Chamber, the Chancellor gave detailed instructions to his secretary to instruct Roger Nowell of Read Hall, near Whalley in Lancashire, a Justice of the Peace, to find out what was going on on the Cliviger wastes.

When Ralph again presented himself at the Duchy Chambers he was closeted with a lawyer who explained the terms upon which he could be granted permission to search for, dig and smelt lead ore, and sell the lead in the open market. Ralph was not put out by the expected duty of every thirteenth dish to the King, and the one tenth tithe for the Church, but he was a little disconcerted by the stipulation that the work had to be done efficiently, and only skilled men employed, so that the mine had always to be in a safe and durable condition, and the miner who first discovered the seam had to be named.

Thinking rapidly he decided to gamble on forestalling any other claims.

'I can name the skilled Derbyshire miners, who I have hired to search for the rake; and, if mine there be, they will be the first discoverers of it.'

'And who will they be?'

'Humphrey Greaves of Wirksworth in Derbyshire and Godfrey Mercer of Rochdale in the Duchy of Lancaster.'

'Very good, I will enter these names on the order papers together with yours and your partner, William Butler. You will all be responsible for the orderly running of the mine.'

Finally the partners were required 'from tyme to tyme to make and yield accomptes upon their oathes, both of the charge expended and profitt raised thereby'.

It was a well-satisfied Ralph Highley who commenced the long journey home to Rochdale, carrying copies of the Orders in Council, which authorized him and his partners to 'finde out, digge for and worke our leade oars within anie partes of our said wastes, and to smelte and refine the same, and then to make sale thereof.'

The 'said wastest' were of course 'our wastes of Cliviger, parcell of our Duchie of Lancaster in our Countie Palatine of Lancaster'.

CHAPTER VI

The Chancellor's Message

All these events took place in the spring and summer of 1627 in the second year of the reign of King Charles I. There was little that could be done in winter time, travel was almost impossible for all except the most desperate of journeys; and, for rich and poor alike, the months from November to April were ones of retrenchment and survival. The best that man could do was to preserve that which he had: the rich could beguile the long winter evenings with music, dancing and song; but the poor, since being excluded from the thane's hall, where they had gathered to work at their many handicrafts, in the light and warmth of the communal fire, and to watch and listen to the entertainment, could only huddle together around a meagre fire for hours of almost permanent darkness. No wonder the coming of spring was heralded with celebration and joy.

However, in 1627, there were still many weeks of good weather available at Thieveley for Godfrey and Humphrey to begin sinking a shaft, and very shrewdly, they believed that it would be the best time, when all the freeholders were fully occupied in preparing for the winter months, and when Robert Hartley's ditch had been accepted as a permanent feature of the Common.

They soon found that the task was different, yet easier, than that in Derbyshire, where it had involved the quarrying of limestone rock. Here, at Thieveley, they found an apparently bottomless depth of blue shale, which yielded readily to their picks, with the ore, or galena, quite easy to separate. The difficulty they experienced was that the shale soon weathered, softened and fell in upon them, so that it had to be shored up and supported with timber frames. However, there was little timber remaining on the Cliviger Commons. Whatever woodlands remained were fenced round in the private holdings of the many freeholders. But in the matter of the small amount of timber at first required by the miners, Robert Hartley was able to help them by his privilege of obtaining kindling and fencing timber from Thomas Whitaker's woods.

The miners had begun their shaft a few yards to the south and a little higher than Robert's ditch, so that their workings did not interfere with its course, nor did the water pour into the shaft. They had the added bonus of being able to wash their ore in the stream of water. After washing, the ore was stored away for safety and privacy in one of Robert's farm buildings.

Alice, however, was not carried away by the enthusiasm of the three men; and, as the small pile of ore increased, so did her forebodings.

'Tha's sticking thi neck out reet,' she warned Robert. 'Old Thomas wi'ant like his wood being teken, and if t'constable finds that pile of ore in our barn – he's bayn to march thi off to t'dungeons.'

'Nay, lass, there's nowt to worry about at this time on t'year, wi' winter coming on.'

'Well, thee get Godfrey and Humphrey to pack that ore o'er to Rochdale afore we get catched.'

But the men were too fascinated by the growing depth of their shaft to waste time packing the ore off to Isaac Clegg in Rochdale, nor would he have been able to take it down to Wirksworth until the following spring. But, because of Alice's forebodings, they were careful to keep the entrance to the shaft concealed with brushwood, and to spread the spoil in hollows on Robert Hartley's land, where it would not be noticed. In this manner they began to enjoy a sense of security, and continued, so long as weather would permit, to sink the shaft, wash and dress the ore, and store it away.

Meanwhile in Read Hall, some nine miles away, at the little end of Pendle Hill near Whalley, Roger Nowell, Justice of the Peace, was a very worried man. He had pondered for many hours over a cryptic message from the Chancellor of the Duchy, bidding him to find out what was going on in the Cliviger wastes. Some years earlier he had been deeply disturbed by the affair of the Lancashire Witches, when he had sent Old Chattox, Mother Demdike and some others to their deaths at Lancaster Castle.

He had not worried much over the old hags Chattox and Demdike, but his dreams were haunted by that fine woman, Alice Nutter, whose only sin had been to defend her freehold of Roughlee against avaricious and vicious neighbours, and by the childish face, and young sexuality of Alison Devizes. The women had been sacrificed to the vanity of James I. To allow them to live would have been a negation of his book on witchcraft, but Roger did not believe that the new King, James' son, Charles I, shared his father's views; or his father's preoccupation with academic studies and debate. But one never knew what was going on in the heads of the men who ruled England in a despotic manner from the capital city. Nor did one know of the stories which were being fed into their ears by sycophants, eager for preferment above their fellow men, and the wealth which came with it. No man, no matter how good and conscientious in his duty, was without enemies working ceaselessly for his destruction; and, as he became older and perhaps less able to defend himself, the pressures became greater. The only respect he had was for his property which became the only guarantee of security in his old age. He could not rely for ever upon the fact that, in the time of the great Elizabeth, his uncle Alexander had been the Protestant Dean of St Paul's, his uncle Lawrence, Dean of Lichfield, and uncle Robert, attorney of the Court of Wards, a most prestigious appointment affecting the revenue of the Crown.

So what lay behind this cryptic message? Was it the first shot in a battle to encompass his disgrace and perhaps the confiscation or his estate? He could not see where he had gone wrong – he had always paid his rents, tithes, subsidies and benevolences. He had even paid the fine which was imposed upon him for not taking up a knighthood, and in his long term of office as a Justice, whilst trying to be fair, his final judgement had always been one which he believed would have pleased the King. In religion his family had adopted the new Protestantism after the dissolution of Whalley Abbey in 1539. They had even bought some of the confiscated lands from the King, Henry VIII. Roger himself, as befitted his position, never failed to attend at the mother church of the great ecclesiastical Parish of Whalley.

He could only believe that the practice of witchcraft had re-established itself, and that a coven was perhaps holding ritual meetings on the Cliviger wastes.

Not many years back a respected yeoman named Giles Robinson, on a journey from Rochdale to his home in the Pendle Forest, had had a frightening experience in the Cliviger Gorge when he had seen Old Loynd, a notorious Cliviger witch, seated astride the Eagle Crag with a huge black cat, whose eyes emitted sparks of fire, seated upon her shoulder. The moment the cat had taken his place, the witch drew a large flambeau, as it were, from the beak of the eagle, and waving it round and round in her hand, flew away as swiftly and securely as an eagle itself, in a north-west direction. 'No doubt to Malkin Tower,' as Giles later asserted.

At the same time Giles' son Ned had been made prisoner by a coven of witches, and only escaped with his life by making a frantic leap to the safe side of the Boggart Hole where two horsemen took the incoherent boy to safety. As a result Giles and his son vowed they would have the law upon the witches. They denounced sixteen women who lingered for years in Lancaster Castle as lawyers contested the case, and four were even at this present moment at Westminster for examination by Charles I, in person. But, unlike his father, Charles did not believe in witchcraft, and the few who had not died in gaol were released. However, this was in the future, and at present Roger did not know in which direction the wind was blowing. Nevertheless the belief in witches, boggarts and hobgoblins was still a firm conviction in the minds of all classes, including the churchmen and the justices.

That dark forbidding gorge, with more than its share of starving paupers, was just the place for such practices. There was a dark recess in the Thieveley hillside, begirt with fallen rocks, but sheltered and covered by a grove of woodland, called the Earl's Bower, which might be the very place.

He would instruct his constable to keep a close watch, and he would question the pinder who rounded up the stray sheep, and the ale-taster who visited all the alehouses, whether they knew of any resurgence of the practice of witchcraft.

However it was with no thought of witchcraft, but of apprehension, that Alice Hartley invited the constable to take a seat by her fireside. Determined to keep him there until she could warn the menfolk, she set ale and food in front of him. To her confusion his conversation turned in a most peculiar direction, about the old women of the parish, and were there any stories going round of milk being curdled, cows being found dead, or even human beings sickening to death. Alice was afraid these things were always happening, but they were God's will and had to be endured.

'Ah but they could be the work of the Devil,' the constable interjected, and Alice began to wonder if the man had become one of the new sect of religious bigots,

Puritan dissenters from the Anglican Church, who were crying out against the wickedness of rich and poor alike.

The constable however, sensing Alice's agitation, and aware of her heightened colour and the brightness of her eyes, was thinking what an attractive woman she was; and, as she brought him more ale and seemed eager for him to stay, he fell into a reverie of delightful anticipation. Many women in the rude cottages which he visited on his daily rounds had been pleased to grant him their favours, although he had never thought of Alice Hartley as one of these. However, his reverie was brought to an end by the abrupt entry of three men, whose clothes and footwear were soiled with blue clay.

The ale having done its work, he greeted them with joviality, and never a thought that they had been employed on anything other than legitimate farmwork; so, from contemplation of the woman, he joined in with the rough joviality of the men.

When he had gone Alice told the three men: 'He gave me a proper fright when I saw him standing at t'door, so I fetched him in, and gi'e him some ale. He were ready for it atter climbin' t'hill fri' t'chapel, and then he started to talk all queer like, about t'owd women and witchcraft and turning t'milk sour, and bewitching t'cows and stuff like that. If you ask me owt we'll a' t'watch him. I doan't like that sort o' fellow snooping around.'

Roger Nowell's constable, pinder, and ale-taster came back with nothing to report, there were no rumours of witchcraft or of anything else amiss on the Cliviger Commons. He could not delay sending a reply to the Chancellor much longer, and he knew instinctively that a report that all was well would not do; it would give the Chancellor the opportunity he needed to get rid of him, and bestow the office upon some younger and more lucrative contender. But all his wit could not devise anything to report, until he remembered his cousin, Thomas Whitaker of the Holme. In the time of Henry VIII, his aunt, the sister, Elizabeth, of the Deans of St Paul's and Lichfield, had married Thomas' grandfather, also called Thomas, and Queen Elizabeth had made their son, William Whitaker, Master of St John's College, Cambridge. Ever since there had been close ties between the Nowell and Whitaker families. They had both become active in supporting the Anglican Church instituted by Henry VIII in place of the Church of Rome, and established securely by Elizabeth and James I. Thomas Whitaker was no fool, he would know if there was anything amiss in Cliviger, and he would most certainly spend an evening at Read Hall on his way to pay his feudal dues to Receiver Assheton at Downham.

This would be on the feast day of St Michael, September the 29th, Michaelmas Day, a quarter day, chosen to give the payment of rents a religious significance, as though blessed by St Michael, and sanctified by God.

When Thomas had been given a sumptuous dinner, and the two men had settled down to smoke pipes and drink Portuguese wine, the talk inevitably turned to the one topic which interested all country gentlemen of that era – the rebuilding, in stone, of their ancient halls. It was as though possession of such a hall gave them the title of Esquire, only one class below that of the peerage;

although the real test was the amount of their income. They had risen in the previous century from the ranks of the small freeholders, by buying up their neighbour's land, and renting it out, by skilful inter-marriage, by farming state monopolies, and finding lucrative appointments for their younger sons. Their old wooden-framed, wattle and daub halls were in many instances those appropriated by the Norman conquerors from the Anglo-Saxon thanes. They were warm and dry, because the wood and daub absorbed the dampness in wet periods, and recovered naturally in the dry; but the problem with stone building, particularly the great castles of the nobility, was condensation whereby the walls and flagged floors ran with water. The only solution had been the hanging of tapestries on the walls, and rushes on the floors. The invention of lime plaster altered all this, and by applying a thick coating on the insides of the walls, stone building could be made as free from condensation as were the old wattle and daub halls.

In the next century the same families, grown even richer, were to employ Italian craftsmen to execute beautiful plaster ceilings, many of which are still preserved. For the rebuilding of the houses, all sites in the Pennines had ample supplies of good stone and timber, and the work could be done by the owner's own men, for little more than their sustenance, but the two great out-of-pocket expenses were for lime and lead. Lead was needed in large quantities, for windows, for sealing the flagged roof, for gutters, pipes and downspouts. Roger was obtaining lime, by the packhorse load from Clitheroe, and lead from the Trough of Bowland, but Thomas, further away in the hills, was having to pay much higher prices.

Mellowed by the wine, he at last unburdened his mind by telling of the discovery of lead ore, by one of his tenants, on the very borders of his freehold land at Thieveley; and of his intention to obtain Ralph Assheton's offices in securing permission from the Duchy to dig for the ore. At his age, he could not face the arduous journey to Westminster. He continued by telling how he had given Robert Hartley a good dressing down for wanting to dig for the ore himself.

Roger was enthusiastic in his support of the idea, even suggesting a partnership; and pointing out that the two of them, possibly with a third gentleman involved, could scarcely be refused a licence.

However, on the following day it suddenly occurred to Roger that this matter of the lead mine on the Cliviger wastes could extricate him from his dilemma in the matter of his report to the Chancellor. On considering the matter further, he realized that here was a way in which he could turn the report to his own advantage. Once again he sent for his constable.

'How is it,' he began, 'that I have always to do your work for you? What did you find out about the discovery of lead on the Cliviger Common?'

'Nothing – I heard nowt about it.'

'No, I thought not, but you have ears and eyes in your head, it's your duty to find out these things.'

'But there's nowt wrong in anyone discovering lead or owt else on t'Common.'

'No, nowt wrong, so long as they report it to the

Justices, so that the King may be the receiver of his own. Now I want you to go to Robert Hartley's farm at Thieveley, and get him to show you this discovery, and I authorize you to dig up and bring me a piece of the lead ore.'

'How will I know what it is? A've ne'er sin lead ore i' mi life.'

'Well it's up to thee to find out.'

Then, all at once, the constable realized how he could get back into Roger's favour.

'I'll tell thee what, I did go up to Thieveley Farm, and I thought there wer summat queer going on, there were three men 'ad bin out diggin', covered wi' blue clay they were. But I questioned 'em, like, and it seems one o't'men were Alice Hartley's brother, and they were diggin' a ditch on t'farm; so there seemed nowt wrong i' that.'

'Well, get thee back to Thieveley tomorrow, and find out what's going on; and tek four of my gardeners wi' thi, wi' strong nobsticks; and if they're digging for lead, tha mun arrest them, and tek 'em to Towneley Hall for Richard Townley to lock up i' t'dungeons, on a charge of stealing the King's ore.'

When the constable had gone, Roger sat, smiling to himself. He was going to enjoy writing his report for the Chancellor; he would even pay the extra for a special express messenger.

CHAPTER VII

The Arrest

Godfrey Mercer and Humphrey Greaves became completely absorbed in the task of abstracting, and dressing the lead ore from their diggings at Thieveley. They had been baffled, at first, by the instability of the blue shale, and the difficulty of shoring it up with roughly dressed timber; but the resourceful Humphrey, who had helped to build log cabins in the Americas, soon came up with the answer. They made the shaft rectangular, and, as it were, built a log cabin downwards into the shaft. They found a wonderfully rich vein, which meant that much of their time was taken up in washing and dressing the ore. The ore was found in a gangue, a stony matrix with the galena encrusted in concentric coverings of hard silicates. The dressing process was one of washing, knocking, and separating. Firstly the sticky shale had to be washed away, then the clean gangue knocked, or broken open, with a hammer, followed by further washing and separating out of the ore. For this work they needed several shallow tubs, a dressing floor, dishes and sieves – all of which had to be made, or adapted, from utensils around the farm. But, with Alice's help, they managed to contrive all which was required for a very simple process, in which it could truly be said that every grain of ore was produced by hand.

But with the cutting and dressing of timber, the digging, the timbering of the shaft, the disposal of the spoil, and the washing and dressing of ore, progress was tediously slow, so that after several weeks the shaft was only some four yards, or two fathoms deep.

These lead mine shafts were called grooves, and their depth was always given in fathoms. It was customary to sink down for some eight to ten fathoms, and then to create a landing, and to tunnel sideways for a few yards before sinking further. A windlass was then erected over the top of the shaft to hoist up the spoil in leather buckets, with a winder, and a carrier on each landing. In this way, ore could be brought to the surface from depths exceeding fifty fathoms, but only by the use of quite an army of winders and drawers – as the carriers were called – and are still called today in the Lancashire coal mines. The miner at the rock face was known as the pickman.

When, billions of years ago, the earth's crust cooled, the great compressive forces of its shrinkage caused it to crack and crinkle – like a shrivelled apple – creating cracks or faults in the earth's surface, with one side of the fault being thrust upwards from a few feet to many hundreds of feet above the other. In this way the Cliviger Gorge was formed with an upthrust of over 1,000 feet creating the near precipitous slopes of Thieveley Scout.

In Cliviger, apart from the main fault which delineates the gorge from Todmorden right through to Burnley, and which the River Calder uses for its bed, there is a subsidiary fault running from the watershed at Crossing-of-Dean in an almost exact east-west direction to Deerplay and Crown Point. As though in honour of Robert Hartley's discovery, this fault is called the Thieveley Lead Mine Fault, and it was at one point where the mineralization had reached near to the surface that Robert had dug his ditch and discovered the ore. The skill, the intuition, the experience, the observation, and above all, the luck of the miner was all concentrated in the task of following the vein, or rake, of ore down into the unknown depths of the earth's crust. It had always been man's experience to find that the deeper he penetrated the richer the deposits. If he were fortunate enough to find the main spout, his fortune was assured. But at a depth where the solidified crust of the earth had given way to the molten core, both the fault, the rock strata, and the lead ore ended abruptly, so that all lead mines had a bottom below which it was useless to probe further. This was the picture which Godfrey and Humphrey, from their experiences in Derbyshire, had in their minds, as they sunk their groove the first few fathoms. It was this picture which drove them on, despite the painful slowness of their progress, to work from dawn till dusk, with the constant promise of an ever-deepening groove. In their own minds they were already 'free miners' on the first step of the ladder from the classless poor, whose only privilege was to work and be ruled, to the class of 'the free' who, in seventeenth-century England, literally owned the earth.

They were not yet deep enough to require a windlass, like those used for deep wells, over the top of their groove. They hoisted out the spoil using a length of rope knotted for handgrips at regular intervals, and with this, one man hauled up the buckets, hand over hand, from the pickman at the bottom of the hole. The pickman also used the rope for climbing in and out – walking vertically up the rough poles which shored up the sides.

The bucket was emptied onto a floor of stone flags – the sorting floor – the galena was sorted out here and put into a shallow tub for washing; this process was known as buddling, and the tub as a buddle. Later buddles were rectangular wooden flumes with a constant stream of water running through, thus carrying and washing the ore from the sorting to the dressing floor.

The two men interchanged the work, for each task exercised a different set of muscles, and in this way they obtained relief without delaying the work. Also too much hauling on the rope brought the skin off their hands. And when they had a sufficient pile on the sorting floor, they sorted and washed the ore and wheeled away the useless spoil to fill in hollows in Robert Hartley's land.

But the day came, with a paralysing shock, when, as Godfrey leaned over the mouth of the groove against the wooden straining bar, with the rope dangling down into the shaft from his hands, he was suddenly seized from behind by two men, to be dragged around to face two other men and the constable. They were all armed with heavy sticks. The constable walked to the straining bar, and leaning over shouted down to Humphrey:

'Now come thee on out, tha'rt under arrest for stealing the King's ore.'

There was nothing Humphrey could do. He was caught like a rat in a trap. But the man still had his mouth, and it had talked him out of many precarious situations in the past.

'Nay, I'm not stealing the King's ore, as the first discoverers of the mine we have the right, as written down by Parliament in the reign of the blessed Queen, so long as we pay our cope to the King.'

'And 'as ta paid thi cope?'

'Nay we havena' selt any ore yet. But, when we has a load, we shall tek it to t'Barmaster at Wirksworth to be assayed and weighed; and he will take his dues, and one-thirteenth for the King, and one-tenth for the Vicar. A've bin doin' it all mi life, and A've ne'er bin arrested yet.'

The constable was clearly confused, but fell back upon his authority.

'Well A've got mi orders from Justice Nowell that tha's got to be teken in for diggin' for t'King's ore on t'Cliviger Common. Tha'll 'av to argue thi case wi' t'Justices. Now are ta cumin' eyout or 'ave we to fetch thi?'

Humphrey swung himself up the rope, and climbed out of the groove; two of the men ran forward to hold him, but suddenly drew back at the concentration of his looks.

'Keep thi hands off mi,' he warned them in a low voice. 'Now,' he said turning to the constable, 'let's go and see this fancy Justice of thine, and let go of that fellow while tha's at it.'

'Nay, tha cannot see t'Justice today. My orders are to lock thee up i' Towneley Hall, until he can decide to see thee, and there should be three a' thee; wheer's t'other fellow?'

'Nay, there's nobbut two un us.'

'Reet, well, come on – let's be goin' – A've to fetch Mr Townley to get thee two locked up.'

Having decided to talk himself out of trouble, there was nothing he could do but concur, so nodding to Godfrey, he set off in the direction of the farm track with the guards crowding round him. They had been promised free ale, and a sixpence each when the prisoners were safely behind bars.

'Na then,' said the constable, 'not that way – o'er here.' And he turned them away from the farm towards Black Clough and Stonehouses Cote, the nearest way to Towneley Hall.

Disturbed by the persistent barking of their guard dog, Alice Hartley came out of the farmhouse in time to see the group of men set off in the direction of Stonehouses. Calling and running she brought them to a halt, and rapidly caught up with them. She had seen Godfrey and Humphrey, and recognized the constable.

'What are thi up to?' she gasped.

'A'm tekin these men in t'dungeons i'Towneley Hall for stealing the King's lead.'

'They've not stolen owt, all t'ore's still here for t'King to tek his share.'

'Aye that's as may be, but it's up to Justice to decide. A've had mi orders to lock 'em up, and A'm cumin back tomorn for t'ore and A'll 'appen be tekin thee in as well.'

'Nay we've 'ad nowt to do wi' it, nobbut givin' 'em a bite to eat, now and then, for t'help they've gi'en us around t'farm.'

'Well, thee stick to that tale, and tha'll 'appen be alright.'

With these wards the constable ordered his men on, and

the party left Alice standing in a temporary coma of despair.

When Robert returned from shepherding on the high moors, he passed by the mine workings, and seeing that everything was left in disarray, he had an immediate premonition of disaster. He ran the last short distance to his home to hear the whole story from Alice's despairing lips.

'Now then, lass, it looks bad, but there must be summat we can do.'

'Nay we munna do owt or t'constable said he'd 'av us i't'dungeons wi' 'em.'

'Well t'first thing we'll do is get all yon ore out o't' turf house and stack it out on t'Common.'

'Nay thou musna hide it, he' cumin for it tomorn.'

'A'm noan goin' to hide it, A'm just gettin' it off our land, so's as they've nowt agin us, and A'll show 'im wheer it be when 'e cums.'

So they worked late into the evening, removing every scrap of ore from their farm buildings, and arranging it in a cache on the Common, as though it had been stored there all the time.

The very act of doing something to safeguard their position helped to alleviate their fears, but neither of them could sleep that night, and were glad when the first rays of daylight flickered over Black Hameldon across the valley. But even then they could not rid their minds of anxiety, the catastrophic turn of events dominated their every thought. They could talk of nothing else, and discussed, over and over again, what they ought to do. The days when every man had his lord, and the great man looked after his own were gone. The common people were on their own, without rights or privileges, to be whipped, and even hung for the most trivial offence. Their only hope lay in the support of their fellow labourers, and their families having influence with some powerful member of the squirearchy. But Robert and Alice realized that they dare not appeal to Thomas Whitaker; and Richard Townley was a remote figure in his fortified mansion at the foot of the valley, spending much of his time at his estate of Nocton in Lincolnshire. He had also remained a staunch Catholic, and because of this, was completely divorced from the Protestant establishment, except when they required his help in the use of his wealth and fortified mansion house, with its several dungeons deep down within the foundations of the massive walls.

They decided that the best they could do was send word to Alice's father, the copyholder Nicholas Mercer in Rochdale, to see if he could enlist the influence of some powerful gentleman. So Robert set off for Rochdale, where he would also be safer from arrest, and Alice awaited the coming of the constable.

Having, with a woman's intuition, seen the designs in the man's eyes – she went outside for the wolfhound, Max, brought him into the house and ordered him to lie down in front of the hearth. And when the constable came straight in, with scarcely a knock on the door, the guard dog sprang straight for his throat, and bore him back against the wall. Alice ordered the dog down, but from then on, with Max baring his teeth at the constable's every move, she was in complete command.

His first enquiries were about the whereabouts of her

husband, and she told him that Robert was out on the Common looking to the sheep. Saying that he had come to arrest Robert, that he had some men outside and that he could wait all day if need be, he sat down in Robert's chair and stared insolently across at her. Noting her nervous agitation accentuating her femininity, he became more desirous than ever for her, and did suggest that if she took him to her bed, he would leave Robert free; but she took up his challenge.

'Tha canna arrest him for he has had nowt to do wi' diggin' for t'lead. Old Thomas from t'Holme 'as warned him as if he so much as hears on 'im diggin' on t'Common he'll tek farm off us, and Robert's not such a fool as to risk that.'

So the constable decided that once again he would have to bide his time, but he vowed that if he couldn't have her soon, he'd have her ducked in the Brun, by Burnley Parish Church, as a witch and a deceiver of men. That would teach her who was the boss in these parts.

'Now thi brother and his mate weant tell us wheer they've hidden th'ore they've getten. Does ta know wheer it is, cos if tha doesna tell me A'll tek that husband o' thine in for helpin' 'em.'

'Nay a doant know nowt about it, we've tellt 'em to keep off Old Thomas' land, except for fillin' in a few holes which were a danger to t'beasts.'

Just then two men came to the door.

'We've fun' a pile o' summat up agin t'farm wall. Tha'd best cum, and look at it to see if it's what tha'rt after.'

The constable went out, and did not return for some time.

'We've fun' what we're after, and it's a good job for thee it wi'ant on t'farm.'

Then when they were leaving, his resentment against Alice having subsided with the success of finding the ore, he shouted back to her:

'If tha doesna want that brother o'thine to starve, tha'd better tek 'em some vittals. Tha can't expect Mr Townley to feed 'em.'

CHAPTER VIII

The Reprieve

Roger Nowell was contemplating his good fortune, at ease, seated before his huge fireplace in a most comfortable chair, smoking a pipe of the very latest tobacco from the colony of Virginia, and sipping a wine from Oporto, which was taking the place of French and Spanish brands.

He had, earlier in the day, sent off his dispatch to Sir Edward Newburgh, detailing his discovery of the illicit lead mine in the Cliviger wastelands, of his capture and imprisonment of the miners and the sequestration of over three hundredweights of lead ore. He had proposed, if the Chancellor be so gracious, that he and his cousin Thomas Whitaker – who held the nearby Cliviger freeholds, and one other gentleman, should form a company to develop the mine under a lease from the Duchy, paying their full dues to the Duchy and duties to the King. He put forward the humble suggestion that, as the common rogues whom he had caught were criminals without rights, in law he, Roger, was the true and first discoverer of the mine.

All that he need do now was occupy his mind and business time to the discovery of a suitable surveyor or undertaker, with the necessary skills, to superintend the management of the mine workings. There were lead mines – not a dozen miles away – in the Forest of Bowland, and the Duke of Cumberland had extensive workings, and a smelt mill at Grassington on the River Wharfe. He would make discreet enquiries, and meanwhile he could only wait, with pleasurable anticipation, for the Chancellor's reply.

Meanwhile, at Thieveley, Alice and Robert continued in an atmosphere of deep anxiety and fear. In an age when even petty thievery carried the death sentence, and men were thrown into prison and hung, almost on suspicion alone, with no proper evidence brought against them, the true enormity of the charge, of stealing the King's lead, with evidence beyond dispute, left them in a state of despair, to which was added a real fear for their own lives, and almost a certainty that they would lose their farm, and with it their home and their livelihood.

Their only relief was to occupy their minds with the farmwork. To their daily tasks was now added the additional one of carrying a basket of food and flagon of ale, with straw and warm covering to counteract the persistent cold and dampness, the six-mile walk, there and back to Towneley Hall. They even had to pay out some of their hard-earned savings to the Townley underlings to gain admission to the prisoners. The Townley servants did not look upon this as an imposition, but as a right, in compensation for the additional work which they had to do, and if they were not recompensed the poor prisoner had little hope of attention. Under the law the prisoner was only entitled to a bare sustenance, just to keep him alive, and this was interpreted as being a dish of water with a hunk of bread daily, and an armful of straw thrown into one corner of a bare stone cell. The task which the servants resented most was the removal of the rough bucket of excrement, which they performed daily, more for their own benefit than that of the prisoner. If the prisoner had no relative or friend, he was indeed in a miserable condition. On the contrary, life for those whose relatives were able to help could be made tolerable. So long as the jailers were bribed, there seemed no limit to the amenities with which he could be provided. Sir Walter Raleigh and John Milton wrote their famous books, *The History of the World* and *Paradise Lost* while in gaol. But the welfare of the prisoner depended upon their families and not upon the state. In addition the final verdict was often influenced by the concern or lack of it, shown by friends and relatives.

The dungeons at Towneley Hall can be visited today, by arrangement, and visitors are shown one cell with a hole driven outwards through the foundations. The curious visitor peers through a distance of over twenty feet to the little hole of daylight at the far end. He is told that this is an escape tunnel, but the disposal of the stonework, for a man confined in a small cell, seems so unlikely that it may be a ventilation hole to dry out and purify the air in these lower regions made when the dungeons were no longer in use. But the hole is significant in revealing, at a glance, the massive nature of the mediaeval fortress, and the hopeless position of any prisoner incarcerated within its depths.

The spirits of the prisoners were revived from the low ebb of their first dreadful night by the food and drink, and indeed by the sight of Alice, as she was allowed into their cell. They were able to ask for more straw and sheepskin coverings so that they could rest in comparative warmth and comfort.

Humphrey was still confident that their plea of being the first discoverers of the mine, and that they would automatically have paid their dues to the King through the barmaster at Wirksworth, would soon bring them their freedom, and see them back at work in the mine with official blessing. Further hope came on the third day when Nicholas Mercer arrived on his way from Rochdale to put their case to Roger Nowell at Read Hall. He had visited an attorney in Rochdale, and ascertained that a statute was passed in the last year of Elizabeth, 1603, setting out the right of the first discoverer of a mine to the first choice of a stake in the mine. There is little doubt that this legislation was primarily to encourage the discovery of gold and silver mines, at a time when the wealth of a nation was judged by its stock of bullion, and gold and silver coinage, to enable England to compete with the immense wealth of Spain. Fortunately for the two prisoners, the statute also covered the commoner metals – zinc, copper, tin and lead which were needed for the manufacture of arms, pigs of lead being issued to every company of soldiers and to every warship, for the casting of bullets, even whilst the battle was in progress.

But Nicholas returned from his visit to Read Hall to tell Alice and Robert that he had not had an encouraging meeting with Justice Nowell. It was the Justice's opinion that the two men had forfeited their right by not registering their discovery, and as men of no property, and common felons, they could expect little mercy from the

law. He was only waiting for instructions from the Duchy
Chancellor before passing the death sentence. It was
agreed not to pass this dreadful news on to the prisoners,
but sleepless nights and a blackness of despair returned to
the Thieveley farmhouse.

Nicholas told them of his determination to go to
Westminster to put his case, and what money he had, with
the Chancellor; but he greatly feared that he might be too
late, that the Chancellor's sentence of death would pass
him on the road. However, with his son's life at stake, he
had no choice but to go.

There came a day when Alice, working in the garden, saw
a party of men approaching down the trackway from
Thieveley Pike. There was one man on horseback, slightly
in front, and followed by a group of men with long staves
leading a few ponies with full packs.

'Oh God!' thought Alice, 'Here comes a man from the
Duchy with more trouble for us.'

In a numbness of despair she stood by the farm gate as
they approached. The man halted his horse in front of her.

'Are you Alice Hartley – Nicholas Mercer's daughter?'

'Yes.'

'Well my name is Ralph Highley – I bring orders from
the Chancellor of the Duchy of Lancaster in respect of a
lead mine on the Cliviger Common, and I wish to discuss
this matter with your husband Robert Hartley.'

Alice's normally colourful face turned pale with fear.

'What do you want wi' him, he's not here, he's out on
t'moor wi' t'sheep? I doan't know when he'll be back.'

'Is thi brother Godfrey and his mate Humphrey Greaves

anywhere about, for A'm looking for them as well; but A would like to talk to thee and Robert first.

'Tha knows full well that Godfrey and Humphrey aint here.'

'Nay a doan't, a've cum all this way to see 'em.'

Alice was clearly bewildered.

''as ta cum to tek Robert deawn to t'dungeons i' Towneley Hall?'

Ralph could only laugh at her question.

'Nay, nowt o't'sort. A've come wi' orders from t'Duchy to start a lead mine up here, and I don't want to harm thee or Godfrey and Humphrey at all – I want 'em to tek a share and help me wi' t'mine.'

'They canna do that – they're locked up i't'dungeons i' Towneley Hall, and me and Robert mun 'a' nowt to do wi' it or Old Thomas Whitaker will put us on t'parish.'

'Now what's all this about? I tell thee tha's nowt to fear from me – in fact if Godfrey and Humphrey 'ave got themselves stuck in jail a'll soon 'ave 'em out.'

'You will?'

'Aye, sure I will, A needs their 'elp, bad, wi't'mine. Now a've ridden a long way today to see 'em, so if a can stable mi horse, and have a bite to eat at your table we can 'appen sort summat out. A'll pay thee well for all tha does.'

Alice opened the gate. Ralph Highley ordered his men to tie up the ponies, and to sit themselves down behind the wall on the Common. After seeing to his horse, he followed Alice into the house, and while she prepared food and drink for him, she told him of the constable's visit, the miners' imprisonment, and the serious charge with the death penalty hanging over their heads.

And much to Alice's bewilderment, as the story unfolded, Ralph became more and more amused, until at the end he was laughing out loud.

'Well, damn me – A've never heard owt so funny.'.

'It's noan damn well funny to me,' Alice replied sharply.

'Ah but it will be when tha next sees t'constable, and tha can laugh at 'im for mekin' a fool of hisell. I have papers here authorizing me to dig for, and smelt, lead ore on the Cliviger Wastes, and they're dated three weeks afore that fancy constable came pokin' his nose in. Now I wants Godfrey and Humphrey for my first miners to sink the first groove, and as my workmen they've every right to 'ave made a start. You just leave this to me, a'll 'ave 'em out o' those dungeons i' no time.'

'My God – I 'ope tha can,' said Alice fervently, and he noted the relief and hope in her face.

'There'll be nowt to it,' he replied, 'just thee leave it to me, and thee and thi 'usband 'as nowt to worry about either, A want thee to help me all tha can, not wi't'mine, but wi' 'ousing and vittals and ale, and things like that; and if tha can board me or mi partner, William Butler, for odd nights we'll pay thee well for everything.'

'A'd do it for nowt if tha can get Godfrey out o'trouble.'

'Nay, lass, we'll pay thi for all tha does. Now wheer 'ave I to goa to get them lads out o' jail?'

'Tha'd a to go and see Justice Nowell at Read Hall – it's a good ten mile away. Tha canna goa today.'

'But a'll go first thing i't'morning, and a'll promise thi this, a'll bring them two men back wi' mi.'

When Robert was on his way home from shepherding, he

saw, with great alarm, the party of men outside the farm, and for a time he scouted round the outside perimeter wondering if it was safe to go in or whether he would fall into a trap, as had Godfrey and Humphrey. But gambling on the fact that the men would not know him, he joined the company, and asked them casually what they were about.

'We've cum wi' Ralph Highley to start a lead mine.'

'Tha's what?'

'A tell thi we've cum wi' our boss Ralph Highley to start a lead mine.'

'And wheer is thy boss?'

'He's in t'heas wi' t'missis as lives here.'

At that, Robert went straight in, for his second surprise. After hearing the news he was only too pleased to go out to Ralph's men, and help them to unload the ponies, to turn them out to pasture and make the men comfortable in the barn.

'Now th'art all reet here, but whatever tha does, doan't set alight to that hay.'

In the morning, after Robert had shown him the mine shaft, Ralph set his men to work building turf houses nearby.

'We wiant do owt wi' t'diggin', until we get Godfrey and Humphrey here to put us in t'way.'

And with these reassuring words he departed on his ride to see Roger Nowell. Robert set off in haste, once again, for Rochdale to try to contact Nicholas Mercer before he began his long journey to London.

After a day of alternate hopes and anxieties, as evening

approached Alice could not restrain herself from going outside at regular intervals to look for the returning travellers, but as so often happens in such cases, she was in the house when Max warned her of someone's approach. Then Godfrey and Humphrey burst in to seize her in their arms and to dance her round the kitchen table, whilst Ralph stood, smiling, in the doorway. It was an uproarious home-coming in which Ralph was the hero of the hour. But when Robert arrived to say that Nicholas had already departed on his journey, Godfrey made up his mind immediately.

'I'm off,' he said. 'I'll get after 'im, and if I keeps goin' all neet I'll 'appen catch him tomorn. I know t'road like palm o' mi 'and, A knows all t'inn keepers on t'way so A'll cetch 'im if it kills me.'

So once again there was hustle and bustle for Alice in packing up food, and once again Ralph came up with the answer by telling Godfrey to take his horse.

'He's done nowt today – nobbut eat oats i'Roger Nowell's stable – so tha can push him hard and take some of the fat off 'im,' he laughed.

So, clad in warm clothing, with a good pack of food, Godfrey set off into the night for his wild ride over the top of Thieveley Pike to Rochdale, to give the good news to his mother to catch up with his father before he had left Lancashire.

Meanwhile, at Read Hall, all Roger Nowell's anxieties had returned. As he had read the order papers which this man Ralph Highley had produced, the whole dreadful implications for him of their meaning sank in. In the papers were the names of Godfrey Mercer and Humphrey

Greaves as first discoverers of the mine, and a full licence for this same Ralph Highley to dig, smelt, and sell lead from off the Cliviger Wastes. There was nothing else Roger could have done, other than give the man written instructions for the release of the prisoners, and get rid of him before his temper got the upper hand.

And now, as he sat in his comfortable chair, he wondered anxiously what the reply to his message to the Chancellor would be. He had no illusions about the ruthlessness of Sir Edward Newburgh, Chancellor to King Charles of His Highness' Duchy of Lancaster.

CHAPTER IX

William Butler Takes Charge

The above events almost brought the year 1628 to a close. Ralph Highley returned to Rochdale, leaving behind assurances that there would always be a meare of ground available for the two miners, and that Robert and Alice Hartley would be well paid for all the help they could give. Godfrey and Humphrey were to carry on with their work, but they must not sell any of the ore, which by grant of the Duchy now belonged to Ralph and his partner William Butler; but they would be paid for the ore, in the Derbyshire manner, when the partners had built a smelting hearth and could convert it into saleable lead. Ralph departed with the smiles and good wishes of the Thieveley folk rounding off, for him, what had been an unexpectedly easy passage, and for them almost a miracle of deliverance. He took his men with him, for in truth he had only brought them, and their staves, in case he had met with a totally different reception.

Shortly afterwards William Butler arrived, and spent several hours watching the miners at work, and studying the lay of the land. After a meal in the farmhouse, he had a long conversation with Robert asking shrewd questions about the names, holdings, and characters of the surrounding freeholders, and of the availability of timber in the woodlands, of the owners of packhorse ponies, and of the nearby smithies.

After he had gone some of Alice's foreboding returned; it seemed to her that the farm was no longer their own, that some sinister power, beyond her control, was taking it over, and Humphrey did not help when he remarked:

'We'll 'ave to watch yon man. He's a different kettle o' fish from that Ralph Highley. A wouldna trust 'im as far as A could throw 'im.'

And later they heard that William had been riding round the district negotiating with the freeholders, and spreading the news of the impending development of a lead mine at Thieveley, financed by himself and his partner. Rumour soon exaggerated the wealth of these go-ahead clothiers from the important and wealthy wool town of Rochdale. And perhaps most surprisingly of all, William had sat long hours with old Thomas Whitaker in the Holme, and at last came to an agreement with him that the partners could build a smelting house on Thomas' freehold land at Thieveley. There were several reasons for this, the principal one being that they were relieved from entering into complicated negotiations with the Duchy to erect a building on the common land. It was far simpler to negotiate with the man on the spot. Another reason was that there was scarcely a square yard of level land available except at the end of the knoll of Dean Scout, where Thieveley Farm was situated for this same reason. A third reason was the availability of the ancient road, the Hacgate as Bacup men called it, or Blackgate as named on the Cliviger side, which climbed out of the

Cliviger Gorge from Crossing-of-Dean, passed Thieveley Pike, to Sharneyford, and thence into William's parish of Rochdale.

William then soothed the Hartleys and the miners, by offering Robert a rent of four shillings a year for building the smelt-house on his tenanted farm, and explaining to the miners that he would pay them day wages for helping to open up the mine shafts, until the smelt-house was in operation, when they could take a meare of land and work a groove of their own. He began to pay them a weekly wage of four shillings each, which, because of the terrible depression in the cloth trade at that time, was considered to be good money. He promised that he would pay them for the ore, which they had already produced, when it was smelted into lead, on an old principle that no man could reasonably expect payment until his produce had been converted into coin.

Godfrey made a journey home to Rochdale to explain the situation to Isaac Clegg, that they were working temporarily for Highley and Butler on day wages, but that their partnership would be resumed when the smelt-house was working and that they would then be able to pay him his share of the ore produced. Isaac was quite content to let the matter rest as a long-term investment.

William Butler turned out to be a powerhouse of energy, with considerable organizing ability. The site of the mine soon became an area of intense activity. In addition to Godfrey's first groove, the sinking of three other grooves – by Hugh Bateman, Thomas Whitaker and Henry Flint, all working for day wages – commenced. In addition, businessmen with capital to invest arrived, and brought with them Derbyshire miners to sink their own shafts by agreement with Highley and Butler – as was the custom in Derbyshire. So there were two systems working, side by side – Highley and Butler sinking three shafts under a management system akin to their factories in Rochdale with men on day wages; and four shafts being sunk by independent partnerships, self-financed, and paid only for the ore they produced. This led to a complicated system of storing the ore in separate batches with each partnership jealously guarding its own. Robert and Alice were brought in to find secure storage space in the farm buildings, and even ended up with ore in the farmhouse itself.

To add to the scene of activity a small village of turf houses sprang up, the married men bringing their wives and children; whilst trollops and desperately homeless women arrived to care for the single men, to share their food and their improvised beds. It was a cruel environment, perched 1,000 feet up on the hillside in one of the wettest areas of the British Isles, but these were desperate times, and there was great optimism that the mine could become an Eldorado.

William Butler encouraged all this development because he realized that if he were to build a smelt mill there must be a sufficient supply of ore to keep the furnace burning continuously. The economy of the smelting of metals depended upon the smelting hearth remaining continuously in a molten state, the cost of cooling down and reheating the hearth being totally prohibitive, so that the furnace had to be kept going night and day, and even at weekends. In Derbyshire and the Yorkshire Dales it was quite usual for one smelt mill to serve all the mines in its area – the only limit being the distance or severity of the route along which the ore had to be brought to the mill by packhorse ponies.

But at Thieveley the nearest mill was at Grassington, some thirty miles away, so the partners considered that they had no option but to build a mill of their own, and expand the mine to keep it running.

With the coming of the spring of 1629 the pace of the work accelerated. The timber for which William had negotiated began to arrive, by packhorse, in a constant stream, to be sawn into lengths, and immediately used by the men sinking the seven grooves. Meanwhile the smith, Nicholas Bailey, from the ancient smithy at Cliviger Mill Bridge, where the Long Causeway crossed over the Calder, was engaged to make and fit windlasses over the shafts. The rapidity with which the shafts were being sunk can be gauged from the fact that candles had to be purchased during the first week of March, and from then on were bought at the rate of two to three dozen a week. Also, during this week, the first windlass was being used, with a local man, John Eastwood, employed as winder.

Bearing in mind the Chancellor's instructions to keep proper accounts, an out-of-work Cliviger clothworker, who must have been taught to write by his master, was engaged as clerk-of-the-works at a wage of six shillings per week, a 50 per cent increase in wages over the other workmen. It is from the accounts of this man, Robert Wilkinson, fortunately preserved in the Public Record

Office, that a week-by-week reconstruction of the progress of the mine may be attempted. His accounts begin for the last week of February 1629.

Meanwhile, Ralph Highley, ranging far and wide on his clothier's business, had discovered a man, Charles Core, from the parish of Bashall Eaves, near Clitheroe, who professed to having worked in the smelting mill on Waddington Fell near Slaidburn; and, taking the man at his word, Ralph sent him to Thieveley at agreed wages of ten shillings a week to superintend the building of the mill. Charles Core, also, started work during this momentous first week in March; and one other event, which passed unnoticed but was of greater significance than all the others, was that two brothers, Edmund and John Milne, were started to bail water out of the shafts. This task was performed during the night so that sinking and ore getting could proceed during the daytime.

The smelt-house was built after the fashion of a seventeenth-century stone barn, and considering that all the stone, including the roofing slates, had to be hewn and fashioned out of the hillside, that all timber had to be felled and shaped by hand from the local woodlands, and that the smith had to forge all the iron work from wrought-iron billets, and that everything had to be carted up the mountainous track to Thieveley on the backs of ponies, the progress was amazingly swift.

In those early days of industrial development most of the rural communities were served by two types of road: one for wheeled transport, and the other for packhorses, known respectively as the broadgate and the narrowgate. From certain place names such as Bradget Hey, there is no doubt that Cliviger had its broadgate, and we have already mentioned the Blackgate which ran by the Thieveley farmhouse. This road is referred to by Robert Hartley, in a petition, as being fit for carriages, so it was obviously a broadgate, and would have crossed the valley floor at the watershed where there was no flooded river to cross. But with Thieveley being part of the domesne lands of the Holme, there was also a track directly from the Holme to Thieveley farmhouse. This track forded the Calder a little to the east of the Holme, and then zig-zagged up the precipitous slopes of the hillside. This was the narrowgate to Thieveley, and was the steep and dangerous track along which the ponies brought all the materials to the mine. During that spring of 1629 there were as many as eight named men with their packponies 'leading' materials of all kinds to the mine. The word 'leading' is interesting as it was still in use in Cliviger up to recently to describe the process of carting loose hay out of the meadows into the barns. But the tractor and the baling machine have now put an end to that.

A skilled dry-waller named Abraham Whitaker, who does not appear to be a near relation of the Whitakers of Holme, but who came from the nearby hamlet of Stiperden on the Yorkshire side of the border, raised the walls of the house in the astonishingly short time of three weeks, so that by the end of March there was the ceremony of house-rearing, in which all the men assisted in the lifting up and setting in place of the roof trees. For this they were rewarded with free ale, brewed by Alice Hartley.

At the same time wood was being sawn, and laths

procured, while slate stones were being quarried and dressed on the lands of Widow Sagar. These must have been the lands of the present-day Sagar Fold Farm. That all this material arrived promptly is proved by the fact that the roof went on within a week of the 'house-rearing'.

By the second week of April two skilled masons were working on the dressing and erection of stonework for the smelting hearth and its chimney, whilst down at the forge, Nicholas Bailey had finished the construction of a pair of bellows, using two cowhides, which had cost the great sum of £3 2s 6d. There is a separate item in the accounts for the sum of 1s 6d for the carting of the bellows for the two miles from the smithy to the mine. This is the equivalent of some £30 of today's money, £15 per mile, which gives an assessment of the cost of transport in the early seventeenth century, before the revolution brought about by the canals.

Meanwhile large quantities of a new type of wood, chopwood for burning, were being delivered, together with a small amount of coal, and three men and one woman were engaged cutting and carting sods. By 18 April the work was complete, and Charles Core, aided by his brother, and with two men working the bellows, commenced smelting.

The smelting hearth was like a blacksmith's forge, except that in place of the iron table there was a stone trough, which gradually filled up with molten lead. When full, this trough held about three hundredweights of lead, which was never removed. The trick was to keep it in a continuous molten state to provide a liquid pool into which the ore finally gave up its lead. The fire, of mixed wood and coal, was lit on the hearth, and an iron pipe, the tuyere, blew the draft from the bellows into the heart of the fire.

The bellows were situated outside against the back wall of the furnace, and were operated by the legs of the blowers as though pedalling a bicycle. This proved to be the Achilles heel of the system, for the smelters required a constant draft, ten hours at a time, for a day's smelting, and such effort was beyond the physical capabilities of the blowers, who had to work harder than galley slaves. One smelter fed chopwood and ore into the fire, whilst the other worked the semi-molten brouse with an iron bar known as a gavelock.

The great hearthstone, in front of the fire, had a worktop, and the skill of the chief smelter was in drawing the molten brouse onto this worktop, and then pushing it on the end of his gavelock into the hottest part of the fire, which should be immediately over the pool of lead in the trough. A groove was cut into the worktop so that when the trough was full the liquid lead ran out, and was directed by a spout into an iron vessel, known as the sumpter pot, which also had a fire burning beneath it to keep the metal in a molten state.

An old man or boy was on hand to ladle the lead out of the sumpter pot into stone moulds, of a standard size, in which it solidified into ingots. These ingots were usually stamped with the name of the mine or a code number, whilst the lead was still soft. The lead would only run from the ore at a certain temperature, and should the heat of the fire drop only half a degree below this critical figure the metal would refuse to run and remain in a sticky spongy mess. The whole skill of the smelter was in maintaining the working part of the furnace at the required temperature, from his experience of judging the heat by the colour of the fire, and manipulating the brouse into that location. Hence the constant altercations between the two men sweating in front of the fire, and the two outside, wet through with perspiration, from their labouring at the bellows. And if the lead refused to run each would blame the other, even to the exchange of blows and the bringing of blood, during which fighting, the fire would die down and many hours of smelting time lost.

Because of the smallness of the operation at Thieveley it was not possible to employ two shifts of smelters to keep the mill on stream night and day, so after a ten-hour day, the fire was banked up with coal, and then completely covered over with damp sods to keep in the heat, and if possible maintain the three hundredweights of lead in the hearth in a molten state. The first task in the morning was to remove the sods and beat up the fire. During the long day's work the smelters were constantly engaged in keeping the fire clean by removing the ash and slag which floated on top of the molten lead in the hearth, and only allowing clean lead to run into the pot. There was also the second fire to attend to beneath the sumpter pot. The quantity of chopwood burned was truly astronomical, as many as twenty horse loads a day.

But despite all these difficulties, a first smelting was accomplished within six weeks of work beginning on the building of the smelting house, a remarkable achievement by any standards, and a tribute to the driving force and organizing ability of William Butler.

CHAPTER X

Trouble at the Mine

Smelting and ore-getting continued throughout the month of May, but as the grooves were deepened, the water problem became more acute, to such an extent that three Milne brothers, Edmund, John and James, were employed on night work in bailing out. The steady flow of packhorses continued to bring wood; two brothers Anthony and James Thomas spent half of each week turf getting, to damp down the fire; and an additional man was engaged to carry the ore to the mill, and presumably to stack the finished ingots, in Alice Hartley's house for safety.

But by the early weeks of June it became obvious to William Butler that all was not well. The costs of the whole operation were far too high; and, even worse, two factors threatened the very life of the mine. Firstly there was this problem of smelting. According to repute a Derbyshire hearth would smelt one fowdre, or fother, that is 19$^{1}/_{2}$ cwt, of lead per day, but here at Thieveley only some eight tons had been produced after six weeks of this most expensive process. Charles Core and his brother were being paid 16s 6d per week in wages, more than double the pay of the miners; and, understandably, William Butler was beginning to doubt their proficiency.

But the smelters maintained that there should be four blowers to keep the blast going, the wood was too damp, and the ore was not like the ore from Waddington Fell – it just would not run. And perhaps worst of all, instead of the anticipated half ton of lead from one ton of ore, they were only converting half of this amount. Isaac Clegg had reported that the ore which he had taken down to the Wirksworth mill had yielded more than half and half. In short, the smelting of lead ore at Thieveley was totally uneconomic.

The second problem was the incessant seepage of water out of the blue shale into the shafts. According to ancient custom it was the responsibility of the mine owner to keep the workings free from water. Otherwise they were abandoned. At Thieveley, as the shafts penetrated below the two-fathom mark, the water threatened to take over. Despite bailing out at night, the miners were flooded out before they could complete their day's work.

The mine had only been in operation for three months when William Butler realized that it could not continue much longer unless some drastic action was taken. He put the seriousness of the situation to Ralph Highley. Here they were with a depression in the wool trade, and the venture which they had hoped would save them was heading for disaster; and, looking over their shoulders was the sinister figure of the Chancellor of the Duchy. He had insisted upon the keeping of accounts so as to be able to abstract his pound of flesh. But would he believe that the mine, far from being profitable, could involve them in a loss. One could not fool around with such powerful men. However, Highley and Butler were resilient and resourceful men, and after much discussion decided upon a plan.

Firstly, they would stop smelting for the time being, and stockpile the ore, until they could discover a better method. Charles Core and his brother would have to go. They would be immediately relieved of all the ancillary costs of the process. Secondly, in order to keep the workings dry, William proposed the sinking of a water groove, deeper than all the other workings. It was hoped that this would draw off the water into a sump, and the Milne brothers could bail out the water with buckets and windlass, like a domestic well with a rope wrapped round a turntree with one bucket descending as the other was drawn up. They could do this during the daytime whilst the miners worked in the other grooves. And if the water would not drain out by natural seepage, each groove would have to have a connection made to the water groove. The only consolation for this work was the hope that more valuable deposits of ore would be recovered.

The partners also agreed that they could not continue the Derbyshire manner of independent partnerships working their own meares of grounds. They firmly believed that the only hope of profit for them was to operate the whole mine under their own management, with men employed, as they were in their factories, for a weekly wage.

The whole operation would have to be under William's strict supervision with the men working to his plan for the drainage of the mine; and, as it was not known whether they would strike ore or not, it was considered only fair to

put them on a wage of 4s 0d a week. All who would not
agree would have to go.

To Alice Hartley the spring of 1629 heralded the
beginnings of a nightmare which was to continue, in
various guises, for the next five years.

The building of the smelt-house on her doorstep
removed whatever order and tidiness which she had
established at the Thieveley farmstead, since first coming
there, with high hopes, when Robert managed to secure
the tenancy. Now all was dirt and dust, with piles of
building materials strewn around, and rough men going
wherever they pleased. Her children loved the disorder
and the excitement, but Alice lost all hope of ever keeping
them clean again. To her they became as the ragamuffins
and street urchins of the nearby towns. Then the little
village of turf houses, which had sprung up on the
Common, offended her Puritan upbringing. A few were
occupied by decent married couples struggling to survive
and bring up their children, but the majority were
alliances of convenience, and even of debauchery, with
men and women alike knocking at her door for ale. And,
sensing her disapproval, they became insolent, and began
to call her Mrs Prim, which some wag changed to Mrs
Pym; and, although the majority did not understand the
allusion, the name stuck. To Alice's mortification they
used it to her face as often as they could; it was 'Yes, Mrs
Pym. No, Mrs Pym,' followed by unprintable obscenities.
They were always telling her where she could stick things
and which part of their anatomy she could kiss.

And although they came to buy such things as milk,

eggs, oats and rye, Alice soon became certain that they were stealing more than they were buying. Anything of household use would disappear at any moment. They even gained Max's friendship by familiarity, and feeding tit-bits, so that Alice was at her wits end to watch, guard, and lock things up. Men and women roamed everywhere with no respect for private rights. Their new water supply was absorbed in the maelstrom of the ore washing, and their house supply was polluted by dirty water bailed out of the grooves.

But all this was as nothing to her misery when the smelting commenced. The smoke and sulphurous fumes billowed down over the farmstead, and penetrated into every room in the house, covering everything with a fine white ash. Before long she found that the vegetables in her garden refused to grow, and the grass and crops of their small piece of ploughland turned a sickly yellow.

She could not help herself from blaming Robert for encouraging the mine. In the evenings she poured out her frustrations, so that in the end relations became strained. They began to quarrel and tempers burst out of control. Robert tried to justify himself by saying that they must make the most of the opportunity to take and save as much money as they could, to buy their own copyhold farm. But Alice could only point out that more was stolen and damaged than was sold, and so far all they were getting was 4s 0d a year for the ore storage, and 5s 0d a year for the ground rent of the smelt-house, which income would not buy them a farm in a lifetime.

Meanwhile, Alice had grown really fond of Humphrey Greave and had considered it her duty to see that he and her brother were properly housed and fed. Consequently she had run the gauntlet of the village trollops to take cooked food to them, and to tidy up the mens' crude abode. And she liked to stay awhile to talk and enjoy their male company. But the women put another interpretation on these visits, with catcalls as she passed by, and Alice blushed at their suggestions because in truth she did find Humphrey's manliness disturbing. But her greatest humiliation came when two women moved in with the men, and turned her back at the doorway.

'We doant need thee cumin' o'er wi' thi fancy food, and if it's Humphrey tha's after, there's nowt for thee theer, A'll mek sure o' that, if A 'as to drain 'im dry.'

And all the women shrieked with laughter, and sent more obscene calls after her as she returned in complete desolation, still carrying the basket of pastries.

'Thi pasties mustn't a bin good enough.'

'Nay it's noan her pastries that wian't good enough.'

'Humphrey's getten another brush to rub,' and so on, until she could escape and hide her misery in the house.

And to add to her mortification she often noticed Robert laughing and talking with the women in what seemed to her, a too friendly familiarity. She began to wonder if she really knew him. Was he just as coarse and vulgar as they? The lead mine was driving another rift between them.

The two women who had taken up with Godfrey and Humphrey caused further trouble. They began to boast that their men were not just common labourers working for day wages, but were free miners who should have a meare of their own in a business partnership; and, to bring this about, they nagged at the men to have it out with William Butler, and get paid for the ore they produced. So when William returned to Thieveley, Godfrey and Humphrey put it to him that they wanted to return to the Derbyshire manner of working in the groove which they had started; but William told them quite bluntly that they could either work for day wages under his orders, or not at all; and think themselves lucky, for he was giving over smelting, so there would be no money for producing lead ore in their own grooves. Humphrey protested that they had a right to a meare of their own, that is, 32 yards along the vein with 8 yards on either side.

'That's as may be,' replied William, 'but tha wiant get any money out o' me for t'ore so tha can tek it or leave it.'

He knew that they were entitled to this meare, but he also knew that two men of no property, living in a sod house with two whores on the Cliviger wastelands, had no chance of taking their case to the Duchy Court in Westminster.

Godfrey and Humphrey were too proud to be browbeaten and to lose face in front of their paramours, so they left the workings and spent the summer days in idleness on the Common, living on their sacks of oats, rabbits and trout from the Calder, waiting to put their case to Ralph Highley. They found however, that William's words were no idle boast. For the week ending 20 June, the smelt-mill furnace was allowed to burn out, the blowers were dismissed, and Charles Core and his brother departed in a rage. There was no longer work for the turf-getters, and the loads of burning wood and coal ceased to arrive. One by one the independently operated meares were deserted, the Derbyshire men disappeared, and the men who were financing them no longer came to follow their progress. Even the clerk Robert Wilkinson was dismissed. The deserted grooves slowly filled up with water.

William himself was as active as ever. When he had first come to the mine, he had brought with him from Rochdale a man called Nicholas Birch and his wife Jenet, to work for a joint wage of 7s 0d a week. They were both excellent workers, and while the husband had been sinking a shaft, the wife had been in charge of the ore washing; and so much ore was produced that she was provided with two girls to assist her. Now Nicholas, and the three Milne brothers, were set to work on what was to become known as the water groove, while other men began to drive connecting galleries from the other grooves, winning what ore they found for Jenet to break and wash. William had by now reduced the workforce to the day workers of his own choosing, and sent everyone else away from the workings, nor would he allow hangers-on to stand around watching, and staring down into the grooves.

When a cleric from the ecclesiastical parish of Whalley came to claim a tithe, he was told that no wealth had been produced. When he asked to be allowed to see for himself, as he was accustomed to assessing the farmers' crops in order to take his tenth, he was again told that there was nothing to see, and was not allowed to poke and pry into the works.

Ralph Highley also played his part well. He told the

various businessmen, who had financed a meare, that there was nothing, only loss, in the digging and smelting of the ore at Thieveley; that they could continue if they wished, but that he and William Butler could not pay them for the ore produced. So, like true entrepreneurs, they cut their losses and withdrew. However, with a totally different object, Ralph went into the Yorkshire Dales to see the successful smelting of ore at the Duke of Cumberland's mill at Grassington; and he obtained a promise from a smelter called Godfrey Wheatley, to come over to Thieveley when they were ready for him.

The hope which spurred the partners on was the fact that, unlike cloth, of which there were mountains in stock and scarcely any demand, there was a shortage of lead and an ever-increasing clamour for more. Wealthy squires, who were extending and rebuilding their halls, artisan glaziers from the great towns of Rochdale, Manchester and Salford, even potters who used lead to glaze their ware, came of their own accord, despite the fearsome journey, to Thieveley to buy at a price of £10 a ton. This would be the equivalent of around £4,000 of today's money. And when the commissioners for the Army and Navy entered the market, the price would rise even higher. So Ralph and William had high hopes for the ultimate success of the mine, if only they could overcome the initial difficulties.

CHAPTER XI

A Surprise Package from the King

The year 1629 was one of the fateful years of English history. It was the year in which Charles I decided to rule his kingdom without a Parliament.

It was quite easy for him to appoint ministers to form the Privy Council, the equivalent of today's Cabinet, and these men could order their work all the better without the constant interference of Parliament. But the great difficulty, as always, was money. The King had no tax-gathering bureaucracy. The money had been collected and delivered to Westminster by the Knights of the Shires, as Members of Parliament were called, and they had been dismissed.

Being desperate for money to pay his soldiers and sailors and to build a Navy to protect his realm from Philip of Spain and the corsairs of the Barbary Coast, Charles summoned Lord Newburgh, Chancellor of his Duchy of Lancaster to his Chamber in the Palace of Westminster. This would be at the time when Highley and Butler were building the smelt-house at Thieveley.

The King explained to the Chancellor the urgent need to extract all possible extra income from the Duchy, which was administered by the Chancellor as a separate kingdom within a kingdom.

'I am afraid that your honoured father, in a like necessity to your Majesty, investigated all possible means of securing his rightful dues from the subjects of the Duchy, by collecting knight's fees, the sale of baronetcies, and obtaining payments for confirmation of freeholds and copyholds, but if Your Majesty will permit me a little time I will investigate all further sources which time and your illustrious father's generosity may have overlooked.'

'It is our pleasure, and indeed our urgent requirement, that you apply yourself with the greatest diligence to this task.'

The tone and look of the King left the Chancellor in no doubt that his own future depended upon the success or otherwise of his investigations. He clutched at straws to preserve his reputation.

'There is, immediately, one little matter, if I may be permitted to explain, which may be of profit to Your Majesty.'

'And what is that?'

'The Duchy Council some time ago issued orders for the discovery and working of a lead mine in the Duchy wastes of Cliviger, in the County of Lancaster. It is my immediate thought that these mines, if successful, could be operated by a Commission for Your Majesty's sole profit.'

'To whom have these orders been granted?'

'Oh – to men of no consequence, clothiers of the town of Rochdale.'

'Why were these concessions granted to men of no consequence?'

'Your Majesty, it was my belief to have men of this description – who seem to have the money and the diligence to search out such ventures – to prove the richness or otherwise of the mine, when we need have no conscience in taking it from them.'

'That was well thought out, Chancellor, we must discover whether this mine may be of greater profit to us. Appoint a Commission to investigate this matter on our behalf, and do this with the greatest urgency, authorized by my Great Seal of the Duchy.'

'I will instruct my secretary to have the documents prepared with the greatest dispatch. Would Your Majesty wish to choose the, er, gentlemen of this Commission?'

'Gentlemen?'

'Your Majesty, if I may humbly suggest, it would not be meet to appoint noblemen to such a matter of trade and industry, and there are gentlemen in that locality who, because of favours granted, would apply themselves more diligently to the task.'

'It shall be as you propose. Prepare a list for my approval, but I warn you – no Knights of the Shires or recusants.'

The Chancellor called for his sedan chair, and made the short journey into London to the Duchy House in Holborn. Here were the chambers of Sir Gilbert Gerard, head clerk to Sir Edward Moseley, Attorney-General of the Duchy, and the offices of their clerks and scriveners. Deep down in the dark cellars was the interrogation room with its torture chamber and dreaded rack.

Sir Gilbert was instructed to draw up an order for the appointment of a Commission to investigate the lead mine at Cliviger.

'This is to follow on the orders which were granted last

year to two clothiers of Rochdale. I forget their names, insolent fellows who rise above themselves, but bearing in mind the recent statute of Elizabeth, confirmed in 1623 by James, we must make due provisions for the first discoverers of the mine. But first you must prepare a list for me to submit to His Majesty, of proposed members for the Commission. I suggest gentlemen esquires with one baronet to take charge, and a man of little account, eager for favour, to be appointed our surveyor. There must be no Knights and no recusants. His Majesty has fallen out with his Parliament, and we must be careful not to upset our Archbishop.'

When the Chancellor had gone, Sir Gilbert asked the Attorney-General to draft out the legal wording of the Commission, and then applied himself to the task of selecting suitable names for the King's approval. Apart from the strictures laid down by the King the trick was to choose men who were under an obligation to the Duchy Council – not particularly for their freeholds and copyholds – but for additional licences or monopolies, which they relied upon to further their ambitions. Such men dare not neglect the Council's instructions. It was not long before he had selected the names of Sir Ralph Ashton, baronet and Roger Kenyon, gentleman. Sir Ralph was a member of the great Ashton or Assheton family which had given its name to many places in Lancashire such as Ashton-under-Lyne, Ashton-on-Mersey and Ashton-in-Makerfield. Roger Kenyon had recently been granted the privilege of farming the markets of Haslingden, Burnley and Colne. Then there was Nicholas Townley of Burnley who had taken a lease on all the glacial limestone deposited in that area, and other gentlemen who were pressing for permission to enclose the wastes, or dig for coal. These men would know on which side their bread was buttered.

Sir Ralph had purchased the dissolved abbey of Whalley from Edward VI and had converted the abbot's apartments to become his family residence. To add status he had then purchased a baronetcy from James I. It did not take Sir Gilbert Gerard and Sir Edward Moseley long to decide that Assheton was their man.

During the early weeks of June 1629 a Duchy courier travelled north to deliver a bulky dispatch case at Sir Ralph's residence. It contained six copies of the King's Commission each bearing the Great Seal of the Duchy. A covering letter from Lord Newburgh, the Chancellor, gave certain confidential instructions to Sir Ralph.

Five of the commissions had to be delivered to the esquires and gentlemen named. Sir Ralph was left in no doubt that he now held the overall responsibility. The other members of the Commission were Richard Shuttleworth Esq., of Gawthorpe, Robert Holt Esq., of Stubley, Nicholas Townley Esq., of Royle, Saville Radcliffe Esq., of Todmorden, and Roger Kenyon, gent., of Parkhead. The interesting fact is that the seventeenth-century houses built by these men in stone to replace the old wooden-framed fifteenth century halls still survive with one exception. Royle was demolished in 1950 because, unfortunately, it was adjacent to Burnley's sewage disposal works.

The Orders in Council were that the commissioners had to assess the richness or otherwise of the mine by personal examination and by sworn depositions taken from Highley and Butler, Humphrey Greaves and Godfrey Mercer, the first discoverers, and as many others with as intimate knowledge of the mine to be of value.

Roger Kenyon was appointed surveyor and given the King's authority to command every person connected with the mine to obey his instructions. All examinations and reports had to be the work and responsibility of at least three of the commissioners, but choice was restricted by stipulating that Sir Ralph and Roger Kenyon must be two of these.

The Commission was dated 23rd May 1629 and was to be completed by Commemoratia Animarum (All Souls Day), the 2nd of November 1629.

There was also the secret and confidential letter, in Lord Newburgh's almost indecipherable scrawl, instructing Sir Ralph, in the event of his esteeming the mine to be rich, that he must be sure that Highley and Butler could be dismissed from the mine for malpractice. Finally Sir Ralph was to burn the Chancellor's letter.

CHAPTER XII

The King's Commission

After carefully studying the Commission, Sir Ralph sent for Roger Kenyon, and informed him that he, Roger, had had the honour of being chosen by the King to be the surveyor of a Commission to investigate a lead mine at Cliviger. He then proceeded to give Roger detailed instructions for setting the Commission in motion.

'We have until the 2nd of November to prepare this report, and it is up to you to see the matter through all its stages; that is the meaning of the word surveyor. We have all the authority of the Great Seal of the Duchy, and force must be used if necessary. There must be no thought of failure. These men in Westminster will accept no excuse. If we fail them they will never forget. Your first duty will be to deliver these commissions to the men concerned, and to arrange a joint deputation to visit this mine and present the King's instructions. Never forget we are the King's servants, swords will be worn, pennants carried, and a suitable number of armed retainers taken along.'

'Will any money be provided for this purpose?'

'Yes, but we shall be the providers. Take my advice and think not of your own fortune, dig deep into your pocket even to the mortgaging of your estate, to perform the

King's service, and to pay the King's debts. Ask nought in return. We pay for our privileges, and thank God for our blessings. Make the matter a success and mayhap we will be rewarded in some way, but if we fail there is an absolute certainty of ruin.'

'But I know nought of lead mining. I am a man of figures and accounts. How shall I avail?'

'You will have to learn, and learn quickly. But I have thought of that. John Talbot of Carr Hall has meddled with lead mines. I will call him to our advice. He will at least put you in the way for a beginning. But if you have the least fear of failure bring your trouble to me and I will do all in my power to have it resolved. Take comfort from the thought that we are all in this together, and will help one another – but the doing is up to you.'

It was a troubled man who directed his horse up Whalley Brow on his way home to Parkhead. He realized that he would have to devote the most of his energies in the next four months to this Commission. And if he did this with success, once the mission was completed and, thank God, there was a fixed date to this, the 2nd of November, he could return to his own business. Meanwhile he would have to deputize the farming of the markets, and leave the building of his house in the hands of his servants. Before his horse had surmounted the hill he had arrived at these resolutions and resigned himself to the task.

For the next four months Roger Kenyon spent most of his life in the saddle. Firstly there were visits to the other members of the Commission, to Richard Shuttleworth of

Gawthorpe Hall near Padiham, to Robert Holt of Stubley at Littleborough, to Nicholas Townley at Royle – near the confluence of the Calder and the Pendle Water, and to Saville Radcliffe of Todmorden Hall. Then he had the difficult task of locating the clothier Ralph Highley in Rochdale, and leaving at his house a summons to be present at the lead mine on a certain day in August. In this he was helped by Saville Radcliffe. Radcliffe was a barrister-at-law and a Justice, and he provided Roger with all the legally worded documents, sealed and signed, to summon men to the meetings.

To familiarize himself with the ground Roger visited the mine itself, and was relieved to find a domicile there where he could obtain refreshments. He arranged with Alice Hartley for the brewing of ale, and the laying in of provisions for the day of the Commission, and left a sum of money with her for this purpose out of his own pocket. He asked her if she knew ought of two men named Godfrey Mercer and Humphrey Greaves. Alice was able to bring these two men into the farmhouse to be questioned, and Roger immediately realized that they would provide him with much of the information he required. He became busy with pen and paper writing down the names and associates of all the men and women who had worked at the mine. It was fortunate for him that his market work had fitted him for a clerk's duties, with portable writing materials and a ready hand.

Then there were further visits to Rochdale to speak with the men who had taken partnerships at the mine, and summonses had to be made out and signed by Justice

Radcliffe, and sent down to Derbyshire to bring back the miners who had been put off the works.

For all these journey's Roger was riding over some of the wildest and loneliest country in England, penetrating deep into the Pennine Hills. He had to find his way along ancient trade routes, such as the Long Causeway over which the Britons, and then the Romans, had travelled from east to west, and which had become the route of the De Lacys in their journeys between their castles of Pontefract and Clitheroe. But of most use to him were the packhorse trails with their firm footing and reliable crossings of rivers, often flooded by summer storms; and on these routes he could be assured of meeting other travellers to ask his way, and to find inns where he could eat and attend to his horse. And to his surprise he found that he was enjoying the work, sustained by the euphoria of being the King's chosen servant, and being given VIP treatment wherever he called. He increased in stature and dignity, and no longer begrudged the money which it was costing him.

When the great day, the 9th of September 1629 arrived, a great assembly of people gathered at the mine, all who had worked there, and many besides. They clustered on the end of Dean Scout to scan the valley; and eventually in the distance, coming from the direction of Burnley via the Long Causeway which crossed the Calder at Cliviger Mill Bridge, they espied a cavalcade of horsemen, a most impressive sight with cavaliers in their finest clothes, followed by retainers in the colours of their masters, and pennants of the Duchy of Lancaster and of Sheriff Assheton flying at their head. For a full hour the crowd at

Thieveley watched the party thread its tortuous way along the valley floor to the Holme, where it halted on the broad flat pasture in front of the Hall to be entertained by Thomas Whitaker and his servants.

After a delay of nearly two hours the cavalcade formed up again and, fording the Calder, took the steep zig-zag trail to Thieveley whilst the crowd on Dean Scout marvelled at a sight such as they had never seen before.

'Santa Maria,' said Humphrey, who had found that it was safe to blaspheme in Spanish Catholicisms, 'it's all that's left of King Charles' bloody army.'

And indeed as the troop came nearer it was seen that the horses were caparisoned for war, the esquires were dressed with their swords, and the infantry wore stout leather jerkins and carried bill-hooks. The whole party drew up in front of the mine, and the proceedings were started by the blowing of a trumpet. The crowd of rough country people perched themselves on the mine workings, while Roger Kenyon read out in a loud voice Sir Ralph Assheton's modified version of the terms of the Commission beginning:

'Charles, by the grace of God, King of England, Scotland, France and Ireland . . .' and ending '. . . know ye that anyone who should dare to resist the working of this, the King's Commission, do so at their peril.'

The constable, who was one of the party, then took over.

'All men and women whose names are called out must step forward.'

A clerk read off a list of names starting with Ralph Highley, William Butler, Godfrey Mercer and Humphrey

Greaves, and as each man stepped forward the constable placed his hand on his shoulder, and ushered him into line.

Roger Kenyon then read out that these named persons were to attend at the Burnley Market Cross at 9 a.m. on the morrow, the 10th of September, and to testify under their solemn oaths to the aforementioned Commissioners in the hostelry known as the Sparrow Hawk, opposite the aforesaid Market Cross, and that their depositions would be taken down in writing and sent to the King's Chancellor of the Duchy of Lancaster. Each person would be given one shilling, and free food and ale after they had made their depositions. Anyone who made a false declaration would be held answerable to the Chancellor with his life.

Highley and Butler were then brought forward to stand in front of the mounted Commission whilst Sir Ralph Assheton told them that from this time on they had to order the mine to the directions of Roger Kenyon, who by the King's command had been appointed Surveyor of the mine, and that they had to yield up to him all their books of accounts, and in every way assist him in the carrying out of the King's investigation.

The proceedings were brought to a close by a ceremony similar to that performed by the Barmaster in Derbyshire in laying out a meare of ground, but in this case the erection of a wooden post carrying a notice to the effect that these lead mines were now under the authority of the King's Commission, with a list of the names, titles, and places of abode of the Commissioners.

The gentlemen then went in to Alice Hartley's table,

and oatcake and ale was brought out for their retainers. The crowd of onlookers lingered on, until the gaily clad Cavaliers came out to remount their horses, and the troop clattered out of the farmyard in fine array. There was then a great demand for ale; and Robert, who had foreseen the demand, rolled out a barrel and collected 2d for every pint. Soon there was much good-natured merriment, and all declared that they would not have missed the event for the world. It had been a better day out than Burnley's annual fair.

Of the six gentlemen chosen for the King's Commission, Sir Ralph Assheton and Roger Kenyon could scarcely evade their responsibilities, but of the remaining four only two appeared willing to contribute a useful endeavour. These were Nicholas Townley of Royle, in Burnley, and Saville Radcliffe of Todmorden Hall, built on the few acres of level land deep down in the ravine of the Yorkshire Calder. Radcliffe, being the only barrister-at-law, volunteered to advise and help in all legal matters which may arise, and Townley very willingly agreed to be the third acting member.

These four were present on 10th September at the Sparrow Hawk, opposite the Market Cross and Parish Church of St Peter alongside the River Brun at Burnley, some three miles from the site of the mine at Thieveley. Sir Ralph, in his 50th year and beginning to be troubled by gout, and Saville Radcliffe, because of the difficult journey, lodged at the inn; Nicholas Townley was only two miles from his own house, and the busy Roger Kenyon had to ride the eight miles home to attend to his affairs at Parkhead.

The witnesses all gathered around the Cross. Gossiping amongst themselves, they were called in one at a time to be sworn in, questioned by the barrister, and have their depositions written down by his clerk. These were ostensibly in reply to seven articles attached to the Duchy Order, but Radcliffe shrewdly instructed his clerk to write down only those replies which favoured the Chancellor's purpose, and there was of course a modicum of browbeating by the Commission to influence the illiterate country people in the required direction.

These men, in their turn, had all the intuition and natural shrewdness of the uncluttered mind, and soon realized what was expected of them. Nor were they prevented from discussing their evidence as each man returned to the eager crowd around the Market Cross.

From the evidence of the Derbyshire miners it appeared obvious to the Commissioners that the mine was rich in a good quality lead ore; and, as none of the seven articles enquired into the difficulties likely to be encountered, the general atmosphere was one of optimism in the mine's future; and the expectation that even greater wealth would be discovered as the shafts penetrated to a greater depth. It was then an easy task to obtain evidence of mismanagement, from disgruntled workmen, against Highley and Butler; and not one of the Chancellor's seven articles was worded in such a way as to enquire into the exceptional zeal and energy with which William Butler in particular had put in to the enterprise in so short a time.

Without revealing the Chancellor's secret letter, Sir Ralph Assheton had had no difficulty in convincing the other Commissioners of the nature of the replies which would bring them the most approval in Westminster, so that they had little difficulty in selecting the material to be attached to the report of their findings.

However before the report was due there was still much work for Roger Kenyon to attend to. The instructions in the Commission were that he had to be responsible for the running of the mine from June to 2 November 1629. He had arrived at Thieveley in June just at the critical time when Highley and Butler had discharged all the free miners and were reorganizing the workings and sinking the water groove to drain the mine. Quite naturally, upon the arrival of the Commission, with the King's authority to supervise the operation of the mine, William Butler had suspended all work and Roger Kenyon was left with the problem of bringing some order out of the ensuing chaos, 'for the better profit of the King'.

In this he was advised by John Talbot. Meares were let off, after the Derbyshire manner, to several partnerships. In this way work was resumed on the original seven grooves with Edward, John Talbot's son, in charge. Highley and Butler were relegated to a partnership in a meare of their own, and it is interesting to note that Godfrey Mercer, financed by Isaac Clegg, was granted a meare, as was Robert Hartley, because the works had been 'troublesome and noysome to his dwelling'. Robert obviously believed that the authority of the Commission would protect him from any retaliation by his landlord, Thomas Whitaker. Realizing the necessity of draining the mine the new management continued the work on the water-groove at their own expense; whilst, pending approval of the Chancellor, Roger Kenyon paid John and Edward Talbots' expenses out of his own pocket.

There was now only one loose end to be tied up, to enable the Commission to make a satisfactory report for the Chancellor, and that was the difficult operation of smelting. As the smelting house clearly belonged to Highley and Butler, Roger Kenyon authorized them to proceed with their original plan, and after repairs and modifications to the smelting hearth, smelting was resumed, but only at the last moment, at the end of October. The smelter was the man Godfrey Wheatley, whom Ralph Highley had persuaded to come to Thieveley for a wage of 6s 10d per week.

With mining, draining and smelting well under way, the Commissioners felt that they had discharged their obligations to the full; and, under Saville Radcliffe's expert supervision, set about the compilation of their report.

CHAPTER XIII

The Commissioners' First Report

Obviously overawed by the Great Seal attached to the King's Commission, the three active commissioners took the greatest care in the preparation of their first report.

This was due on a date specially chosen for its religious implications, the Commemoratia Animorum, or All Souls Day, the 2nd of November. Any misrepresentation, on such a day, would be immediately apparent to the host of saints and angels and there was no knowing how they would react.

The documentation which the Northerners sent down to Westminster was in four parts. Firstly, a covering report signed by Sir Ralph Assheton and Nicholas Townley; secondly, an explicit and detailed account of all the action taken, as detailed in the previous chapter, by the surveyor Roger Kenyon; thirdly, a complete transcript of all the depositions taken in the Sparrow Hawk; and lastly a considerable collection of accounts.

In his detailed report Roger Kenyon gave the Commissioners' joint conclusions and replies to the seven stipulated articles, as follows:

1. Godfrey Mercer was the first discoverer of the mine.

2. Since the beginning of mining, in March 1628 to November 1629, 15 tons of lead worth £150 have been produced, but that if Ralph Highley 'had done his best to advance the profitt of the Myne I conceave there might above three tymes soe much have been gotten.'

3. One ton of ore will yield a half-ton of lead at a cost for smelting of about 30s.

4. The nature and condition of the mine is considered to be very good and likely to continue long.

5. All recommend the Derbyshire manner of working.

6. Highley and Butler have deceived His Majesty by concealing the true worth of the mine.

7. Roger dare not estimate a weekly, monthly or yearly profit after only two months' experience, but believes that the mine could be worth £100 a year to the King.

Roger concluded in the following words:

I find (in this unsettled tyme of the manner of workeing) much debate, variances and contecions to arrise amongst the workmen. I appeased as many as I could. But there will remain a multitude of differences in accomptes, allowances and other variences to bee determined and decyded by this Honorable Court or by the Commissioners from the same aucthorised to examine and end them. I have left divers persons workeinge in certaine meares assigned them, vizt. George Casson and David Goodwin in one grove, Godfrey Mercer and Isaac Clegge in an other grove, Thomas Whittacres and his partners in an other grove, one Thomas Cocroft and his partner in another grove, and in an other grove Roberte Hartley whoe deserves more favour than others, for that the Workes are troublesom and noysome to his dwellinge house, some sinckinge and some gettinge, besyeds Highley and Butler theire groves, who before the end of this tearme will have gotten good quantities of Oare. Alsoe I have intreated the before named Edward Talbott to contynue amonst them to directe them and take theire accomptes till your Lordship and the Courts' further pleasure bee therein signifyed to mee or them. I oabserve that Raphe Highley and his partners, from the begininge of the Worke, which was from secundo Marcii, 1627 (28) till decim. Septembris, 1629, beinge about Nynteene Monthes, all the Workemen gott but about Elleven Tunne and a halfe of Lead. And since the first sittinge of this Commission, vizt., decimo Septembris, 1629, till secundo Novembris followinge, beinge under two Monthes, there is gotten soe much Oare as will make about three Tunne and a halfe of lead, and yet but about the same number of Workemen employed. Thus much in dutie I thought good to certifye to your Lordship, together with an Accompte or Decleracion hereunto fixed showinge what moneyes is alleged to have beene spent and what profittes receaved for or concerninge the said Mynes, and the severall persons desireinge Recompence, etc. All which I humbly submitt to your Lordship's consideracion and further Direccion. And myselfe ever more to bee Your Lordship in all dutie to bee commanded.

Rog. Kenyon.

Burneley the seacond of November, 1629.

Special mention should now be made of the fact that all concerned, the deposers, the commissioners and their advisers, recommended that, under the King, the Thieveley Lead Mine should be operated according to the Derbyshire system.

This system had been painstakingly developed over the past 300 years, as the only practical manner in operating so random, risky and often nebulous a venture as a lead mine. Originally introduced from Germany in the thirteenth century, it was first ratified by Edward I at an inquisition at Ashburne in 1288; and again by Henry VIII, in 1513, when a standard dish for measurement of ore was placed in the Moot Hall at Wirksworth where it remains to this day.

The essence of the system was that meares of land should be let off along the vein of ore to partnerships of free miners. These partnerships found all their own materials, employed labourers, sank the shafts and extracted and dressed the ore, for sale at an agreed price per dish to the mine owner.

The mine owner was responsible for the drainage of the mine, the provision of access roads for packhorse trains, the carriage of the ore, and its final smelting into lead.

The King, as Lord of the Manor in which the mines were located, had his lot and cope. The lot was a fraction of the dressed ore, usually every thirteenth dish, hence the unlucky number; and the cope was a duty paid by the mine owner of 4d per two horse-loads of ore, about 5 cwt., delivered into the smelt-house. The lot compensated the King, as the mineral owner, for the loss of the ore, and the cope authorized the mine owner, in place of the King, to smelt the ore into saleable lead.

A number of articles ensured that the mines were run in a safe, efficient and law-abiding manner, and the whole was supervised by an official known as the Barmaster. He operated from the Moot Hall in Wirksworth, and was assisted in the settlement of disputes by a jury and a court, the Barmoot.

Humphrey Greaves had been correct in asserting that the first discoverer of the mine was entitled to the first two meares. The landowner, in Thieveley's case the King, was entitled to the third meare, and all subsequent meares were 'freed' by the Barmaster to partnerships of free miners.

The freedom to prospect for metals, and to open up new mines, was known as the 'liberty' of the King's Field, always provided that the discovery was immediately registered with the Barmaster.

The question then arises, who was the Barmaster for a new and isolated 'field' such as the Cliviger Common. The answer of course was the Chancellor of the Duchy of Lancaster, as Ralph Highley had so shrewdly guessed.

The Commissioners had been much exercised in the additional question as to whether the laws and customs of the Derbyshire Field were applicable in Cliviger. Saville Radcliffe's legal mind considered Derbyshire as a precedent, and gave his whole-hearted support to the active commissioners in restarting the mine in line with the ancient liberties, laws and customs of Derbyshire.

But, of course, with Highley and Butler still operating the smelt-house, all that the King would receive was his lot and cope, as though from a privately owned mine; and, as will be seen from the Chancellor's replies, the King, not unreasonably, as both Lord of the Manor, and owner of the mine, wanted much more.

CHAPTER XIV

Robert Hartley's Petition

The arrival of the King's Commissioners in Cliviger was the greatest event which had happened in that remote and hidden parish since the Norman Conquest, and the takeover of the old hundred or wapentake of Blackburn by the alien Roger of Poitou, the building of Clitheroe Castle by Robert de Lacy, the setting up of the Norman Honor of Clitheroe, and the inclusion of Cliviger within its manor of Ightenhill.

Consequently the spectacle of the Commissioners, with their cavalcade, and the subsequent enquiry in the Sparrow Hawk, alongside Burnley Market Cross, had provided an almost endless topic of conversation in the parish. Talk and gossip, along with rough sport and bawdiness, were the palliatives of the common people. But nowhere was there more talk than around the mine itself, of the events, and of speculation of what might happen in the future.

Robert and Alice Hartley talked of little else during the times when they rested by the fireside. At first Alice had poured out her forebodings, and grumbled at their loss of privacy and the contentment which had been hers before the discovery of the mine. And there is no doubt that she could not help blaming Robert for setting the whole thing off. In defence he pointed to the growing collection of coins in the secret hole which he had dug beneath the hearthstones. In this age coin of the realm was of inestimable value.

For hundreds of years the people of Cliviger had provided for all their own wants. They had built their own houses, produced their own food, made their clothing and footwear, and all the crude implements to farm their land. They had paid the miller with his share of the meal, the church with the tenth of their produce, and the lord and landlord with their labour. They had rarely handled the coin of the realm, for this coin was in very short supply.

The supply of coinage, minted by the King, could never keep up with the twin demands of inflation and an ever-expanding economy. Furthermore, because of inflation, the intrinsic value of the metal in the coin was greater than its face value, so that the King had to lay out excessive sums of money to purchase gold and silver to mint into coinage which was of less value than the parent metal. This coinage was then introduced into the economy as wage payments to his army and navy. But there was never enough. Hence the great desire to capture the Spanish treasure fleets, and to discover gold and silver mines at home. The ancestor of Sir Ralph Assheton, Sir Thomas Ashton of Ashton-under-Lyne, had even been commissioned, by Henry VI, to work on the transmutation of lead into gold and silver. It is ironical to note that modern government, have achieved a similar effect by a wholesale substituting of an inferior metal for the coinage. But in Charles' reign the coinage was so valuable, as metal alone, that unscrupulous men debased individual coins by scraping slivers of the metal off the circumference and melting down these accumulations. It was this malpractice which led to the provision of serrated edges, and every man had a right to refuse a coin from which these serrations had been removed. The debasement of the coinage became a very serious crime. Modern governments expatiate their debasement by a promise to guarantee the coinage.

This scarcity of coinage, and the fact that so little of it ever fell into the hands of the poorer classes, led to a race of men eager for trade and barter, but so reluctant to part with even one penny of coinage, that they would deny their families every simple requirement, and even starve them of food. Men of this ilk still persisted in the Pennine Hills right up to the present age, of affluence, of prodigality, and the Welfare State.

Consequently Robert Hartley could point with some satisfaction to the growing hoard of coins in his secret hideaway. Ralph Highley had paid all which he had promised. And then a class of people had arrived for the first time in Cliviger, the wage-earning industrial worker, eager to exchange his wages for ale. As Dr T.D. Whitaker of the Holme so bitterly complains nearly 200 years later, of his own parish of Cliviger, in his monumental *History of the Parish of Whalley*:

> In joy or sorrow, for business or dissipation, the riot of a marriage feast, the maudlin solemnity of a funeral, the senseless noise of a parish meeting and never-ending jollity of a wake, omnes codem cogemur, all fly to the place

which affords at once accommodation and freedom, oblivion of care, or a vent for mirth, which removes at a distance the control of domestic authority, or the voice of conjugal reproach – everything ends at an alehouse.

Such is the strength of our Anglo-Saxon inheritance that the same can be said for the present day, a further 200 years on from Whitaker's writing.

There was a statutory price for ale of 2d a gallon, so there was no bickering over a price. This allowed Alice a handsome profit. But wise government also insisted upon a standard, and every high-constable had his ale-tasters to protect the buyer. However there was no need for an ale-taster for Alice Hartley's ale, she had only one standard, and that was excellence. The brewing of ale became their most useful source of income from the mine.

The arrival of the Commission brought further additions to their savings for Roger Kenyon paid handsomely out of his own pocket. Robert was able to put their grievances to Roger, and, in an effort at compensation, he was given one of the deserted grooves to work for his own profit. At this time his landlord Thomas Whitaker was failing rapidly; he died in 1651, and Robert believed that he had nothing to fear from Thomas' son, 27-year-old William. Robert bailed the water out of the groove, and with his young sons to help haul up the baskets and wash and clean the ore, he soon had his own little cache of ore, a commodity equally as valuable as the King's money.

Immediately after the reading of the King's Commission in September, Humphrey Greaves, who had grown wise to the ways of princes, ready for a change, and tired of his strumpet, decamped for Derbyshire. Godfrey, pointing out that Humphrey had been named as one of the first discoverers of the mine, tried to persuade him to stay. But Humphrey averred that this was all the more reason to go. He preferred independent anonymity.

'That's all we'll get, bits of paper with our names on and empty promises with no money at t'back on it.'

So Humphrey went back to the private mines in Derbyshire where he said he would be able to see the man with the money in his pocket, and demand and get his just rewards; either that, or a bloody nose.

Godfrey, bereft of companionship, returned to Rochdale where Isaac Clegg, once more putting money in his pocket, sent him back to work the meare which Roger Kenyon had allotted to them. Isaac brought a miner, Frances Leigh, from Ashford-in-the-Peake to work with Godfrey; and they were assisted in the hoisting and clearing of the ore by a woman from the camp. There is no record of this woman ever being paid, and no doubt she worked for her keep and share of the men's lodging, the rough turf house on the hillside,

When Roger Kenyon, weary from his journeying, knocked at her door and asked if he could sit by her fireside, Alice Hartley experienced an uplift from her depression. Here was a gentleman, a man of courtesy and good manners, treating her as an equal, and a person of some consequence. She, in turn, was elevated in her demeanour, and felt in no way inferior. Roger Kenyon found a deep sense of peace and security sitting by her fireside in contrast to the mud, rain, and vulgarity outside, and partaking of excellent ale and freshly-baked oatcake.

She is a fine woman, he mused, fit to grace any man's parlour, to attend to his wants, and warm his bed. So a great ease developed between them, he confided to her his problems and fears of the great task put upon his shoulders by the King, and to her it seemed almost unbelievable that the dreaded King's Majesty had come into her lonely wattle and thatch farmhouse high up on Thieveley Scout above the Cliviger Gorge.

In her turn she told Roger of all her frustrations since the discovery of the lead ore; of Thomas' threat to evict them; and all that had happened since Ralph Highley's arrival, taking away her peace and happiness. Roger was a sympathetic listener, and quick to reassure her that he would do all he could to alleviate any nuisance that the mine might cause. Consequently when Robert came in Roger was prepared to listen attentively to the details of Robert's point at view. He took out his writing materials, and made a few notes.

On his next visit, Roger explained that he had given much thought to the Hartleys' problems. They occupied a key position and could offer very essential services to the Commission so he felt that they should have compensation and be rewarded. Unfortunately he himself had no power to make hard and fast arrangements; he could only make recommendations to the Duchy Chancellor. However, he was sure that due notice would be taken of these, and he was sure that compensation would be paid, and he himself would see that they were paid for all services.

In the matter of the great inconvenience they had suffered up to date, during Highley and Butler's managership, this was a more difficult matter as their claim was against them, and not against the King. However, in order to help in every way, he had drafted out the wording of a petition to the Chancellor, who in authorizing Highley and Butler, must accept a degree of responsibility. The greatest difficulty, however, was that for a petition to be recognized by the Council and Court of the Duchy, or indeed any petition to any authority, it must be presented by the petitioner in person. The common law of England placed great emphasis upon the presence of the actual flesh and blood of the body of any petitioner, plaintiff or accused, on the rough and useful principle that: no body – no case. He, Roger, would happily write out and provide the necessary document, but Robert would have to deliver it himself to the Chancellor in Westminster.

To Robert and Alice this was a daunting proposition. They had never in all their life travelled beyond Rochdale to the east, and Burnley to the west. There were fearsome difficulties and unknown terrors beyond the safety of their parish boundary.

Robert, being the man he was, took up Roger's suggestion. The journey to London presented great difficulties, but it was at once a challenge and an adventure. Although travel was inordinately expensive for the rich, the poor, provided they had the necessary shilling to frustrate the vagrancy laws, could travel almost free of charge on their two feet. And Robert believed that, active husbandman as he was, he could work his passage with the regular packhorse trains or drovers of cattle which converged on the capital. He would only need money in the city itself, and he was prepared to invest a little from his savings. The greatest urgency was to be on his way before winter brought greater hardships. He planned to do the round trip in the last two weeks and first two of September and October, whilst the mellowness and fruitfulness of autumn still touched the land, with an abundance of food in the countryside.

The petition had all the evidence of Roger Kenyon's tidy mind. It was based on the fact that the smelt-house and the ore dressing floor were on freehold land rented by the petitioner. Damage to the freehold land as a result of the workings on the King's wastes were that water had been diverted from its true course and springs had been polluted. The diverted water had washed away the carriage way which served his farm. The 'noysomeness of the smoke' from the smelt-house had destroyed all growth in his garden, and had taken away the colour of the grass and corn from the farmland. Finally the workmen did trespass all over his freehold land.

When Robert had gone, Roger smiled quietly to himself at the success of his scheme. Now perhaps he would be the more intimate with Alice in her loneliness. But being of middle-age and weary from all the travelling and contentions, he would not press his suit with the impetuosity of youth, and then only if the woman herself were willing. If she were not he would content himself with second best, enjoy the aura of her womanliness together with the peace of her fireside, her cakes and her ale.

And that was all Roger was able to enjoy on the few occasions that he was able to visit Thieveley, for he found

Godfrey Mercer, her brother, living in the farmhouse, Humphrey Greaves, not liking the turn of events, having returned to Derbyshire.

Roger had an uncomfortable feeling that his designs had been foreseen by the astute country folk, and so in an attempt to retrieve the situation his attitude became one of studious formality. Then, he consoled himself, after the 2nd of November the whole business will be finished and I will be done of the affair.

CHAPTER XV

The King's Second Commission

However, far from being able to forget the Cliviger mine, Roger soon found himself saddled with complete responsibility for the project. With amazing speed the Commissioner's report of 2 November was answered by orders dated 3 December. These took the form of a second Commission from 'Charles, by the grace of God, Kinge of England, Scotland, France and Ireland, Defender of the Faith', in which the six Commissioners were ordered to operate the mine for the King's profit. This new Commission was again stamped with the Great Seal of the Duchy of Lancaster, so that it could only be disobeyed or neglected under a charge of treason and a penalty of death.

Accompanying the Commission were a covering letter from the Chancellor, and Resolutions of the Council giving exact instructions upon how the mine was to be operated.

The covering letter complimented the commissioners 'wherein you have with soe much care and diligence and exactness attended and performed the service' and then continued 'upon the perusal of the proofes of the several miscarriages and false dealings of Highley and Butler I have with the advice of the Attorney and Counsell of the Dutchie discharged and cast them absolutely out of the worke and resolved to make a tryall how we may best way bringue the cleere entyer profitt to his Majesties' Coffers'.

And so the commissioners were well and truly 'hoisted by their own petard' but without the freedom and independence enjoyed by Highley and Butler. From now on the sinister figure of the Chancellor would always be in the background, and instructions arriving from Westminster which were out of tune with the realities on the bleak Thieveley hillside. The first set of Resolutions of the Council were typical. They completely ignored the commissioners' recommendation that the mine be run after the customs of Derbyshire. The Council's instructions were explicit 'by setting soe many skillfull and expert Myners to work, whoe are not to be recompenced by any allowance of Oare or Lead by the dishe or otherwise, but to have such fitt wages by the daye or weeke as they can be agreed with for'. A feudal and autocratic Chancellor in London was still working on the assumption that the upper classes were prepared to sacrifice their time and money, possibly their lives, for love of the King, and that the lower classes were still the serfs and villeins of the early Norman Conquest who could be driven to labour for their mere subsistence.

According to the Resolutions, Highley and Butler were only to receive the value of the ore and lead produced up to 2 November 1629 and that only to a limit of £150. It is no exaggeration to say that the mine and smelt-house were stolen from them, for the King paid nothing and yet took possession of the mine. It was nationalization without compensation.

Roger Kenyon was specified to run the mine with only promises of payment. Indeed Article 5 reads, 'the Commissioners and the Surveyor and their necessary agents Shal be rewarded out of the cleere proffittes arising to his Majestie in such manner as the Chancellor and Counsell shall finde them to deserve'. So the inference was clear: if there were no profit there would be no pay.

Money to run the mine until sufficient lead could be sold was to be obtained from 'the particular Receavor of his Majestie of the Dutchie revenue of the Countie Palatine'. This receiver was another Ralph Assheton who lived at Downham Hall, near Clitheroe, and was a cousin of Sir Ralph of Whalley Abbey. But because the King had dismissed Parliament, receiver Ralph had no authority to collect the King's subsidy within the county so that for the moment his title had little substance.

He was unable to provide money of the sums required to pay for men and materials until an adequate amount of lead had been sold. In addition he was very much diverted by a distressing affair of witchcraft. His son had died recently, allegedly bewitched to death by a certain John Uttley who was at present on trial for his life at Lancaster Castle.

Consequently Ralph of Downham had little time to spare, or even patience, with Roger Kenyon's requests for cash to pour into such an unlikely venture as a lead mine in the wild wastelands of Cliviger.

So once again Sir Ralph of Whalley had to call together the six Commissioners to try to make the best of what for them was a very poor prospect: to have to find cash to run this venture for the King at a time when their own resources were stretched as they were embarked on ambitious schemes of rebuilding their houses and laying out elaborate domestic offices, outbuildings, home farms, pleasure gardens and plantations of woodlands.

In the days when they had had to take their resources to the wars of the warrior kings there had always been promise of rich booty, glory and honours, but this low-class affair of a lead mine had no such compensations.

CHAPTER XVI

Roger Kenyon's Troubles

Roger Kenyon was not a businessman of the type of the new entrepreneurs, the clothiers, manufacturers, ironmasters, and mine owners who were rising rapidly from the lower into the middle classes, where they now threatened the age-old supremacy of the landed gentry. He was an administrator, a land surveyor, market supervisor, a man of figures, who freely admitted that he had no knowledge of industry and in particular of lead mining.

But under the threat and authority of the Great Seal he had no choice but to obey. He had wrestled with the affair by restoring the mine and smelt-house to working order but this had only filled him with forebodings of the difficulties entailed. And now all the problems which had caused Highley and Butler to close down the mine were laid upon his doorstep.

Even worse, as he read the Resolutions of the Council, he realized, with growing despair, that all the good work which he had done in letting off meares to partnerships of free miners had now to be undone with all the unpleasantness and difficulties which that entailed.

All he could do was dismiss these men from the mine without redress, a most unpleasant task which could quite easily have lead to violence in those rough and ready days. Furthermore he had to shoulder the responsibility upon himself because, in order to protect the privilege of his market franchise, he dare not in any way put the blame upon the King or the Chancellor. There were too many informers, and too many ears, eager to retail gossip back to Westminster, spurred on by jealousy and the desire for the privileges for themselves.

Roger had even to dismiss Godfrey Mercer and Robert Hartley from their meares. Godfrey had a legal right to his portion of the mine, but nevertheless he and his partner, Isaac Clegg, were dispossessed.

After clearing the workings of the free miners, Roger had to find men who were willing to work for a weekly wage. This would be for six days, each of eight hours' labour. None of the skilled Derbyshire miners would agree to stay, so Roger was left with an odd assortment of inferior and untrained workers, and consequently he was only able to proceed with three of the original seven grooves, the most important of which was the water-groove, for the draining of the mine. One groove was worked by the ever-present Nicholas Birch, whose wife Jenet was responsible for the ore washing, and the third groove was worked by a man called Henry Hayworde. These two men had labourers to lift the ore to the surface, an operation known as drawing and winding. Nicholas Birch's groove was called the Cope Groove. Hayworde had taken over Godfrey Mercer's groove, which was still named Godfrey's Groove, in the accounts.

The all-important water-groove was being excavated by a man named Joe Cresswell; and, while the mine was being restarted, presumably with little production of ore, Jenet Birch was drawing and winding in the water-groove, proving that she was a woman of determination, not frightened by any task, or any labour.

We now find a graduation of wages, according to skill, the miner or pickman was paid a weekly wage of 5s, the unskilled drawers and winders 3s, boys 2s, women 2s 6d, and highest of all 7s for the skilled-work timbering of the shafts.

Although not yet recognized by the Council, Edward Talbot was the overseer of this work, and was still receiving his wages from Roger, as his acting deputy on the spot. There was also the expense of his lodging at the hostelry in Holme Chapel.

It can now be seen that owing to the interferences of the Council the production capacity of the mine had been reduced from seven grooves to three, and these mined by unskilled workmen, ex-weavers and clothiers, and that the incentive motive of working for oneself had been removed from the workforce. They had become mere wage-slaves, a condition little better, and some might say worse, than that of the serfs and villeins of the Middle Ages, or the plantation slaves of the Americas. The serfs and slaves were at least fed and housed by their masters, and lived in far kinder climatic conditions. From 1500-1700 England was subject to a cold period, sometimes referred to as 'the little ice-age' by weather historians, so that in 1630 the rigours of the climate at Thieveley must have been very severe.

The second effect of the Council's resolutions was to completely undermine the authority and credibility of the

Surveyor, Roger Kenyon, and his overseer Edward Talbot. In the eyes of the workmen they became men who did not know their own minds from one week to the next, and could not therefore command respect. And once this assessment was accepted it became almost impossible to change. The management became a subject of contempt and ribaldry, to be gone along with but not taken seriously.

Apart from the administrative troubles, Roger was also deeply concerned about the two practical difficulties of the mine, the same two which had brought work to a standstill under Highley and Butler – the problems of flooding, and of smelting of the ore. The water-groove was not a success. It still required the unceasing labour of human muscle, by day and night, to lift the water out of the mine. The use of men, other than slaves, for such a purpose could never be an economic proposition. John and Edward Talbot recommended the driving of a drainage tunnel into the hillside, known in those days as an adit or sough, but Roger was appalled at the magnitude, and expense, of such a task.

The poor smelting results were still blamed upon the inadequate blast of the bellows, and here again it was man's inferiority as a workhorse which was the cause. The smelters blamed the blowers; and the blowers, in their turn, blamed the bellows. They were too stiff to operate, and they leaked too much air. Roger decided to have a new pair made, with softer and more supple leather. He even engaged a reputable shoemaker to choose the best quality hides. The smith at Cliviger Bridge was set to work making this new pair of bellows. Meanwhile the smelter Godfrey Wheatley was kept occupied in sorting, splitting and storing specially dried burning-wood, and in making alterations to the smelting hearth. But his wages and board had still to be paid.

Once again a stream of packhorses was converging on the mine, daily, bringing timber, for supporting the shafts, burning-wood and all other necessities. And again everyone had to be paid. Money supplied to Edward Talbot, for this purpose, was constantly running out, and urgent messages had to be sent to Whalley for more. A servant of Roger Kenyon's, called George, became a regular courier between Whalley Abbey, Parkhead, Nicholas Townley's house at Royle, and Thieveley. But despite this, the plea was always for more cash.

The only remedy was to generate cash at the mine, and this could not be done until there was lead for sale. To aggravate matters, because of the depression in the cloth trade, the demand for and price of lead was falling. Customers went away, refusing to buy and saying that the Thieveley lead was too expensive, when one had to add the cost of transport from so difficult a location.

Nevertheless, to ease the cash shortage, it was considered essential to start up the smelting hearth. Smelting was attempted once again with the new bellows but still with very poor results. Edward Talbot became convinced that it was the nature of the Thieveley ore which was at fault, so two horse-loads of ore were sent for a trial smelting at the Duke of Cumberland's mill at Grassington in Wharfedale. The report came back that the 4 cwt., 3 stones and 10 pounds of ore had run well and yielded 2 cwt., 3 stones and 14 pounds of best quality lead.

Apparently, then, there was nothing wrong with the Thieveley ore, it was in fact of a very high quality.

Not only was the smelting uneconomic but it was found that the miners were not producing enough ore to cover the wages of themselves and their labourers.

During his hasty visits to the mine, in which he only wished to rest by Alice Hartley's fireside, Roger had to tramp around the mud and slime of the workings, climbing up and down ropes, exhorting Edward Talbot, and the workers, to greater efforts. But apparently there were a hundred reasons why the ore was not coming to the surface: the shafts were in deep water, the sides were falling in, the early timbering was rotten and needed replacing, and so on. All plausible excuses which Roger could not decide were genuine or not. And as soon as he left, or Talbot's back was turned, the workers downed tools and sat on their backsides, in the warm galleries, sheltered from the weather and cheered by the candlelight.

Then, to complete Roger Kenyon's despondency, he was involved in a distressing accident. He had been detailed off by Sir Ralph to take John Talbot, Edward's father, to view the smelting house and offer his advice. 'And in the way passinge over wonderous steepe hills his horse fell upon him and brooke his leg in soe dangerous manner, the bone startinge out of the flesh, that he may never walk thereon again.'

On top of the shock of the accident Roger had to ride for help, have a litter constructed, and the injured man carried to the Holme, to be cared for by Thomas Whitaker's household. Edward had to leave the mine to attend to his father's business and carry him safely the long and difficult journey back to his house Carr Hall at Wilpshire, alongside the main road from Blackburn to Whalley.

With the allegiance of the middle classes to their joint survival, Sir Ralph and Roger believed themselves responsible for John Talbot's great misfortune, and that it was their duty to support him through it. It was one more financial burden heaped upon the rest. The mine was exacting its price of human suffering, and there were many, even in the pulpits, and such as Alice Hartley, to say that it was God's vengeance upon them for digging into the bowels of His Earth, and interfering with His Handiwork.

But, for Roger Kenyon in particular, the troubles thrust upon him by this most unwelcome Commission from the King were only just beginning.

CHAPTER XVII

The First Quarterly Report

To the Chancellor and Council of the Duchy in Westminster the operations of the mine seemed so delightfully simple: dig out the ore, smelt it into lead, sell the lead, pay the workers, and send the profit down to the King. But the stark realities on the exposed hillside, over 1,000 feet above sea level, in a typical winter of 'the little ice age', were vastly different. The miners, cold and undernourished, living in their turf houses without windows or doors, with only rough worn-out worsted hanging over the entrance to keep out the piercing east winds which impinged directly upon the hill with unabated fury, or those climbing the precipitous hillside in the darkness from their single-roomed cots in the valley, were glad to get underground to the comparative warmth of mother earth, and the comforting glow of the candles. However these were not dry rocky caverns, but timber-supported tunnels through a sticky blue shale which ran with water, so that they could not keep the dampness out of their clothing, or out of the wrappings round their feet and legs. Consequently they were more concerned in finding a comparatively warm and dry hole for themselves and keeping a little fire going of peat and off-cut timber, than of getting ore for the King. Fire was their only luxury, and they huddled round its life-sustaining warmth, maintaining their spirits with banter, bawdy talk, and laughter at the efforts of Roger Kenyon and Edward Talbot to produce the all-important lead. And at pay day they gathered in a menacing group, like a pack of wolves, round the young Edward Talbot, snatching the money out of his hand until he scarce knew who had been paid, and finally left them with the money to sort out and quarrel over amongst themselves. The only comfort for him, in his loneliness, and at times his fear, was in the farmhouse kitchen.

Before March had reached its end, with spring and the new year in the offing, the Commissioners were at their wits' end to know what to do. Each week the mine was swallowing up money, as though it were poured into the holes in the earth, and the smelting house was costing more to run than the lead which it produced. And staring the Commissioners in the face was the realization that in a few weeks' time they had to send their first quarterly report and their accounts to Westminster. This was in accordance with one of the Resolutions of the Council.

Realizing that some drastic measures had to be taken, they decided to call in experts, private mine owners who were running their ventures at a profit, and pay them for their advice. On 8 April 1630, a meeting of the four active Commissioners, which included Saville Radcliffe, and three mining men, was held at the Sparrow Hawk in Burnley.

The experts called in, besides John Talbot who was to have his terrible accident during these investigations, were a Mr Warburton, and a Mr Bardsley, overseers for the Duke of Cumberland's extensive lead mines in the hills above Wharfedale. The expenses and fees of these men were paid for their long journey to Burnley, and for staying for two days to view the mine.

As a result of these deliberations a new course of immediate action was agreed upon, if only to stem the disastrous outflow of cash.

> ... when wee observed that the payment of wages and providinge timber and other necessaries for them exhausted from his Majesties purse more moneys than the Oare gained would countervaile, wee plainely perceaved that wee weare in no course for his Majesties benifitt, men of theire qualities, workeinge under the earth, where no eies can discover theire painfull or loiteringe labours, weare not like to raise profitt to theire Maisters unles they worke for themselves at theire owne charge. Wee therfor resolved to putt in practise some other course for a perfecte triall of the Mynes with least lose to the kinge that wee could devise and especially nowe the dayes beinge longe and the tymes very seasonable for the purpose. Wee therefore appointed a generall meetinge at Burnley (a towne neare to the Mynes) Upon the eight of Aprill last, where accordingly wee mett, and in the meane tyme for our better informacions what to protect and how to make our best bargaine, wee sent for to come unto us thither some verie expert men in Mynerall affaires (casuallie them in those partes). And after long debate and treatie with the workmen (a generacion of dangerous condicioned people to deale with) wee resolved on this course:- First to discharge them all from day wages after one weeke from that tyme and to give them and all others (come who come will) libertie to worke upon theire owne charges and to

provide worke loomse, timber for theire groves, ropes, and all other materialls, untill the Oare bee ready for smeltinge at theire own charges, and to have all they gett to themselves upon theise tearmes:

Then having explained how they had installed free miners after the Derbyshire manner in the liberty of the field 'to goe soe deepe as may make an absolute and perfect tryall of the Myne' they go on to the twin difficulties, which so bedevilled Highley and Butler, of drainage and smelting:

And because they are troubled with water, and never able to make anye such tryall as afforesaid unles it bee taken from them, wee undertooke to make (on his Majesties charges) a sough or trenche, by them called an Audit, of some three score yardes deepe under the earth, or more or lesse as occasion may happen to require, by that meanes to issue and convey the water away from them, which worke we have alredye caused to bee begunn on, and doe nowe purpose to go on with the same.

Regarding the difficulty of smelting:

we gathered the fault to bee in our smeltinge house and uncertaine blast, the Bellowes beinge blowen by men and not by Water Wheele, soe wee resolved to keepe the oare in store till it might bee more comodiously smelted, though his Majesty for the presently out more money. Wee conceave there is noe way for his Majesty to helpe this, but eyther to build a smeltinge milne upon some water neare unto some store of woodes, or else to have an undertaker to smelt it at a certaine rate by the Tunn of lead. There is a gent., Richard Townley of Townley, Esq., who hath a great deale of freehoulde land of his owne neare adioyninge and in it a convenient water to build a mylne on, and hath woodes of great extent at hand. Hee is best furnished eyther to buy the oare of the kings and smelt it for his owne sale or to build a milne and provide a smelter and smelt it for the kinge at a certaine rate in the Tunn of lead, or else to graunt his Majesty a convenient place to sett a milne uppon and to furnish his highnes with wood at reasonable prices.

However Richard Townley, who had chosen to live on his estate of Nocton in Lincolnshire, leaving his brothers, Charles and Christopher, in residence at Towneley Hall, was a noted papist and recusant.

In days of bitter religious persecution a recusant was an outlaw, shunned by the establishment, and not allowed to take any part in the public life of the nation. At this time the King's favourite, Archbishop Laud, was arraigning great and small alike before the despotic court of the High Commission. Consequently the Protestant Commissioners were afraid to meet with Townley, and suggested that the Chancellor night conduct the negotiations himself in London.

The lengthy report then continues with the Commissioners' deliberations upon the various petitions, of Robert Hartley and of the original miners Highley and Butler, Mercer, Greaves and Isaac Clegg. They describe the distressing accident to John Talbot:

> that hee yett lyeth in great ieopardie whether hee shall ever recover it to walke thereon againe or noe. Yt hath cost him much money, and his estate is very meane to support it, hee is modest in makeinge sute to your Lordship, neither shall wee further preesse it for him than your lordship's owne noble disposicion.

Ralphe Assheton. Nic. Townley. Rog. Kenyon. From the

accounts attached to the above report, the King came out as a loser by £22 7s 9d, which in today's terms, corresponds to about £9,000, for only three months' operation of the mine. Also this did not cover any remuneration for the Commissioners, or wages for the surveyor, Roger Kenyon. In a covering letter the Commissioners justify their new arrangement quite logically:

> Wee cannot conceave what great hurt may nowe come to the kinge whilst wee receave Oare for the money that is paid. There wilbee nothinge wantinge but number of workemen, wherein if gaine bee found they will flocke unto us fast enough. Thus farr wee have gone, and according to our duties to his Majesty and the trust reposed by your lordship have done our best to advance the service; if any dificiency hath beene it was for want of skill (the employments beinge out of our elements) not endeavor.

CHAPTER XVIII

The Reorganization

Attached to the report of 3 May 1630 there was an almost poignant letter from Roger Kenyon to Sir Edmund Brewster, Clerk to the Council. One extract indicates Roger's depression: 'I have had much labour about them and yet all will (at present) produce no good effect. The myners are worse than divells, they will deceave any man though hee still looke upon them. I would rather wish any employment from the Court, more in my element. I am much discouraged to take such paines, and yet the King to bee a loser.'

One can sense that it is almost with despair that Roger set about the task of making the third reorganization of the mine in less than a year of being given the active managership. His only consolation was that he was well backed up by the remaining Commissioners. He had now to dismiss the wage-earners and set up partnerships of free miners in the grooves. Again it meant many hours in the saddle.

These miners worked at their own charge and were paid for the weight of washed ore delivered by them to the smelting house. Edward Talbot had the task of both assaying and weighing the ore presented, and then, by some means or other, getting it smelted into lead and sold for a price which would bring a good profit to the King. The most difficult task, and the one open to great abuse, was the assaying of the ore. Short of examining every piece with an expert eye it was virtually impossible to say that that which was presented by the miners was the required galena. There were a whole range of compositions associated with the ore: metallic salts, silicates, an inferior ore called binge, and a material called blende, from the German *blenden*, to deceive. Some of these such as fluorite or fluorspar blende or zinc sulphide, and calamine, were valuable if they could be recognized and separated, but all that the eye of Edward Talbot could do was reject the obvious blue shale and dirt, and take the rest in good faith. The partnerships were paid £3 a ton, today's equivalent of £1,200, so it can be seen that considerable sums of money were involved, and a considerable incentive was there, both to produce, and at the same time to cheat.

Roger and Edward were helped in their reorganization by the willingness of some of the miners to group into a partnership and continue to work in the same grooves. This indicates that the workers, the men who should know, were satisfied with the richness of the mine; and that the ore was sufficiently available for them to make a profit under the Derbyshire system. Consequently four of the workers – Richard Royle, Thomas Whitaker, Joe Cresswell and Nicholas Birch – took over two grooves and employed six boys at 3s a week as drawers, and two women, part time, as washers.

The second partnership was more of a capitalistic

venture financed by two gentlemen working one groove, and employing a pickman at 5s 6d per week, a boy Sutcliffe at 3s a week, and Gascoigne's wife washing at 4s a week. They were greatly troubled by water, so only produced one ton of ore in the month from 16 April to 16 May 1630. In comparison the first partnership had delivered 8 tons, worth £24.

The gentlemen involved were John Talbot (of the broken leg), and a new and interesting character, Thomas Cockcroft. He came from his estate of Greenwood Lee, part of the beautiful valley of Hardcastle Craggs, near Hebden Bridge. He had proved to be the best buyer of lead, and in addition was eager to become involved in the mine itself. John Talbot, despite his accident, was probably content merely to finance the venture, and leave the supervision to his son, Edward, Roger Kenyon's deputy at the mine.

Because of the failure of the water-groove, the Commissioners promised the free miners that they would undertake a new method of keeping the grooves free of water. This new Project recommended by the experts was to drive a horizontal tunnel from lower down the hillside at right angles to the fault, in which was found the vein of ore. It was hoped that when this tunnel struck the fault the water-table in the region of the mine would be lowered by the water draining away down the fault and out through the drainage tunnel. This was very advanced practice for the year 1630, possibly the first or at least the second example in England of a method which was later to become standard practice wherever mines were wrought in the hills and valleys, be it in Wales,

Derbyshire, the Lake District, or the Yorkshire Dales. If it were a drainage tunnel it was called a sough or an adit, but if used for bringing the ore out of the mine it was called a level. These levels were, in later times, fitted with rails and the ore run out to the dressing floors in very sturdily built wagons. In some cases where the flow of water was excessive, a sufficient depth was maintained by means of a dam and sluice gate to float the ore out in narrow boats. But at Thieveley the tunnel was meant only to be a drainage sough. The ore had to be wound up the shafts by turntrees to be delivered to the dressing floor.

The Commissioners put this project into operation with great vigour. A man named James Fairbanks undertook to dig an open trench which would spill the water over the precipitous sides of Dodbottom Clough. And when this trench had reached its maximum depth in a deep cutting, a man named Gervase Gascoigne contracted to drive the sough into the hillside for a price of 8s per fathom. The strata through which he had to tunnel was the Accrington Mudstone, a soft rock from which the finest bricks in the world, the Accrington 'Iron' bricks, are made. This was a comparatively easy rock to cut, but had the disadvantage that it was not self supporting and had to be shored up with timber. It is believed that the smallest tunnel which it was practical to work, and to ventilate, with men lying on their sides, would be one of about 30 inches square. There would be a pickman at the rock face, tearing out the rock by candlelight, and men loading the spoil into sledges and dragging them out to the spoil heap, all on their hands and knees. They must surely have worn leather kneecaps.

One can but be amazed at the fortitude of such men, prepared to burrow into the unknown hazards of the hillside without benefit of any rescue service.

James Fairbanks started on the open trench immediately after the meeting of 8 April, and this enabled the tunnelling of the sough to commence by 16 May. Work on this sough continued, at the King's expense, without remittance throughout the summer of 1630.

Also during this summer a third attempt was made at smelting in the Thieveley smelt-house. This was sparked off by a letter of 18 July from John Talbot, a letter which was also a very touching rejoinder upon his plight following upon his accident on the Thieveley hillside.

John Talbot to Roger Kenyon, 18 July, 1630:

To his vere good Master and approoved good Frende Mr. Ro. Kenion at Parkeheade his house be these deliverd.

Good Sir, Myne opinion is that (if yow be satisfyed that those bellowes that are to be boughte bee of Carre his beste makinge, yt is better to buye them, beinge both very durable and wille rightly serve your turne, than to bee at charges of mending your owne and in doubte whether they will serve well when yow have doone or noe; besydes the losse of tyme, which is precious unto yow. Mr. Butler of Newcastell and all the bests leads masters I knowe have fetched theire bellowes from Carre, and the pryce aboute £6 or 20 nobles, as I remember. Yf your smelter have bene used to a foote blasts then no doubte of his welldoinge. I gave my smelter a noble a tunne and founde one to helpe him and foure blowers or treaders to whom I gave an other noble so that my leade lay me in a marke a tunne besyde my chopwood, which musts be cutte to the syze of the smelters harthe, otherwyse theare willbe eyther more wood spente or lesse leade runne.

I comend my lame legge to your charitable consideracon, and would be gladde to knowe my falte, that I mights (if I coulde) amende it for sure so kynde a master woulde never have forsaken so lovinge a servants without some more than ordinarie cause. And since I coulde not doe any servyce I am now yt semeth in the case of Aesop's dogge. And the worlde takings notyce of the smale accompte I am made of, every knave doth now grossly abuse me, so that I am earnestly to intreat you out of the true love I have ever borne you that you woulde be pleased to see me, in hope that my greefe havinge bene suche in respects of your absence (as I veryly thinke) hath hindered my legge for mendinge so faste as yt woulde have doone by your kynde visites. So. now I may by your presents not onely fynde more ease but also that by your good advyse I maye better helpe my selfe againste myne adversaries. And thoe I have not so good legges as heretofore, I have the same harte serve and pray for you and yours, and ever reste your poore, oblyged, cripple and lovinge servante.

Carre, the 18th of Julye, 1630.   J. Talbott.

As a result of this letter, on 24 July, Roger Kenyon began a journey on horseback to Shiregreen near Sheffield, to place an order for the third set of bellows to be tried at the mine. He stayed the Tuesday night at Halifax, journeyed to Sheffield on the Wednesday, placed the order with a deposit of five shillings on the Thursday, and was back at Halifax for the Friday night. Here his horse needed shoeing, at a cost of sixpence. Thos. Carre did not waste much time either, for the bellows were delivered to Thieveley during the week beginning 7 August.

A Robert Whitaker undertook the carriage of the bellows from Sheffield, and one wonders whether these were transported on poles across the backs of ponies, or whether he was able to make the journey, it being summertime, with a horse and cart. Whatever the method the charge was sixteen shillings which was the equivalent of four weeks' wages for what may only have been a four-day journey, there and back. Thos. Carre accompanied the bellows to superintend their installation at Thieveley, and the total cost of the whole operation came to £8 19s 6d.

Having lost confidence in the first two smelters, Charles Core and Godfrey Wheatley, an approach was made to a smelter, William Badger, from the Duke of Cumberland's mines at Grassington, where a sample of Thieveley ore had so successfully yielded a good return of lead. Being given 1s 6d, a lad was sent, using his wits and his tongue, to find his way to Grassington, to guide William Badger back to Thieveley. On this journey the boy would have walked over 60 miles, slept under the hedgerows, and only spent his money on food and ale.

The smelter was apparently satisfied with the smelt-house, for it is recorded that he worked at Thieveley from July to September at a wage of 6s 8d per week. He was present while the new bellows from Sheffield were being installed, and no doubt a trial run would be made with Thomas Carr, the bellows maker, supervising the four men who were engaged for the arduous task of treadling the bellows.

Despite this, however, the smelting of two tons of ore only yielded 600 pounds of lead, and that only at a totally prohibitive cost in burning wood and labour. It is probable that by the first week in September the smelter's exasperation had reached such a pitch that he threw up his job, for William Badger walked to Kenyon's house at Whalley to demand his money, which was always overdue, and then disappears from the accounts, the third smelter to do so in less than two years.

One can imagine Roger's despair as, badly needing the money from the sale of lead, he watched the disgruntled smelter set off on his return to Grassington, along that age-old trade route through Gisburn, Gargrave and Cracoe.

CHAPTER XIX

Edward Talbot

B ecause of subsequent events, it is now necessary to say
something about the young overseer Edward Talbot.
Talbot is one of the illustrious names in English history.

In the year AD 1280 Edmund de Lacy of Clitheroe
Castle granted much of the glorious valley of the River
Hodder to a branch of the Talbot family. Here was
beauty, fertility, and some of the finest fishing and hunting
country in the Kingdom. The Talbots established
themselves in the valley, and were confirmed in the
possession of Bashall Eaves and Mitton near Clitheroe by
Edmund Crouchback, youngest son of Henry III and first
Earl of Lancaster. During the ensuing centuries, the
Talbots built halls and developed estates; on the Ribble at
Salebury and Dinckley; and at Slaidburn at the head of
the Hodder Valley. During this period they occupied
nearly every office of importance, in the Honor of
Clitheroe, for the great Dukes of Lancaster, as park-
keepers, foresters, seneschals, and constables of Clitheroe
Castle. In 1589, after the death of John Talbot of Salebury
Hall, there was an inquisition-post-mortem which
revealed that he had a family of illegitimate children,
referred to as born ante-matrimonium. The eldest, John,

was slain on 27 June 1568 in an affray by John Dewhurst, his mother's lawful husband. The second son, Robert of Ribchester, married a natural daughter of Sir Richard Houghton, the one who entertained James I at Houghton Towers when the King is reputed to have knighted the loin of beef. This daughter was one of a family which Sir Richard had had by a servant woman, Ann Brown.

Now the reason for the success and survival through the centuries of certain families is because of the care which they took in the succession, always passing on their estates intact to the eldest son. But this did not mean that they neglected the younger sons, or even their daughters. They were provided for in many ways, by purchase of lands, by lucrative employments, and most of all by judicious marriages. And, taking their cue from Royalty, the upper classes even looked after their illegitimate children. They were 'legitimized' within one generation by grants of land and by well-connected marriages. The large family of the love-children, Robert of Ribchester and Margaret of Houghton, were baptized as legitimate Talbots, and took their place, as became their fortune, in the ranks of the Lancastrian middle classes.

The eldest of this new Talbot family, John, occupied land within his grandfather's desmesne of Salebury, and built himself a house, Carr Hall, at Wilpshire near Blackburn. And when lead and silver were discovered in the hills flanking the Hodder, the true-blue Talbots called upon the inferior branch of the family to soil their hands with trade and industry. In this way John Talbot of Carr Hall became involved in the Talbot lead mines in the Trough of Bowland and on Waddington Fell, and so became the man appealed to by Sir Ralph Assheton to advise the King's Commission upon the development of the Thieveley Lead Mine. John seized upon this opportunity to place one of his younger sons, Edward, in a position connected with the establishment and the Crown. It would be a great help if the lad could make his own way in the Government's service. Roger Kenyon greatly valued John Talbot's mining expertise, and was only too glad to have John's son in regular attendance at the mine, so that he was quite prepared to take the young man, at his own expense, to act as his deputy whilst he, Roger, attended to his own businesses. But, understandably, he could only pay Edward a small wage, and the barest minimum for his keep. He had hoped that Alice Hartley would be able to accommodate Edward, but Alice and Robert, shrewdly assessing that there would be no profit for them in the arrangement, pleaded with some truth that there was no accommodation for a third adult in their single-roomed farmhouse. Consequently, Edward was lodged at the inn of Holme Chapel.

Prices for accommodation were controlled by edict at 1d per night or 6d per week for a feather bed, 4d per week for a flock bed, 6d for a meal, which included all a man could eat of the finest victuals, and 5d per night for the care and feeding of his horse. It can be seen therefore that Edward's costs for his own and his horse's keep was 12d per day, and this was the exact amount which Roger Kenyon allowed to him. In explaining this to the Chancellor, Roger writes: 'The Clerke of the Workes doth think this but smale allowance, beinge but at the rate of twelve pence per diem upon his owne table, yett the comodity arriseinge no better to his Majesty as yett we durst not presume to allow more, as the profitt increaseth your lordship may consider of this as you think fit.'

And so the young Edward Talbot settled in to a lonely and impecunious life in the remote and almost uncivilized valley, sitting out the long evenings in the kitchen-parlour of the inn. Soon, however, strangers arrived enquiring for him, seeking his company, and buying him ale. And because he could not treat them in return they soon had the advantage of him, for each had come for his own purpose, to take meares in the mine, to buy lead, or to offer their expertise.

This was the nature of Thomas Cockcroft's arrival and his open Yorkshire demeanour, his ready confidence, and even readier purse soon won the young man's esteem, so that he accepted Thomas' generosity and was persuaded to join in a partnership in a meare of ground. However, the young man was astute enough always to put his father's name to all written documents.

Another individual who sponged upon him was a certain Lawrence Watmough whose grandfather Hugh Watmough had been the priest at the Holme Chantry Chapel. Lawrence Watmough had woodlands, he had also discovered outcrops of coal, and he had already supplied wood and coal to Highley and Butler.

He was anxious to maintain his sales to the new management, and he also pestered the young gentleman to use his influence to obtain for him an alehouse licence to open the first tippling house in the Cliviger township. That Edward Talbot had difficulty in refusing these requests, is revealed by a letter he addressed to Roger Kenyon on 16 May 1630, 'Good Sir, these maye be to intreate your favour in a businesse concerning a lisence for bruinge. There is a frend of myne, one Lawrence Wattmough he keepes the Coale pitts and is very sufficient for keeping ayle and hath kept verye good order, and a man in no greate neede but desires a license and will pay for it, and withal will keepe good order and bring good suratie for the same. So I did presume to intreate your vavor and furtherance in this cause.'

But during the long evenings at the inn Edward became convinced that he was not like the other frequenters of the inn. They appeared to be completely absorbed in their gambling, their card games, and their ale and apparently oblivious of the women who served them, or prepared food over the kitchen hearth. But he himself could raise little enthusiasm for their rough sport, and had to admit to himself that it was the womenfolk who excited his interest. He could not help being affected by their every movement, as though they emanated waves which both attracted and disturbed him. He had constantly to drag his eyes away from watching them. There was one young woman, Meg, who wore a kirtle laced across her bosom. She was a maiden of great capabilities and energy, and in bustling around the home the laces supporting her breasts loosened, and her skirt swung open revealing no petticoat beneath, with tantalizing glimpses of her bare legs. Professing an interest in the malt house, and the brewery, Edward sought her company, and found himself enthralled by her femininity and particularly the subtle aromas of her healthy young body.

During the evenings when there was no other company in the parlour, the host, who had begun to value Edward, not for the money he spent, but for the custom he attracted, would sit with him and try to amuse him with bawdy talk.

'It bi'ant right,' he would get round to saying, 'for a young gentleman like yourself to go to his bed without a woman. Just thee say the word an' a'll slip one atween the blankets for thi.'

But Edward always laughingly refused. He had been warned by his father of the horrors of the pox, when a man became a social outcast, to die a slow death of rejection and ostracism by everyone he knew and loved. But perhaps the main reason he rejected the offer was because he could not afford the almost certain doubling of his board. And so he existed in a life rendered disturbing by the almost impossible demands of his employment, and the twin frustrations of a relative poverty and a nagging sex starvation.

However, much of this was changed in one evening of encounter and debauchery on the day he arrived back at the inn to find two middle-aged cavaliers installed in obsequious splendour in the parlour. All other company had been banished into the barn and cow shippon, which served as a part-time tippling house for the inferior locals.

The two newcomers were seated at the round gate-legged table behind the finest meal that the house could provide. Edward stammered his apology and made to withdraw, but one of the men jumped up, bowed, and invited him to join with them at their meal.

'I am all dishevelled from my duties at the mine.'

'It matters not – we are men of the world and have supped at many a table covered with the mud and blood of the battlefield. Your honest condition offends us not at all and there are no ladies to turn up their pretty noses, so sit down, man, and enjoy your just rewards, this house's truly excellent mutton and beef.'

After a lengthy meal during which they tasted everything which the innkeeper brought – enjoying some and rejecting others – with praise for mine host, or hurling the offending dish at him as he fled out of the room, and his wife bustled in to clear up the mess, Edward again excused himself. His mind was on the bill of fare, but the taller man of the two stood up, and, placing his hand on his sword, ordered him to stay. Seeing the temper in the cavalier's face Edward could only reply, 'Good Sir, I had no thought of insulting you, I wished not to intrude upon your privacy.'

'I will be the judge of that, and in the meantime you are my guest, so forget the maid who may be waiting for thee under the chestnut tree. I will provide you with better sport than any you can contrive for yourself.'

He called out through the doorway, 'Mine host.'

The innkeeper came hurrying in.

'Keep us this jug filled with ale and that fire burning brightly and let's see no more of thine ugly face. Send us the comeliest wench that thou canst find – from the village if need be – to wait upon us. We want no old hag turning our blood cold and the ale sour. Aye, and make sure she is clean and smelleth sweet even if thou has to wash her thyself, and powder her with lavender. Now get thee gone and see that thou pleaseth us well for your reward shall depend upon it.'

He helped the innkeeper out of the room with a well-aimed kick up his backside.

Shortly afterwards Meg entered the room carrying a copper jug of ale. She curtseyed and placed the ale on the table.

To the sweet smell of her luxuriant hair, Edward detected the aroma of lavender, which all innkeepers kept to sprinkle in the beds of those guests who had ladies in their company.

'Go tell my serving man to bring all my pipes and tobacco, and a bucket to put in yonder corner,' the cavalier ordered curtly.

CHAPTER XX

The Orgy at the Inn
and its Aftermath

When the pipes and tobacco had been brought, the cavalier ordered Meg to sit on a tuffet by his side; and then, with kindness and gentleness in his manner, showed her how to fill and light the pipes.

'Now lass, thinkest thou can keep us well supplied?'

'Aye, my lord, that I can,' the girl replied, and her eyes shone with eagerness.

From then on my lord took little notice of her except now and then, almost absent-mindedly, to run his hand over her, as a farmer assessing a prize beast.

'I brought this tobacco over myself from our colony at Jamestown. It is the only good thing to come out of that God-forsaken place. A Norfolk man, John Rolfe, the same who married the Indian princess Pocahontas, brought the seedlings from Trinidad. I was on shipboard with them in 1616, when they came over to England. Rolfe was more worried about his baby son than the princess. He seemed to make nought of her station. But she was a fine woman; had been taught the English and brought to Christianity by a cleric, Alexander Whitaker.'

'Aye,' Edward broke in, 'I have heard something of the

tale. His cousin Thomas Whitaker, who owns lands hereabouts, is building a new stone house, at the Holme, just beyond the old chapel. The tale is often told, but we never really knew the true story.'

'Well I can tell thee chapter and verse for I saw most of it with mine own eyes.'

As they smoked the pipes and wetted their palates with ale, the cavalier kept his audience enthralled with tales of the infant colony of Virginia and the girl listened to every word, yet never allowed them to be kept waiting for ale or tobacco.

And as the evening progressed the cavalier's hands became more bold. Though not interrupting his talk, he deftly untied the laces across her bosom, and gently lifting out her breasts, put in a little aside:

'If a man wisheth a long life he should only take two drinks, his mother's milk and good ale – especially if he goeth abroad – for there the water will bring on strange fevers, the wine, and fiery spirits made from the sugar cane, will rot his guts, and he will die, with half the women in his life unserved.'

A little later he filled his tankard, and turning to Meg, said 'Now, lass, it is thirsty work for thee sitting by this fire, stand up and let us see thee drain this ale.'

Meg stood up and tipped back her head so that her long hair, which he had loosened, fell down halfway to the floor, and as she drank he stroked her hair and loosened the remainder of the laces which held her dress together, and fondled her.

'Gentlemen,' he said, 'the lady is eager for our favours – it would be churlish of us to keep so fine a wench in further suspense.'

He stood up, and began to unbuckle his sword belt.

'The only occasion when a man is justified in laying aside his sword is to reward the ladies for their care of us. Now, men, off with your swords and let's see what thou art made of, and who is the better man at a sweeter contest than swording. Take your places at the table.'

The second cavalier, who knew the drill, cast off his sword, loosened his breeches and stood at his dining place by the round gate-legged table, and Edward, taking his cue, did likewise.

Meanwhile his lordship had taken the girl in his arms and was bringing the hot blood to her face with his kisses. When his companions were in station, he lifted her onto the table edge and entered her until she moaned in ecstasy; and then, when she cried out with her orgasm, he spun her round the table to his companion, who, soon having his will, sent her to Edward who could scarce entertain her for a second such was his excitement, before having to despatch her back to the cavalier.

'Nay, gentlemen, thou'st will have to do better than that to please the wench.' And he held her until she again cried out with delight.

And so it went on until the second cavalier could continue no longer.

'I am done,' he said and collapsed back on his chair with laughter and took up his tankard of ale.

'Now it is between thee and me,' said his lordship, his eyes blazing into Edward.

But a young man's ardour is soon spent, and ere long Edward had no more to offer.

'Now, sweet child – have you done also?'

'Oh no, sir, durnt thee leave me.'

He continued with her, counting her orgasms as the hot flushes engulfed him. He was a man who had learned to control his emissions, and had acquired the power of self-hypnotizing himself into a state of *erectus permanus*.

But, at length, sensing that she was satisfied he gave her his bolt, but still holding her, said:

'Well, lass, didst ever know a man like me?'

'No sir, I never did, and mayhap never shall. I would follow thee to the end of the world.'

He let her go and placed her on his chair by the fire. Filling a tankard he handed it to her, and while she drank he laced up the dress which he had previously undone. It was as though he could not do enough for her. But he was still the stage manager, producer, director and principal actor rolled into one.

'Now, Ned lad, tell mine host we require supper, the best he can provide, and for four – remember that, for four on pain of his life.'

The host and his minions quickly laid supper for four, and during the meal his lordship waited on Meg as though she were Charles' French Queen, Henrietta Maria.

'And for thy reward, lass, thou cans't sleep in a warm bed by my side,' he assured her.

In the morning Edward Talbot was called as usual to make his way with thick head, and unsteady legs up the steep track to the mine. After supervising the weighing and storage of the ore he sought comfort in the farmhouse kitchen.

'I was drinking late last night,' he told Alice, 'with two

gentlemen, and today I am fit for nothing – my legs will scarce hold me upright.'

'Well sit thee there and I'll mix thee a warm drink with some herbs. We call it the hair of the dog that has bitten thee.'

After the hard life outside, and the company of the crude and belligerent miners, it was a great comfort to sit by her fireside and be waited upon. But he was startled from a half-sleep by an imperious knocking on the door. The cavalier and his companion strode into the room.

'By Jupiter, man – I thought thou wouldst have had enough of ale, and womankind, last night.'

'Nay,' Edward denied, 'I was just resting awhile afore the next weighing of the ore.'

'Aha, and chosen good company withal.' The man's keen eyes were fixed upon Alice until she blushed and curtseyed.

'Can I get you some ale, sir?' she recovered her composure and command of her own kitchen.

'That you can – it has been warm work climbing yon hill, and looking for that young fellow in the mud and mire of the mine.'

After the two men had satisfied their thirst, he turned to Edward. 'Now, in the King's name, I order you to show me all there is of his Majesty's mine.'

Edward had no thought of challenging the authority which characterized every one of this man's actions. He took the two men on a tour of the grooves, the washing and dressing floor, the smelting house, and, way down the hillside, the digging and driving into the hillside of the sough. And he was ready to answer all their questions

which were mainly about the weighing, recording of the
ore and the keeping of the accounts for all the items
which were arriving daily at the mine on the backs of the
packhorse ponies.

After a meal in the farmhouse, which the cavalier paid
for with a golden coin, the two men mounted their horses
for their journey over the pike to Rochdale. So that there
was no danger of them losing their way, before nightfall,
across the wastelands, Edward acted as guide as far
as Sharneyford at the watershed between Bacup and
Todmorden. The cavalier's parting words were brief.

'That lead mine hath only three prospects for thee, the
girl at the inn, the husbandwife at the farmhouse, and the
labouring woman who washeth the ore.'

With these words and a wave of his hat, he was gone
over the high moorlands which led down into the Wardle
valley.

'The husbandwoman in the farmhouse, aye.' Edward,
in his loneliness and frustration at the mine, had
constantly sought her company, and had lusted after her.
But she was always busy about the household, occupied in
some urgent task, such as turning the malt, pressing the
cheeses or churning the butter. As she had to Roger
Kenyon, she offered him great comfort at her fireside as
she considered was his right as a gentleman. And then the
coarse folk around the mine had begun to talk freely of
these occasional visits to the farmhouse.

'He's off in to Mrs Pym, to get his stick varnished,' they
gibed even in his hearing, and there were smirks and
knowing looks when he reappeared. 'She's having to make
do w'it young bull since Humphrey went a whoam.' But

161

before the coming of the cavalier, Edward had hesitated in nervous lack of confidence, and hopes of intimacy had receded further into the background, as he drooled over Alice at the mine and Meg at the inn, in a state of sexual starvation.

But, after the orgy at the inn, something of the boldness and recklessness of the cavalier had entered into his nature. 'The woman who washeth the ore'.

Yes, Jenet Birch was a fine woman. And not just in body alone. She had a natural ability to master any task, as we have seen, either drawing and winding or washing the ore in preparation for the smelter. Edward had gradually found himself relying upon her in the assaying and weighing and in the allocations to the various partnerships. She seemed to have the whole business at her fingertips.

When women are scarce in a company of men, even the plainest acquire irresistible charms. But as the lascivious eyes of the cavalier had discovered, Jenet Birch was far from being plain. In the hot summer sunshine, glad of the cool water which perhaps purposely she had splashed over her scanty clothing as she washed the ore, her nakedness was all but revealed.

Edward, his passions stimulated rather than appeased, could not take his eyes off her as he hovered around the dressing floor. And when he stood at her side, scarce able to keep his hands off her, she turned to him and murmured quietly, 'Why doesn't tha do summat about it, instead of just standing there staring?'

It was the invitation he had almost desperately been wanting for, to spark off the fire.

He picked her up and carried her to the grassy bank behind the smelt-house where he experienced the body-shattering thrill of pent-up anticipation and lust released, followed by the rapture which only a generous and vibrant woman can give. Jenet was all these but she was also an ambitious woman and from that moment on she and not Edward Talbot became the real overseer of the mine, as he, almost with the balance of his mind disturbed, became besotted of the three prospects bequeathed to him by the visit of the King's inspector.

CHAPTER XXI

A Rude Shock
from the Chancellor

Once again the acknowledgement of their report came back to the Commissioners all too soon, and instead of being complementary upon their efforts, it was an ill-tempered rebuke.

'I am a little astonished that contrary to the directions and instructions sent unto you from mee by his Majesties Command, you have entertayned and employed all workmen in such a course (as we conceave) as is likely to prove most prejuditial and disadvantageous to his Majesties proffitt'.

He commands that the workmen be returned to a wage-earning system, but he does concede that 'the craft and idleness of workmen' could be discouraged by some form of piecework, 'rateably or proportionately to the quantity they shall daily or weekly gett'. He quotes the Commissioners' own evidence in their first report from the deposition under oath of a miner, Frances Leigh, 'That there might be gotten by two workmen in one groove, one Loade of Oare a day and so proportionately six loades a week'. He remarks that this 'maketh the accompt now returned from you appear more strange and displeasing to his Majestie in regard that it reduceth these Mynes to the same ill-condition that they were in before in the handes of the said Highley & Butler'.

He concludes this part of the rebuke 'his Majestie will by no means endure the governing of the Mynes in the way you are now in, nor the introducing of Lott & Cope and the Customs of Derbyshire into this which is entirely his owne'.

And then, surprisingly, he orders Roger Kanyon to take a journey into Derbyshire, ' . . . and att your retourne thoroughly to waigh and consider by what means you may reduce these, his Majesties works to the best order and disposition'.

This, of course, the Commissioners had already anticipated by calling in the experts from Bowland and Grassington, but the Chancellor in an ill-considered fit of temper had rejected their efforts.

The only concession he was at present prepared to tolerate was the introduction of piecework in place of daywork. It is remarkable that nearly 400 years ago the Chancellor was advocating this almost certain source of industrial trouble, only solved in modern times by elaborate procedures of work-study, rate-fixing, and shop-floor agreements, only suitable for mass-produced items, and never for so chancy a venture as lead mining.

It was as equally unfortunate for Roger Kenyon and Edward Talbot that they should have the responsibility for administering the system. The age-old Derbyshire manner, which the Chancellor so dogmatically rejected, had been evolved to ensure a harmonious working arrangement between capital and labour, and had acquired a tradition of fair play which ensured its ready acceptance even in the most cantankerous disputes. It was the hammered-out formula for peaceful industrial relations – an employer's charter and workers' rule-book rolled into one.

But worse was to follow. The Chancellor finally accuses the Commissioners of adopting exactly the same tactics as Highley and Butler in concealing the true richness of the mine, and in magnifying the difficulties so that they could eventually obtain a cheap lease of it, and all that the King would receive would be the duty – his Lott and Cope – on the lead produced. The Chancellor concludes with the threat that all at the mine can only disobey the King's commands 'att their perrills' – this from a feudal privy Councillor, backed by a monarch who believed implicitly in the Divine Right of Kings, could only mean one thing: death or imprisonment in the Tower.

Consequently, after the Chancellor's latest strictures, the Commissioners resorted to guile. Once again they dismissed the various partnerships of free miners and shut down all work except upon the water-groove and the adit, on the pretext that until the mine was drained, they could not employ workmen on day wages or piecework.

Gervase Gascoigne continued his intrepid tunnelling into the hillside whilst the ever-willing Nicholas Birch sank the water-groove, and the redoubtable Jenet worked at the turntrees winding up the spoil, and sorting out and washing any ore which came up. It is interesting to speculate upon the method used to ensure that the adit was driven along exactly the correct line to meet the water-groove which, after all, was only some six feet square.

It is probable that some sighting point was used on the

opposite slopes of the Cliviger Valley to start off the trench and tunnel in the correct direction, and then the tunnel kept straight by sighting along a line of candles.

Whatever the method, it was successful, for as the adit approached the lead-mine fault, ore was brought out from the entrance and carried back up the hill for Jenet to wash, and in what must have been a momentous encounter, Gervase at last broke through to meet Nicholas in the water-groove. Again, one marvels at the fortitude or foolhardiness of these men. The final breakthrough could have been fraught with peril if the accumulated water in the mine had burst in upon the helpless Gervase buried 200 feet beneath the earth. With remarkable cleverness he must have run the tunnel on a slight up-grade to drain away the water, and again the untutored Nicholas Birch must have known how to sink his shaft below the expected breakthrough to form a sump hole in the bottom of the mine, and so prevent poor Gervase from being drowned like a rat in its hole.

But all this is to anticipate, for the adit was not to be completed for several months yet.

Meanwhile, having cut the workforce to a minimum, which also reduced the drain upon their finances and improved relations with the Receiver, Roger Kenyon set off on his tour of the lead-mining field in Derbyshire. Not surprisingly, in his absence, Edward Talbot, true to his inheritance from the love-child of two of Lancashire's most dynamic families, pursued with great ardour the girl Meg at the inn and Jenet at the mine. His amorous adventures added just that touch of spice which had been lacking in his early days at the mine.

The long summer evenings were passed in eager anticipation of the hour when Meg would slide into his bed, and yet such was the appetite of youth that, in the daytime, he was ready for Jenet at any time – and sometimes two or three times – upon the hill.

But pleasure has to be paid for in cash or in kind. His meagre salary from Roger did not enable him to pay the extras which the hostelier placed upon his bill, or enable him to lavish any gifts upon Meg – gifts which he was sure she deserved. At the mine, Jenet was of that ilk who wanted nothing for her generosity, except domination over him. So long as he ran the mine with her approval, she was satisfied.

His newfound success with the women brought with it a confidence in his dealing with the men. He issued orders easily to the labourers in the mine and had little hesitation in concluding bargains with the clothiers and chapmen who sought him out at the inn.

He lost all sense of conscience in making deals which diverted a little money into his own pocket, and no longer hesitated at taking hospitality and even gifts of money from his business associates. The shine in his eyes was all for Meg and for Jenet as he lived through a summer of make-believe. But the euphoria, the confidence, and the feeling of infallibility was only akin to that of the inebriate. The stark realities were totally different. The world smiled at his foolishness. The workers at the mine sniggered behind his back, and took every advantage of him. The dealers soon found that he was easy meat once they had bought him ale and greased his palm with silver.

*   *   *

Within the Thieveley farmhouse, Robert and Alice Hartley were able to add to their hoard of gold and silver coins. Robert, having been told that he could no longer occupy a groove as a free miner, redoubled his efforts to find ore within the confines of his farm, and at places on the wastelands away from the mine. He had a little success where the lead-mine fault crossed a mountain stream in a clough, then called Black Dike, and now called Black Clough. He carried the ore home on his back to add to his accumulation.

Alice, however, was still disenchanted with the mine and still looked back with longing to the days before it disrupted her life. The offensive huddle of turf houses still overlooked their farmstead upon the slope of Dean Scout, and its inhabitants, though coming to buy her ale, treated her with derision.

The only compatible visitors were Roger Kenyon and the young Edward Tolbot, and even these had to be kept in their place. She had been particularly worried by Edward coming in at all hours to sit by her fireside for hours at a time, talking to her and watching her about her work with desire in his eyes. When she knelt down at the hearth to attend to the cooking, the atmosphere had been electric in its intensity, and she had been aware that one false move would precipitate a crisis which may have gone beyond her control. And then he became involved with Jenet Birch and, although he still used her fireside to while away the long hours of boredom, the intensity had gone out of his demeanour. And Alice was in no small way piqued that he had obtained consolation elsewhere, so that any need he may have had for her was no longer critical.

When the smelting furnace was relit and the sulphurous fumes blew low over the house and penetrated every ill-fitting door and window, she could not restrain her anger and frustration, so that Edward no longer called in, spending more time with Jenet upon the moor.

In her frustration, Alice railed at Robert and at everyone who came to the door, until she was in danger of becoming a sour and disgruntled woman with a bitter edge to her tongue – such as Shakespeare labelled a shrew – until, little by little, the insidious rumour began to circulate round the miners' camp: 'Mrs Pym is a witch.'

As the summer progressed, the demand for cash once again exceeded the supply. At pay-day, Edward was again surrounded as by a pack of hungry wolves, and it was the strong-minded Jenet Birch who protected him from their fangs.

'There,' she said, taking the money out of his hands, 'this is all there be, and I'll divide it equally among thee.' And, so saying, she went from man to man. 'A shilling for thee and a shilling for thee . . . ' until the money was all gone and each had had an equal share. Edward then, in desperation, had to send a message for more to Roger Kenyon. In the absence of a universal postage system, the gentry carried letters for one another, and a man named Frank Braddyl of the influential family of Portfield, near Whalley, must have been on hand to carry Edward's letter.

Edward Talbot to Roger Kenyon, 3 Sept. 1630 – carried by Frank Braddyl:

> To his esteemed very good frend Mr. Roger Kenion at his house neare Walleie these.

Good Sir, Willme the Smelter beinge comne to yowe, since he went the workmen desired me to send to yow for their moneths paie, the months end being upon Saturdaie the furth daie of September. For the reason is the scantnesse of victuals and being not in creddit in the contrie they can gett nothing without moneie, and is verie unable to worke without, as Francke Braddell can tell you scant the contrie is.

The moneth charge I have sent you by Franc Braddell. Wee alsoe want wood, sire, for our grooves for the last weeke hath made us verie wett and we have had a great storr with the audiat, Garvis havinge driven soe far without tymber, and besids hath lost some levaile in the strikinge thorowe. Alsoe I am in debt for candles that wee have had this moneth. Sos wishing you to lett me knowe how wee maie commpasse some wood, for if wee have not wood wee can not sincke. For Nic Bertch in his sincking he goes downe fast but he must have tymber, and also Cassons shaft, having beene in Davies and Cassons hand, have sett verie slowelie to tymber, see that now wen the wete hath comn to it, it is verie ill to keepe upp without tymber, the toes beginning to rise, and as wee have beane tymbering to Fridaie a pece of earth fell and hath hort one of our men, but god be praised is reasonable well, soe fearing to trouble with this scrowle, and to heare your resolucion, I remaine yours to his power.

Ed. Talbott

Thiefley this instant Fridaie being the third date of September, 1630.

Roger could only send money of his own, as, remembering Sir Ralph's advice, he deemed it politic to beggar himself rather than displease that conclave of sinister men who held power in Westminster.

CHAPTER XXII

The Commissioners' Reply

The thoughts of the Commissioners, during the summer of 1630, were channelled more into schemes of mollifying the Chancellor's displeasure than in attending to the real management of the mine.

They had, by now, realized the mess which their first optimistic report had got them into. The Chancellor's dream of instant riches must be tactfully dispelled without inciting his further displeasure, and so, in the short term, they planned a summer report to educate the Chancellor in the real difficulties – the ones which had almost ruined Highley & Butler, and which they had now to overcome. But, at the same time, they were sufficiently realistic to plan, in the long term, for the ultimate success of the mine.

Firstly, Roger Kenyon paid a ten-day visit to Derbyshire, and during this time, his investigation into the lead mining industry there, and the subsequent paper which he wrote, was so comprehensive and practical as to indicate that he was, indeed, a man with a very clear and logical mind.

If the Chancellor had troubled to read this detailed report, he ought thereafter to be completely familiar with that which the Commissioners were constantly advocating – the Derbyshire manner of operating the mine.

However, not content to take the evidence of the Derbyshire field alone, Roger also toured the mines in Staffordshire, and upon returning home, took a journey into Wharfedale to study the operations at Grassington, at present being developed by the Duke of Cumberland. Here was the water-powered smelt-mill on the banks of the River Wharfe which had so successfully smelted the Thieveley ore. Again he found that these mines were operated in the Derbyshire manner.

Having laboured continuously during the summer months of 1630, being scarcely out of the saddle nor his hand out of his purse in journeying the length and breadth of the South Pennines – a roadless wilderness – wrestling with problems of which he had no previous experience, Roger Kenyon was at last able to present sufficient information to his fellow Commissioners for them to compile a report which they hoped would mollify the Chancellor's spleen.

There is little doubt that the advice of the barrister, Saville Radcliffe of Todmorden Hall, was used in compiling the report for the summer quarter of 1630. Roger Kenyon's detailed findings were attached, and on account of his extended journeys, the Commissioners were not able to despatch their reply to the Chancellor's accusations until 26 October 1630.

After describing the reorganization of the work on day wages with a total concentration on the draining of the mine, they declare: 'now it is in a faire and perfecte course for a triall of what value it wilbee, which may require a good tyme yett ere it bee fullie discovered'.

They then describe their abortive attempts at smelting

the ore in the Thieveley smelt-house. Despite employing several experienced men, and three different bellows – the last made by 'one Carre – a man famous for that trade' – and again using an experienced smelter from the Earl of Cumberland's works in Yorkshire, the results were so poor that 'we left it off, and are satisfied in our judgement that there is noe way to melt it but by Water Blast'. Once again they suggest that the Chancellor should negotiate with the recusant Richard Townley for him to build a water-powered mill on the River Calder immediately below the mine.

Having attached Roger's special report and, as they say, taking the advice of Mr Walter Bardsley, 'who is employed in the King's Silver Mynes in Bowland neare unto us', they then became sufficiently bold to recommend the Derbyshire manner of paying the miners with the King to have every ninth dish of ore.

In the privately owned mines in Derbyshire, the King only received a duty of every thirteenth dish, but as owner of the Thieveley Mine, they considered that every ninth dish would be a fair division of the wealth of the mine.

They justify this division by explaining that 'if the Myner have not a share in the oare more or less their worke for the most part wilbee carlessly performed, let what eyes look upon them that will'.

They very skillfully explain away Frances Leigh's deposition that he, with the help of one man and a woman, got a load of ore per day:

> It is a common thinge in all Lead Mynes that sometymes the Workmen will gett more oare of a daie than at another tyme in a weeke . . . Wee argue thus not to deprave the

Myne, but to show that the deposicion or opinion of one or two men cannot assure anie owner of oure certainty thereof; whosoever medleth in this kinde must hazard . . . they can conclude of nothinge further than they see at the pointes of theire pickes.

They reply simply and with dignity to the serious insinuation of deceit: 'wee should much dispise to be soe disloyal to his Majestie to whom we owe ourselves and all our true labourers, or so perfidious to your Lordship that under him trusted us'.

CHAPTER XXIII

The Husbandwife
in the Farmhouse

During the winter months, endurance was, and still is, the essence of life at Thieveley. The elevation and severity is such that even trees refuse to propagate and grow. Here is a northerly facing hillside offering no vestige of shelter from the persistent north-east winds, which blow directly from the Arctic.

Visitors from snow-bound Canada have said that they could not endure the winters experienced by the inhabitants of Bacup, only three miles over the Pike from Thieveley. The winter winds, laden with moisture from a storm-tossed northern ocean, cut the skin as with a knife, and chill the body to the bone. It is this damp wind which keeps Britain treeless above the 2,000 feet contours, yet forests flourish in abundance at 6,000 feet in other countries. Such is the severity of winter at Thieveley that the tree-line is below the 1,000 feet level.

In such a climate, at a period when England was experiencing its 'little ice age', work continued throughout the winter of 1631 at the mine. One recompense for the miners was that conditions underground were more or less constant all the year round, but for those workers above ground, the winders, and ore washers, with only rough wooden windbreaks, life became almost unbearable, a trial of endurance and survival. Such was the reluctance of the upper classes to mollycoddle the lower, that all surface works at lead mines were without shelter, even up to the decline in the 1870s.

Nor were conditions much better for the womenfolk in the turf houses. Centuries of hardship had instilled into the lower classes the basic instincts for survival, the three essentials of which were food, fuel and shelter. The construction of the turf house had been perfected to such a degree that it has been said of them, whereas the lord shivered in his castle, the stone walls running with condensed water, the villein was warm and dry in his mud hut. The reason was the absence of condensation, and of all openings except a doorway, which was hung with discarded woollen cloth. The staple commodity of food, oats, was treasured in a stout wooden chest, and supplies of kindling wood, and of dried peat, sufficient for the longest winter, were stacked as a windbreak just outside the doorway. Water was carried as required from the nearest well or spring. The same set of clothing was worn all winter, day and night, and never washed, being dried on the body every evening whilst sitting around the central fire, the turf house having the wonderful ability of absorbing the resulting fug into its walls, and at the same time maintaining a warm and dry interior.

One better than the turf house, and still superior to the castle in its kindness to the human body, was the wattle and daub house, with one or two rooms, and sheltered beneath the cover and warmth of a thatched roof. Such was the nature of the Hartley's farmhouse, one better up the social scale than the primitive, but only temporary dwellings, of the mine-workers.

From knowing no other life Alice and Robert Hartley thought nothing of the winters, they were the natural order of their lives. The hardy mine-workers inured themselves to survival, between the mine and their peat fires. But to Edward Talbot, forced to spend all the daylight hours on the hillside with little physical activity, or absorbing interest, life during the winter months became almost unbearable. Physical discomfort was added to boredom and sexual frustration.

With the work fixed into a monotonous routine, most of which was being deftly carried out by Jenet Birch, his life became dominated, as the cavalier knew it would, by the only three prospects of life at the mine. However, even in this respect, there was no continued serenity.

In the beginning, when Meg had crept secretly into his bed and given him all the eager joy of her young body, life had assumed a new dimension causing him to whistle and sing in exuberance during his early morning walks to the mine. But such idyllic happiness can rarely last and his was broken one evening by the innkeeper closetting him in the parlour in feigned severity. He had only just discovered the young man's deceitful behaviour in respect of the girl Meg. True she was a foundling, placed with him by the magistrates, but he loved her, and looked upon her as his own daughter. He was only waiting to find a suitable husband for her, for which there were high hopes, among the sons of the yeoman farmers in the valley. If it became common gossip, as was imminent, that she was being seduced almost nightly by the young gentleman at the inn, what hopes had he of contracting a betrothal to one of the young freeholders who could offer her a farmhouse, a family, and a respectable life? Now if Edward would compensate him for this loss of a daughter's prospects for the time that he stayed at the inn, perhaps the whole affair would soon be forgotten, and some day Meg might find the husband she deserved.

The man shed his crocodile tears, while Edward writhed in discomfort. He would gladly have given the man double board, in return for Meg's exquisite comforts, but he could not. Roger Kenyon could not spare him another penny, and his father John Talbot was lying disabled, unable to look to his own affairs, let alone subsidize his son.

Yet he was too proud to tell the landlord of this. It would have meant a complete loss of face, but what else could he say? He could only fall back upon the ancient practice of the upper classes, to rant and rave, and tell the man to remember his station, to keep his own staff under control, and not threaten him, else he would hear from the magistrates. He hated himself for his infidelity to Meg, and afterwards had to endure the accusing look in her eyes, but there was nought else he could do. The landlord departed in a rage, and from then on there was a serious deterioration in Edward's table and the quality of his accommodation.

The effects of all this, upon Edward, was to inculcate into his nature a cynical attitude towards the power of money, and to persuade him into a justification of taking that which he considered to be his own fair share. The means were so readily available in his position of trust. Roger Kenyon had recently fallen a victim to the distressing complaint of haemorrhoids, and was unable to travel on horseback, so that he had had to place more reliance than before upon Edward, particularly in the payment of money both for wages and the purchase of materials. It was a simple matter for the young man to divert some of this into his own pocket; and for him to cover himself by a falsification of the accounts. As few of the recipients of money could read or write there was no system of written receipts. Every transaction was by word of mouth and sealed by a clasp or smack of the hand. It was a simple matter to book down higher payments for ore, for wages, or the carriage of timber to the mine. Every penny overbooked was a penny for his pocket.

The innkeeper's strict supervision of Meg rendered Edward more dependent than ever on Jenet's favours, which he had enjoyed frequently during the mild autumn days. He had no need to worry in the least about any possible resentment from Nicholas Birch as it was considered an honour to have one's wife noticed by one of the the ruling class. But the onset of winter imposed a severe physical restraint upon the convenience of the act of intimacy with Jenet on the bleak hillside.

The only concession of the management of the lead mines to the winter weather was to discontinue ore-washing from November to April, and this mainly because the necessary water supply and dressing floors were frozen solid. The boys and women were found work underground drawing and winding, so that all the men could be concentrated upon getting ore, or in driving new shafts and levels. Consequently Edward was left almost alone on the surface. The smelt-house was cold and deserted, and the only break was the occasional arrival of a packhorse team with timber to shore up the grooves. Deprived of any interest and activity in his work, Edward's mind and body was almost completely dominated by his needs for the company and solace of womankind. With Meg zealously guarded at the inn, and Jenet working underground with the men and boys, he found himself falling once again under the sway of the cavalier's second prospect, the husbandwife in the farmhouse.

In his loneliness and boredom the attractions of Alice Hartley's warm kitchen became irresistible; and, each day, after resisting the temptation for as long as possible, he found himself inevitably sitting at her fireside, and enjoying the nearness of her femininity as she moved about the farm kitchen. It was not that he was a lecherous or an inprincipled ruffian, it was inevitable that his inheritance, his enforced idleness, and the demands of his body were almost beyond his control. But he was restrained from making any physical advances towards her by the almost constant presence of her children, and the fact that Robert Hartley may walk into the house at any moment.

And so he had to content himself with talk. She was a woman to whom he could unburden himself of his frustrations in his employment at the mine, and confide in her his hopes for the future. Alice, being aware of his liaison with Jenet, and resentful of it, treated him with a studied politeness, but could not resist thoughts of winning him away from the other woman for herself, so her attitude towards him varied from cool aloofness to compassionate tenderness, and both treatments drove him to the limits of his forbearance. The attraction of her womanliness and the comfort of her kitchen compared to the bleak wintertime prospects outside completely unbalanced his judgement so that his first priority became, not the efficient management of the mine, but how soon he could escape to Alice's company. And, of course, once again this did not go unnoticed; the workers joined in the conspiracy and despatched him off to the farmhouse as quickly as possible, so that they could please themselves what tasks to perform, or even whether to perform them at all. When a packhorse train of timber arrived they sent the carrier to the farmhouse. 'He's in theer, doin' 'is courtin',' they explained gleefully, and gathered round to watch Edward's embarrassment as he came out to attend to his duties. Jenet Birch withdrew her friendship, smiling confidently to herself. 'Let him waste his time with Mrs Pym, he won't get far with her, it won't do him any harm to go without for a bit, and when spring comes I'll soon have him eating out of my hand.'

But the impasse was solved in a manner which the two women on the hill could not anticipate, and most satisfactorily for Edward, by the girl at the inn, for, once Meg had recovered from her adoration of the cavalier, all her affections had been fixed upon Edward. Shrewdly allowing the innkeeper's rage to subside, and lulling the old woman, who had been set to watch her, into a false sense of complacency, she was soon able to slide out of her bed and steal silently, like a ghost in the night, through the labyrinth of the house to Edward's bedroom, where she was welcomed with a paroxysm of delight. Although Edward begged her to stay with him she had the good sense to return to her room before falling asleep, and being inevitably discovered. In this manner, with great cunning, she outfoxed the innkeeper, and his duenna, and gloried in the passion with which she was able to give herself to the equally eager young man.

In consequence, though still seeking the comfort of the house kitchen, Edward was enabled to keep his impulses under control and develop that sort of relationship with Alice which, apparently of the greatest friendliness, often drives a woman, despite herself, to thoughts of resentment and revenge.

CHAPTER XXIV

Edward Talbot's Journey
to Westminster

The Chancellor's action upon receiving the latest report from the mine was to write a personal letter to Roger Kenyon, and, of course, this letter coming from so powerful a personality caused Roger considerable disquiet. The letter instructed him to smelt the ore into lead, to convert the lead into cash, which Roger was to hold personally as Treasurer – and, after paying all the costs, to send the balance to the King. This was apparently a move to by-pass the Receiver, but it was of little consolation to Roger who had failed miserably in all his efforts to smelt the Thieveley ore into lead. Without lead, there could be no cash, and this meant either badgering the Receiver or his fellow Commissioners, or else straining his own finances to the point of bankruptcy.

It was this worry, on top of all the travel on horseback in all weathers that had so completely undermined his health that he had, indeed, only a few short years to live. The Chancellor also called for an up-to-the-minute report of the present state of the mine, and left no doubt that he expected it to be in a perfect condition for the regular extraction of large amounts of ore. It all seemed so simple to him from his chambers in Westminster. But, to Roger, it was a daunting and almost impossible task, unless worked in the Derbyshire manner with partnerships of free miners sinking their own grooves. But the Chancellor would have none of this. Roger's whole life – from one of prosperity and contentment farming his Lancashire markets and developing his estate at Parkhead – had been turned into one of thankless and almost hopeless labours which, it seemed, could only lead at the best to the ruin of his fortune, and at the worst, to imprisonment in the Tower, and of course, although he did not know it, his very life was being sacrificed by the hardships and anxieties of his labour.

But being a man of great mental resources, he soon decided upon a plan to, in some way, bring home the realities of the situation to the Chancellor. He therefore penned a lengthy reply and despatched it post haste to London using the young Edward Talbot as his courier.

He refers only briefly to his own illness which has prevented him from attending personally, and suggests that the Chancellor can obtain a true assessment of the mine from Mr Edward Talbot 'who best knowes the state of the workes and who hath been clerk and overseer thereof and paid the wages since wee were first emploied . . . he can informe your Lordship in any thing touching the whole state and condicion of the Myne'.

Roger then puts on record, with no word of complaint, that the flow of money from the Receiver has dried up, that he – Roger – is now paying out of his own pocket, that the Commissioners have abandoned all hope of smelting by foot-bellows in the Thieveley smelt-house, and a third and new difficulty: that the freeholders in the area are refusing to part with their rapidly diminishing stands of timber.

As a solution to these difficulties, he again suggests that the Chancellor should entreat with Richard Townley, 'who has both a river and extensive woodlands', for the building of a water-powered mill, and that the officials of the Duchy use their authority – authority which Roger did not possess – to commandeer timber from the copyhold lands in the district, for without timber, work at the mine comes to a halt.

Finally, Roger protests his own shortcomings in the skills of mine management, and beseeches the Chancellor to use his influence in the Duchy lead-mining fields to choose a fully qualified man to take over as Surveyor – a man with all the necessary experience and able to give his full time to the venture, for 'the Sommer comeinge on, the daies growing long, and the earth like to be drie, yt is the tyme to go effectually on with a full triall and discoverie of the myne by employment of manie people in the worke'.

During the winter months he explains: 'Since our last retorne to your Lordship there hath not been much oare gotten because our resolucion was onlie to go on with the sough and the sinking of two shafts downwards to trie the workes. The number of Myners was usually nine persons in all.'

The mission to London was a further boost to the ego of Edward Talbot, and the excitement of the long journey with the many nights talking and drinking with fellow travellers in the inns, and the encounters with courtiers in the corridors of Westminster Palace was in stark contrast to his hitherto secluded life in Lancashire. He looked forward to recounting his experiences to his paramours, and particularly to Alice Hartley, who, of the three, was likely to be the most impressed, being a woman, as Roger Kenyon had assessed, who could quite gracefully rise from the lower to the middle classes.

It was now the springtime of 1631 and the Chancellor did not despatch Edward back to the mine until the end of May. During his time in London, Edward was questioned closely and shrewdly by the Chancellor and then called to attend at a meeting of the Duchy Council. He was then kept in London whilst new resolutions were drafted for him to carry home to the Commissioners in Lancashire. That Edward had conducted himself well in the halls of the mighty is revealed in these resolutions, which completely ignore Roger's request to be superceded by an experienced Derbyshire miner, but again confirm Roger as Surveyor with, for the first time, Edward as his official overseer at a salary of £20 per annum. The new resolutions agree to a complete change of policy which authorized Roger to pay the miners a sum, not to exceed 12d, per dish of ore, more or less in the Derbyshire manner, with cash to be generated not by the sale of lead but by that of ore.

The subterfuge adopted by the Council to relieve the Commissioners, and in particular Roger Kenyon, from having to finance the mine out of their own pockets, was to co-opt the Receiver, Ralph Assheton of Downham, as one of the active Commissioners, presumably as Cashier and Accountant. But instead of relieving Roger, this action only aggravated the situation, for the new Commissioner only operated in an autocratic manner from Downham Hall, and even made considerable charges – which were all debited against the mine for every consignment of cash delivered to Edward Talbot at the mine. Previously, the money had been supplied at the expense of the long-suffering Roger Kenyon acting as cashier, courier, accountant and paymaster, all rolled into one.

CHAPTER XXV

A Visitation of the Plague

It was a great relief to the Commissioners to be done with the problem of smelting the Thieveley ore, although the lesser one of finding a customer for it at a reasonable price was not simple. The nearest smelting mills, those in Yorkshire, were over twenty difficult miles away, and the cost of packhorse transport of so heavy a substance again reduced the price at Thieveley to an uneconomic amount.

But fortunately, the energetic Thomas Cockcroft of Greenwood Lee in the Hebden Valley, some five miles distance, had an even better river than Richard Townley, together with the necessary woodlands. This was in the beautiful vale of Hardcastle Crags, which is today in the ownership of the National Trust and a popular tourist area.

Thomas Cockcroft, being a staunch protestant, made negotiations with him straightforward. It was soon agreed that he should build a water-powered mill, and at the same time undertake to collect all the ore from the Thieveley mine at a price of £3 per ton.

And so it appeared that most of Roger Kenyon's difficulties at the mine were solved. The drainage sough was almost completed, and with several partnerships of free miners sinking shafts, a good supply of ore could be immediately converted into cash from Thomas Cockcroft's ready purse. But this ill-fated mine seemed dogged with misadventure. It almost seemed, as Alice Hartley and the rough country folk believed, that it was God's vengeance for interfering with His handiwork. It did appear as though the hand of fate was against all the Commissioners' work, when negotiations with Thomas Cockcroft were broken off in a most unexpected manner.

The parish of Heptonstall, in which Thomas' land was situated, was isolated by, of all things, a visitation of the Bubonic Plague. This was so fearsome an event for any township as to bring it under regulations set out in King Charles' orders of 1625 to isolate the outbreaks in areas and then eliminate the disease within these areas. Travel to and from an infected parish was forbidden; the doors of infected houses within the parish were marked with a red cross and the words 'Lord have mercy upon us'.

When the inhabitants had died, or the lucky ones recovered, these homes were fumigated and then closed for six weeks. The state recognized its responsibilities and provided food and care, while the Justices were made responsible for the burning of all infected material and for the regular collection and deep burial of the dead.

In the years 1631 and 1632, sporadic outbreaks occurred in the North, the worst being at Preston where 1,000 people died and the remainder fled from the town.

In 1631, twenty-one people died in Heptonstall, and such was the dread of the plague that people in the neighbouring parishes lived in great fear and vigorously enforced the King's regulations.

Consequently, Thomas Cockcroft was imprisoned within his own lands for an indefinite period, and there was not only no hope of sending for the Thieveley ore, but all negotiations were completely suspended. Indeed, the panic was so great that the Commissioners dare not travel even to the mine, and the local inhabitants of Cliviger were so fearful of the miners – whom they thought of as nothing less than savages – that the mine itself was isolated on the Thieveley hillside.

In the whole of Lancashire, and the West Riding, the summer of 1631 was one of fear, fear of the plague. The people of each parish felt that they were beleaguered with the dread affliction on all sides, and expected it to strike almost daily. Commerce and industry were at a standstill. None dare travel, and if they had, they would have been driven back whence they came with stones and vituperation. None cared for the loss of their livelihood so long as they were spared their lives. The little community at Thieveley was thrown back upon itself, to sit it out in two camps: the farm and the mine, united against the common enemy but divided amongst themselves.

At the farm, Alice Hartley guarded her brood, forbidding the children to go near the miners, and constantly hectoring Robert, who yearned for the male company and liked to laugh and joke with the women, to keep his distance. Because of her sharp tongue, a certain coolness had developed between them, and, to escape, Robert would take his pick and spade and search for lead in Black Clough, away from the mine. Meanwhile, Alice kept watch over the farmhouse, serving the mine women with butter, oats and ale, over the dividing wall, and shouting abuse at anyone who trespassed into her domain.

She made rush candles, mixed with dried herbs and onion leaves, and had these constantly burning in the farmhouse so that their pungent smoke filled the room and wafted out whenever the door was opened.

The only exception to her strict ban was Edward Talbot. He was a gentleman, and could not possibly carry a plague which had been sent by God to punish the miserable poor for their sins. And when the miners' wives saw him disappear through the grey smoke at the open door, they shook their heads and murmured amongst themselves, 'He is bewitched – God only knows what she is doing to him.'

And then they laughed and cheered up. 'So long as the witch is here, the plague will noan cum. The divil looks after his owan.'

And for Edward Talbot, it was exactly as the cavalier had said, the mine had only three prospects, and with death all around, he was determined to enjoy them all. Throwing his inhibitions aside in the current atmosphere of 'eat, drink, and be merry for tomorrow we die', he would take Alice in his arms and kiss her on the lips. She on her part, similarly affected, as women are in times of great danger, yielded to his embrace, but as soon as she felt his ardour rising, would push him away and fly to some household task. Then he would sit by the fire and savour thoughts of her attractions until he had to go to attend to the mine.

Then there would be another embrace as she pushed him out of the door. It was a dangerous game, but they were caught up in its excitement. She would have been as disappointed as he if he had failed to press his suit.

Once outside, he would go to the weighing and storing of the ore with Jenet Birch, and, aroused by Alice, partake of her generosity in the isolation of the smelt-house. And to please her, he would be liberal in the assessment of the money due for the ore, and made sure that she received her increased wages whether she put in the hours or not. It was only a matter of a few pence and could easily be accounted for in his book-keeping.

CHAPTER XXVI

1631 – The Summer of Fear

It so happened that there had been time, between receiving the new resolutions and the outbreak of the plague, for Roger Kenyon to let off a few meares along the lead-mine fault to free miners.

Thomas Cockcroft, allegedly in partnership with the injured John Talbot, but more likely with Edward Talbot, employed miners in two grooves – the Watergroove and the Cope. It is probable that these men worked in galleries which were now free of water as Nicholas Birch was still sinking the Watergroove to meet Gervase Gascoigne in the sough.

The indomitable Jenet did the winding for her husband as well as separating and washing any ore which he sent up. The most of her efforts were required in winding up water buckets to prevent her husband from being drowned out at the bottom of the shaft which was now approaching 200 ft in depth. On account of this, her wages were raised from 2s 6d to 3s per week, which may not sound much but, relative to the values of the day, was still a rise of 20 per cent.

A Rochdale miner, George Casson, in partnership with a David Goodwin, worked a groove – henceforth named in the accounts as Casson's Groove. A third free miner also appears in the form of the ex-smelter Godfrey Wheatly, from the Forest of Bowland. He worked a groove now named Godfrey's Groove, and also showed enterprise in constructing a device called a 'buddle' for reprocessing the waste material from the spoil heap. This was in the form of a long wooden trough of running water. The spoil was raked along it and the heavy ore sunk to the bottom and was trapped by a wooden dam across the trough.

He was, of course, paid the agreed price of 12d per dish for all the ore which he produced either from his shaft or from the buddle.

Also before the plague, Gervase Gascoigne had completed his contract on the sough, taken his money and departed. A man, Humphrey Griffiths, but always referred to in the accounts as 'the Welshman', was taken on to complete the drainage of the mine by connecting up the various shafts to the sough. He was booked down at a wage of 3s per week at the King's expense so that he was not paid for the ore which he sent up. And so it can be seen that Edward Talbot required a steady supply of money to pay the free miners their 12d per dish, to pay the wages of the men, women and boys employed directly by the King, and to purchase the necessary supplies of timber. To set against this expenditure was the growing pile of ore which had originally been stored in the farmhouse, but which was now locked up in the smelt-house. The responsibility for this cash had now been moved from Roger Kenyon to the Receiver, who reluctantly sent along meagre amounts, and at the same time, made a percentage charge for each delivery.

However, with the mood of optimism effected by the arrangement with Thomas Cockcroft that he would soon be moving and paying for the ore, advertisements were displayed in other mining areas for the taking up of meares in this new and potentially rich mine which was now drained and in a good condition for a fair trial.

That the coming of the plague prevented the arrival of any further partnerships, and, as the regulations came into effect, the community described above became isolated in its hamlet of turf houses on the Thieveley hillside.

For them, 1631 was a summer of terror, terror of a comfortless death which would come like a thief in the night. None knew where or when it might strike next, and every morning, each man looked fearfully at his neighbour as they started work. But when the sun came up and the plague had not arrived, they laughed and joked and sang their ribald songs with the joy of life, until once again, with the falling darkness, their fears returned.

The Commissioners dared not visit the mine and were even reluctant to send or receive messengers. Consequently, it is not surprising that Edward Talbot felt alone and deserted, or that he should throw in his lot, endeared by Jenet's warm embrace, with the mining community on the hill. And as they became familiar with fear, their boldness returned and mysterious visitors arrived and departed in the dead of night, bringing supplies of much-needed food and comforts in exchange for ore.

Even Thomas Cockcroft was able to organize a surreptitious, delivery of ore to Grassington to be smelted for him into the lead which he so urgently needed for his new house at Greenwood Lee. It is not known whether

Edward was aware of these illicit deals, for there is no record of them in his accounts.

Meanwhile, the Senior Commissioner, Sir Ralph Assheton, was having troubles of his own. Now an old man with many of the infirmities of the landed Squires, he had nevertheless been compelled to journey to London and made to stand in humiliation before the dreaded Ecclesiastical Court of the High Commission by the upstart favourite of the King, Archbishop Laud, on a petty charge of having let off some of the glebe lands of Whalley Church without the sanction of the Archbishop.

After a lifetime of allegiance to the monarchy, his treatment in London was such as to win him over to the fast-growing movement against the autocratic rule of the King and the arrogance of his favourites. For the present, however, his presence in London prevented him from participating in the 1631 report of the state of the mine. His place was taken by the Receiver, signing himself as Ralph Assheton Junior. This autumn report records the breakdown of negotiations with Thomas Cockcroft on account of the plague and explains that the ore is being stockpiled at the mine, pending Cockcroft's release, as no-one else will offer a comparable price.

With regard to the visitation of the plague, they write: 'and the said infection soe increased in the said parish of Heptonstall, beinge the verie next parish to the myne in the later end of the yeare wee durst not adventure to come amongst the Myners. Who are a careless, stragline companye, not regarding what companye they come in and not without fear did we admitt Mr Talbot to come unto us from tyme to tyme, whoe is dailie amongst them.'

With regard to increasing the number of miners they explain: 'the Countrie hath been so infected with the plague all this Summer, as well in Lancashire as Yorkshire, almost on everie syde of the Myne that none was admitted to come thither from places suspected, and from remote cleare places none durst come for feare of infection, such fearful reportes of danger in these partes were spread farr and neare'.

CHAPTER XXVII

The Agreement with Richard Townley

It would appear that the Chancellor was not discouraged by the Commissioners' latest report, with its account of set-backs and delays caused by the plague. His reply was so prompt that one wonders at the means of communication over a roadless distance of over 200 miles. There is little doubt that he must have used the established network of King's Messengers. In an almost immediate reply, dated 20 December 1631, he instructed Roger Kenyon to take on as many good miners as would come, as soon as the plague should abate. He also instructed 'Cousen Aston', the Receiver, to supply Roger with all the money he should require; and, in addition, the sum of £40 in part recompense 'of your paynes and care taken'. This was apparently the first and only time that Roger received any recompense for his years of labour at the Thieveley Mine.

On 25 February 1632, the Chancellor is again addressing himself to Roger Kenyon, noting that no agreement has yet been concluded with Thomas Cockcroft; and instructing him to conclude an agreement for the sale of all the ore to Mr Richard Townley of Towneley Hall.

Even by the fourteenth century the Townley family, with de Lacy and de la Legh blood in their veins, was firmly established at Townley, and during the fifteenth and sixteenth centuries, they built the splendid fortified mansion house, Towneley Hall, which is today the showpiece of the modern town of Burnley. During all these earlier times they were close to the warrior kings of England, and several members were knighted for bravery on the field of battle in the French and Scottish wars.

The fortunes of the family reached a first zenith under John Townley (1528-1607), and then suffered a temporary decline due to their staunch adherence to the Catholic faith. John was imprisoned for years during the reign of Elizabeth, and was only released, old and blind, at the age of 73 on condition that he remained within 5 miles of his house at Townley. Henceforth he was remembered, in the family as 'The Martyr'. Under James I, his son, Richard (1566-1629), had two-thirds of his estate confiscated and sold to Ralph Assheton of Great Lever near Bolton. This is where the Townleys' first tenuous connection with the Thieveley Lead Mine begins, for this Richard Townley had married the daughter of Ralph Assheton, and the sale of his lands to his Protestant father-in-law was only a device for keeping the estate within the family. This Ralph was to become Sir Ralph Assheton Bart., the Commissioner for the mine. The eldest son of the above marriage, another Richard (1593-1635), paid the enormous sum of £213 6s 8d yearly for his refusal to attend the Protestant Church, which in effect meant that the greater part of the rent roll of his estates was confiscated.

When the Commissioners for the mine realized that this Richard Townley was the holder of the only land in Cliviger suitable for the provision of a water-powered smelt-mill they were at first reluctant to enter into negotiations with so notorious a recusant. At this time recusants were outcasts of society, and forbidden to hold public appointments, so that it became a delicate matter to enter into negotiations with one, and perhaps open to misapprehension when he should also happen to be the nephew of the senior member of the Commission. That is the reason why the Commissioners first passed the matter over to the Chancellor, while they played for safety by negotiating with the protestant Thomas Cockcroft.

But upon receiving firm instructions, in writing from the Chancellor, Roger Kenyon, no doubt advised by the barrister Saville Radcliffe, entered into immediate negotiations with Richard Townley. The matter was however complicated by the fact that Richard was a bachelor, and almost a recluse, living on his estate of Nocton in Lincolnshire. It is most probable that Roger, aided by Saville Radcliffe, drew up the agreement in close negotiation with Richard's younger brothers, Charles and Christopher, for Charles was soon to inherit the estate, and Christopher to become involved in the management of the Thieveley Mine.

Despite the cruel treatment of the family by three generations of the Monarchy, Charles was later to become a staunch royalist; and in the not-so-distant future, Oliver Cromwell was to conduct Charles' wife over the bloody battlefield of Marston Moor in search of his body, which was ultimately buried on the battlefield itself.

Roger Kenyon acted with a speed that would put modern administrators to shame, for an agreement was drawn up, signed, witnessed, and sealed by 25 March 1631, and this in the complete absence of good roads, postal services, or telephones.

In this agreement there were six items comprising 'articles of agreement had and made betweene our Sovereign lord the Kinges Majestie upon th'one partie, and Richard Townley of Townley in the Countie of Lancaster, Esquire, upon th'other partie . . . for the sale of his Majesties lead ore there already gotten and hereafter for certain tyme to be gotten'.

The principle items stipulated the price of the ore at £3 3s 4d per ton, to be collected by Mr Townley from the mine, payment to be made monthly and that 'the Ore shall be . . . carefullie delivered, well dressed, washed etc., workemanlike as in such cases in other places is usual, and not full of earth and rubbish, which were as well in abuse to his Majestie who buyes it by the dish . . . for prevention of which abuse the Commissioners have admonished Mr Edward Talbot Clerke of the said Workes'.

That it was expected that the mine and the arrangement for the Townleys to smelt the ore should go on for many years is indicated by the agreement being made to include Richard Townley, 'his heires, executors, administrators and assigns' and also 'the Kinges Majestie, his heires and successors'.

And so, by this document, were the vexatious problems of cash for the mine, and the difficulties of smelting, satisfactorily concluded.

A letter from the Chancellor is now given as indicating that Roger Kenyon's diligence and proficiency is fully appreciated by him, although not sufficiently to bring forth a second payment for his services but only a promise of still more work in the future. Roger was indeed ensnared by his own ability.

The Chancellor's letter is also interesting in agreeing to a wage inflation of 25 per cent, brought about by the scarcity of labour due to the ravages of the Plague. However he greatly regrets this, and hopes that the extra 3d per dish will soon be removed.

The Chancellor to Roger Kenyon, 2 July 1632:

To my lovinge Freind Mr. Roger Kennyon at Whalley in Lanc.

After my harty Comendacions, I received your Letter of the 7th Maye last, together with the Articles of Agreement with Mr. Townley, and doe well approve of your doings therein, and shall desire you this Summer to proceed as affectually as possibly you can, and to endevour by all waies you shall thinke convenient to advaunce the workes and encrease the number of Myners as much as you maie, though for the present with that advaunce of 3d. in the dish wages being now necessitated to it, which I hope will hereafter bee taken of againe, otherwise the King's profitt and benefitt will bee much diminished; but you must submitt to such Courses (wherein I am confident of all your Cares) as in your judgements shall conduce to the making a full and absolute tryall to what consequence of profitt and advantage to his Majestie the said workes maye arrive att.

And therefore shall desire to bee Certifyed of all particulers of your proceedings in this Busines at the begining of Michaelmas tearme, and then I shall take order for the renewing your Comission for a longer tyme and for such further directions therein as the Busines shall require from mee.

And soe I rest your loving Freind,

Dutchie Howse, 2 July 1632.   E. Newburgh.

CHAPTER XXVIII

The Conspiracy

By the summer of 1632, the plague in the northern counties had subsided as mysteriously as it had appeared. It was said to have run its course. But the even stranger conundrum of the bubonic plague is that after the Great Plague of London in the year 1666, it has never since appeared in Britain.

Despite the disappearance of the plague, the expected rush of miners to Thieveley did not take place. This non-arrival was later attributed to a conspiracy of Messrs. Highley and Butler, the original owners of the mine. These two energetic men had not lost faith in the mine, and after being frustrated in all their attempts to obtain a just compensation for its loss, they hatched a plot to enable them to become, in effect, the beneficial party at the mine. Having been, themselves, defeated by the twin problems of flooding and smelting, they watched from nearby Rochdale these difficulties being gradually overcome by Roger Kenyon's diligence. And now was the opportunity of poetic justice to obtain compensation at the King's expense.

Their ingenious plan was to become the chief recipients of the mine by becoming the effective owners of all the meares being worked along the rake of the vein of ore. The depth of their conspiracy is quite surprising, and has much in common with the modern attempts of shop-stewards to control the nationalized industries. Indeed, the proof that a conspiracy did, in fact, exist is provided by the thoroughness with which it was prosecuted.

A third member was a man called Joseph Duerden. He was sent down to Westminster to purchase the office of Barmaster to the Blackburn Hundred within which lay the Thieveley wastelands. The Barmaster was the King's official appointed in lead-mining areas to stake out the meares of the free miners, to collect the King's Duty, and to settle all disputes.

The Chancellor, never averse from selling an office, no matter how spurious, to the highest bidder, probably quite unwittingly fell in with their scheme by accepting Duerden's ready money.

Duerden then arrived at the mine to show his credentials as Barmaster to Edward Talbot, and to take away from him the authority of allocating meares to incoming miners. He brought with him one of the early miners, Hugh Bateman, whom he installed as his resident deputy at the mine.

Meanwhile, Highley and Butler, buying Mercer and Casson much drink in the alehouses in Rochdale, had bargained for possession of their grooves. It will be recalled that Godfrey Mercer, as the original discoverer, had the right to the first two meares, and Casson, along with Goodwin, was sinking Casson's groove.

The only grooves not now under the control of Highley

and Butler were the Cope and Watergrooves operated by Cockcroft and Talbot. However, Cockcroft was isolated in Heptonstall and the young Edward Talbot was so utterly bemused by the new turn of events that the conspirators openly boasted in the Rochdale alehouses that they were again in control of the mine.

Bateman's function was to spread discontent at the mine about the difficult conditions in the sticky blue shale and the uneconomic return of 12d per dish of ore. He was sufficiently successful in this to have the price raised to 15d.

Highley and Butler then proceeded to line up spurious partnerships under their control, for whom Duerden would stake out meares at the mine. But before their schemes could come to fruition, conditions at the mine degenerated to near anarchy.

Everyone pleased himself whether he worked or not. Casson and Goodwin remained drinking in Rochdale, their grooves derelict and drowned out. There was a fall of earth in the sough so that once again the water-groove was flooded and Nicholas and Jenet Birch had to bail out the water so that, at least, Cockcroft and Talbot's grooves could produce some ore. The only other ore coming to the storehouse was that produced by Alice's husband, Robert, in a mine of his own discovery in Black Clough, a few hundred yards away from the main mine shafts.

In recognition of his zeal, and to compensate him for the damage done to his farm, the Chancellor had issued a separate authorization for Robert Hartley 'to worke, search, digge, and gett lead oare . . . deliveringe all and everie parte of the care unto his Majestie's Surveyor . . . in a place where no ground was alreadie broken by anie other workman'.

Thomas Whitaker having died in 1631, Robert was now prepared to gamble that, with Roger Kenyon's protection, and the Chancellor's authorization, he had little to fear from Thomas' son, William. However, his wife did not share his optimism in this respect. And it was Alice Hartley who also revealed the conspirators' designs to Edward Talbot, and through him, to Roger Kenyon and the Commissioners.

Disgusted by her brother's complete neglect of his opportunities, and his drunkenness under the sway of Highley and Butler, with female perspicuity, she divined the nature of the plot, and once she was assured, did not waste time in revealing to Edward the nature of the conspiracy which had undermined his own authority.

The Commissioners were not slow to realize the seriousness of their position. They took sworn depositions from the miners whom Highley and Butler had suborned and sent an urgent report to the Chancellor to have Joseph Duerden's credentials quashed. But a great deal of damage had been done, and upon the ailing Roger Kenyon, dragging his unwilling body up to Thieveley, the truly appalling state of affairs at the mine was revealed – the most serious, of course, being the collapse of the sough. Not for the first time Roger began to have doubts about the suitability of Edward Talbot as his deputy and overseer at the mine. However, Roger was able to assert his authority, and with characteristic clarity of mind, immediately switched work to repairing the sough. In this he discovered the Welshman to be a tower of strength and ingenuity, so that Roger promised him the meares which Highley and Butler had attempted to take over, once the drainage had been restored.

Having, as he believed, restored order, Roger rested for a while in the farmhouse, and as he watched Alice prepare food, contemplated upon how fine a woman she would be to grace his new house at Parkhead. He complimented her upon her acuity in revealing the conspiracy, and added that Robert was doing a fine job in winning ore for the King from Black Clough.

CHAPTER XXIX

The Battle in the Inn

Before leaving the mine, Roger gave what he considered to be a reprimand to Edward, together with firm instructions for the reorganization of the mine. But that young man, so bemused by his amorous adventures, and believing in his own mind that he had striven manfully in the almost impossible conditions imposed by the plague, followed by the conspiracy, did not attribute any blame to himself. Consequently, Roger's reprimand fell mainly upon deaf ears; discipline was not restored; and with the mine mainly run by such strong personalities as the Welshman and Jenet Birch, Edward's attention was soon fully diverted by other circumstances.

During the time of the plague, overnight visitors to the inn had virtually disappeared, driving the innkeeper into a black mood of truculence and desperation. A state of coolness had developed in his relationship with Edward which was not conducive to convivial evenings over a tankard of ale in the parlour – so that the inn was, for the most part, only inhabited by the two men studiously avoiding one another, and a bevy of womenfolk with little to do, yet constantly reproached that they were not even earning their keep.

And their only divergence was to exacerbate the differences between the two men, as Edward remained foolishly gay and self-satisfied, with the landlord as gloomy as the proverbial bear.

Edward, with his inherited gift of being able to fall under the influence of whichever female was available, passed his evenings in good spirits in anticipation of the moment when Meg would slide into his bed. In the mornings, when he climbed the steep pathway to Thieveley, his body began to thrill to the thought of Alice Hartley, and by the afternoon, he was more than ready for Jenet Birch's favours – and, of course, to the intuitively endowed countrywomen both at the inn and the mine, his obsessions were like an open book.

However, at the inn, in such a close-knit and emotionally disturbed household, his liaison with Meg could not continue indefinitely. Inevitably the night arrived with a thunderous banging upon his locked bedroom door.

'Now then, what's all the banging about?' Edward shouted from his bed.

'As ta getten Meg in theer?'

'No, I'm trying to get a night's sleep!' Edward lied, meanwhile rapidly struggling into his clothes.

But Meg, clad only in her nightdress, could only remain within the bed.

'Na let me cum in and see for misell – she biant nowheer else in t'house.'

'Thee get thyself back to bed, and let me finish my night's sleep.'

'A will if tha'll just let me 'av one peek atween tham blankets.'

'Clear off with thee – I'll do nought o't'sort. Now go on – I can't stay awake all night talking to thee.'

But the banging on the door recommenced and it was almost as though even the stout bars on the oak door would give way.

By now Edward was fully dressed. He whispered to Meg to wrap herself in a blanket, then taking up his sword he withdrew the bars and opened the door.

The landlord rushed in and then stopped, confronted by a fully-dressed young man ready with his sword, and a girl holding the bedclothes around her almost naked body. Behind him a bevy of womenfolk in hastily donned shawls peered inquisitively into the semi-darkness of the bedroom, their faces illuminated by the innkeeper's lantern.

Recovering his composure mine host turned his wrath upon Meg.

'Now get thee back into thy oan room – A'll deal wi' thee in t'morning if not afore. It's a good beating tha'll be getten.'

At these words Edward's temper flared up. He sprang at the stocky figure of the innkeeper, twirled him round, and with his sword's point bringing blood from the man's backside, hurled him out onto the landing amidst the scurrying and screaming women.

With eyes blazing, and almost berserk, Edward chased them all down the stairs into the kitchen-parlour.

'Now stay there or get thee back to bed, and if anyone interferes with me A'll kill him,' he shouted.

And there was little doubt that he meant it.

Edward returned upstairs, took Meg back to her room,

and stood guard while she dressed. Then they returned to his room where he collected all his personal belongings and the account books of the mine into a leather bag. Beneath the eyes of the terrified women, now attending to the landlord's wounds, they unbarred the great door of the inn, saddled and bridled Edward's horse, and with Meg riding pillion set off into the night.

In those days rough tracks ran through the woodlands from farm to farm, and were considered to be public rights-of-way. They were the beginnings of England's network of winding country lanes, which the modern motorist finds so intriguing, or so infuriating, depending upon the nature of his journey. One such track ran from the hamlet of Holme Chapel to an ancient farm called Lightbirks, and onwards up the valley to Crossing-of-Dean at the watershed of the Lancashire and Yorkshire Calders.

Edward knew this track well, for he regularly purchased timber and coal for the mine from Lawrence Watmough of Lightbirks and it will be remembered he assisted Lawrence to obtain a licence to keep an alehouse.

It was to this newly-opened alehouse that he took Meg, and knocking up Lawrence, announced that it was now his turn to do Edward a favour, and accommodate him and the girl with a reasonable bedchamber. There was then much bustle at the house as the sleeping accommodation was rearranged, and Edward and Meg could once again settle down in blessed security.

However it was illegal for alehouse keepers to accommodate guests, particularly if there were the slightest suggestion of immorality.

But in the morning Edward and Lawrence agreed upon a scheme that Edward was to be a partner in the alehouse, and Meg to be one of the servant girls. They did not expect this arrangement to go unchallenged by the innkeeper, who, apart from his fury, and belief that he owned Meg as a waif almost given to him in slavery, had in the first place resisted the opening of the alehouse, and was determined to bring about its closure.

So it was not long before an earlier acquaintance, the Constable, arrived at Lightbirks, and this became only the beginning of a very difficult time for Edward Talbot.

CHAPTER XXX

The Surrender and Afterwards

At Thieveley Farm relations between Alice and Robert Hartley were almost at breaking point. Robert's early interview with old Thomas Whitaker had hit him, like a blow across the face. For the first time since taking the farm, he had realized the dangers of being a tenant, that, unless he complied with his landlord's every wish, he was in constant danger of being cast homeless and desperate upon the parish. And the older he became, and the larger his family, the greater would be his servitude. From an ebullient and fun-loving young man he would grow into a sour and taciturn old man. Consequently his crusade for freedom, to buy the freehold or copyhold of his own farm, dominated his every waking hour. It became almost an obsession, which had temporarily unhinged his mind, for he believed that the lead mine was perhaps his only hope of ever climbing out of the deadly trap of class distinction. Whereas other men consoled themselves in the alehouse, he flung himself into the task of finding lead ore with an almost frightening zeal. Each morning he took his pick and shovel, and disappeared into the wasteland and only came home, tired, wet and dirty, to eat and to rest. Once he had ploughed the half acre of land on the gentle slope in front of the house he left Alice, and the children, to run the farm. On top of all her housework, the butter and cheese-making, the brewing, and baking, Alice had to drive the children to the feeding of the cattle, the milking, the care of the pig, and shepherding of their small flock of sheep. It may have only been on a small scale in the nature of family subsistence, but every one of the many and varied tasks required her personal attention if disaster were not to overtake their crops and animals, and they themselves to go hungry and cold in the wintertime.

It was this constant daily grind, and Robert's apparent detachment in his obsession with the lead mine that was turning her from an affectionate helpmate, into a cantankerous shrew. For whenever they were together she could not help but rail at him for his neglect of the farm. It was useless for him to point to their growing jackpot beneath the hearthstone, to explain that all his efforts were for the security of a farm of their own; to her it was the present that mattered; and she did not like the loneliness of her task nor the proximity of the alien mine. But perhaps his most grievous omission was his neglect of her emotional and physical requirements as a woman, her need to feel his strong arms around her. It is not surprising then that she should look forward to Edward Talbot's entry, when he smothered her with his passionate kisses and pressed her to his eager body. She would indeed have been cold and inhuman if she had not responded to such an assault upon her sexuality. It became daily more difficult to push him away, to prevent the hot blood rising to her face, and the insistent pangs of desire overriding her conscience. And when he was not there she wrestled long and earnestly with her marriage vows – keep thou to him only – and yet looked forward to the morrow when he would return.

Even while Edward was flying from the inn, the tension between man and wife had snapped; and, suffering her unfair reproaches on top of a fruitless day, Robert could bear no more. His temper flared up beyond his control, and after he had called her every foul name he could lay his tongue to and beaten her, he dragged himself away into his bed. Alice sat for the night, in her fireside chair, and vowed that Edward Talbot would not go away disappointed in the morning.

With almost cold-blooded determination she laid the scene, even to sending the children away on an errand, and when Edward came eagerly into the house and took her into his arms, from behind his back she slipped the bolt into its socket on the door jamb and led him to her bed.

After months of waiting, her surrender took Edward into a paroxysm of delight. She was all and more than he had hoped for, and when they were finished the hot words of love poured out. From that episode on Alice Hartley became the never-to-be-forgotten woman in his life, the one who was to haunt his dreams until he died.

But such is man's gregarious nature that by the afternoon he was lying with Jenet Birch in the smelt-house store, and in this manner, within twenty-four hours, did Edward savour the cavalier's three delights; and, as though that man had baited a trap for him, these twenty-four hours were the zenith of his life at the Thieveley Mine. From that day on it was all downhill.

*　　*　　*

By the following day the story of the fight and Meg's abduction from the inn had spread, with consequent exaggeration, all over the parish. One of the sluts from the mine settlement, sensing with a woman's intuition Alice Hartley's emotional involvement, had gleefully recounted the story to her with no detail left out. Then she plunged home the dagger. 'My, what a man he be, lying every afternoon wi' Jenet in t'smelt-house, and every neet wi' Meg deawn at th'inn. I shall a t' tree 'im out mi'sen one of these days.'

It was worse than a blow across the face; Alice's heart died within her, and when the woman had gone she staggered back into the house and almost collapsed into her chair.

She was still sitting there when Edward burst in ready and willing for her caress, but in an instant he knew that everything had gone wrong. He could only stand and take that which was coming to him. In a flat monotonous voice she reproached him for all he had done to her, leading her to believe she was the only love of his life, when all the time he was playing fast and loose with servant girls, and the common women at the mine. She was deeply humiliated and wondered how long it would be before the locality was laughing and sniggering about her.

He had hoped she would understand the difficulties and loneliness of his life in the valley, miseries which he had so often confided to her. But she would have none of his explanations and apologies and after staying for what he considered to be a decent interval he made his escape.

When he arrived home at Lawrence Watmough's

alehouse, the Constable was waiting to hear his account of the affray with the innkeeper.

He admitted wounding the man but said that it was only a mere prick brought about by the invasion of his privacy.

'More likely in the abduction of a female for carnal lust,' the man sneered.

'Not at all, I was protecting the woman. The man was going to beat her.'

'But you've taken her away from the guardian she was placed under by the vestry.'

'Nothing of the sort – the girl is over eighteen, and came of her own free will to work here for Lawrence Watmough at the alehouse.'

'Well that's as may be but I'm off now to report the whole matter to t'Justices.'

But the unfortunate Constable got nowhere with Justice Nowell.

'Is the man seriously wounded?'

'Aye, he has a nasty wound in his buttock.'

'Is he confined to his bed and unable to look to his business?'

'Oh no, he's still about his work.'

'Then a prick up the backside will teach him to respect his betters, and not to interfere with a gentleman's pleasure. Have you ought else to report?'

'Yes, there are strong rumours of witchcraft in Cliviger. It is said all o'er that the woman Alice Hartley at Thieveley Farm is a witch.'

'Oh, and what are they saying about her?'

'That she was in league with the Devil at the time of the

plague making noisome brews and strange vapours. Then they say she has bewitched this same Edward Talbot, and the surveyor, Roger Kenyon, and has cast the evil eye upon the King's lead mine. She has bewitched the ore so that the lead will not run, because the smoke had turned her oats yellow.'

'These are serious charges – have you found aught to substantiate them?'

'Only in respect of this man Edward Talbot who is verily bewitched and knows not what he is doing.'

'Well then, perhaps you have done well. Look into this matter further – we must protect this poor young fellow from her machinations. Bring me a full report of all that you find.'

So, once again, Alice Hartley found the Constable insolently walking into her farm kitchen, and stretching himself out before her fire. But all he found was an attractive, though embittered, woman supervising her children in the efficient running of the household and its appended farm. He went out to the small community around the mine and listened to their gossip.

There, he was told that there was little doubt that Alice was a witch. She had even spirited away the lead ore from beneath the picks of those who had offended her, and placed easily gotten lodes for those in her favour. She haunted the mine by day in the form of a huge hare, and by night, silently, as a broad-winged owl. And she had turned everyone else's ale into vinegar so that they had to buy hers, and their wages were disappearing into a pigskin purse which she always carried slung around her waist.

For the time being, he hung around the mine, annoying Alice in her kitchen as he deliberated in his mind what to do. He found Alice a strangely different personality. He sensed that the fire had gone out of her and perhaps – just perhaps – he may yet have his way with her. At last, he decided to delay his reports for the present. Once she was in the hands of Justice Nowell, and perhaps in Lancaster Castle, he, himself, would have lost all chance of having her.

CHAPTER XXXI

The Receiver Bewitched

Across the horizon to the north of the Thieveley mine the sleeping lion, Pendle Hill, broods over a countryside which in the year 1612 was the setting of England's most notorious witchhunt, at the end of which several unfortunate women were found guilty of witchcraft, and condemned to death at Lancaster Castle. During their trial one of the beldames, Old Chattox, testified that Mother Demdike had bewitched to death Richard Assheton of Downham Hall, the brother of Ralph, the King's Receiver.

And when in 1629 Ralph's son, also named Richard after his late uncle, began to behave strangely, and exhibit fears and hallucinations about an old countryman named Utley, it is not surprising that opinions were soon expressed that the boy was bewitched. When accused, Utley, foolishly believing that he would be able to extract from the Asshetons that which all men desired, money, admitted the charge saying that the boy had ridiculed his ragged and unkempt figure when he came begging at the back entrance of Downham Hall. If he could be provided with money, and fine clothes he would soon have the boy well again.

Meanwhile Richard had gone steadily worse, and his

nurses in desperation could only quieten him in his wild rambling and nightmares with copious doses of belladonna. It is not surprising that he should then refuse his food, and become rapidly emaciated.

It became a matter of urgency to get Utley into the bedchamber to remove the spell, but before he could be rounded up in his new-found wealth and fine clothes the unfortunate boy was dead.

Ralph Assheton, convinced that both his brother and his son had been killed by witchcraft, hounded Utley to his trial and execution at Lancaster Castle. This was during that period of 1629-30 when Roger Kenyon had so urgently needed his help in financing the King's lead mine.

Utley was hanged for the practice of witchcraft, a not uncommon occurrence in the Reformation period fraught with religious schisms. Witchcraft, as an offence against the state, was first recognized in the year 1563 by a statute of the fifth reign of Elizabeth when the Protestant hierarchy of the day, of whom the Dean of St Paul's, Alexander Nowell, uncle of Roger Nowell of Read Hall, was a prominent member, greatly feared that the enemies of the young queen, well supplied with money by that other claimant to the throne, Philip of Spain, might encompass her death by witchcraft. 'Those who shall use, practise or exercise any Witchecrafte, Enchantment, Charme, or Sorcery, whereby any person shall happen to be killed or destroyed, their Concellors or Aiders shall suffer paynes of Deathe as a felon or felons.'

It would appear then that this Act was aimed more at the procurers of the witch, and to deter them the dread sentence 'payne of death' meant all the horrible ritual and public spectacle of the day. But all that Elizabeth's Act amounted to was that witchcraft could be accepted evidence for murder, and the witches were then tried, not as witches, but as murderers. The vast army of witches, at least one in every parish, were in their day practising witch-doctors, using herbs, spells and incantations in an attempt to make an easy living for themselves. These creatures were now only at risk if their patient were to die, and malevolent enemies to persecute them.

Thirty years later, in Scotland, James VI, convinced that his enemies had connived to drown himself and his Swedish bride, by the employment of sorcerers to conjure up a fearful storm, off the coast of Norway, becoming obsessed and terrified of witchcraft, made a deep study of the subject, and published his pseudo-scientific work *Daemonology* in 1597.

In his book he advocated as tests the finding of the witchmark on the body, where the devil had entered, and the rejection of a witch by the pure element, water, used in baptism, as certain proof of a contract with the Devil. *Daemonology* also listed a whole range of witches' practices which a court could accept as evidence.

Although the unfortunate Lancashire witches had no idea of the purpose of their questioning it was all directed at substantiating their guilt, one by one, according to the tenets of James' book; such as, the use of evil spirits in the form of a 'familiar', usually a small animal or bird, the use of parts of a dead body, the making of clay images, the seeing of spectres by the bewitched, the use of the 'witch's glance' and the bleeding of the corpse in the presence of the witch.

James also postulated that the use of torture was justified in any battle against these machinations of the Devil. When he became King of England James' first act was to repeal that of Elizabeth, and substitute a much more comprehensive law which demanded that any practice of witchcraft, whether or not it resulted in harm or death, was punishable by the death sentence.

The great army of witch-doctors were now constantly at risk, and the era of the parish witch-hunt was on.

After the furore over the death of his son had died down, Ralph Assheton was again able to settle down to his work as Receiver for the County Palatine of Lancaster, and to give his mind to the affairs of the King's lead mine at Thieveley, of which in 1631 he was appointed a Commissioner in place of his Uncle Ralph who had been summoned to London to stand at the court of the High Commission.

The Receiver's reward for his often unpleasant task, in which he had to cover the county with a band of armed followers, was a percentage of the money collected and delivered to Westminster; and he had been much irritated by the demands of Roger Kenyon for money to run the mine. However upon being appointed a Commissioner he hit upon the scheme of charging his percentage 'for portage' of the sums now regularly supplied to Edward Talbot.

It was inevitable that in his rounds of the country he should assimilate all the local gossip, indeed that was one of his tasks, and he was rewarded generously by the Chancellor for any useful information which should lead to confiscations or fines, consequently it was not long before he heard the rumours of witchcraft at Thieveley.

Here was a subject in which he was not only an authority but had had some success. Here was also an opportunity to put that insolent fellow, Roger Kenyon, in his place. Calling upon Roger at Parkhead he demanded to know how the surveyor of the mine could hope for any success when the very ore was being spirited away from beneath the picks of the miners by witchcraft. A well-known witch, Alice Hartley, was practising her evil arts at the mine, and must be arrested immediately.

Roger, rapidly failing in health as a result of his fruitless labours for the mine, resenting the high-handed strictures of the hated tax-collector, and whose only hope of comfort at the bleak and desolate mine rested in Alice, was outraged. His temper, until now kept in check in his dealings with the Receiver, flared out.

'Stuff and nonsense,' he raged. 'You should have more sense than listen to the idle gossip of whores and trollops. The woman is of the greatest respectability, the wife of a good husbandman, and what is more fit to grace the parlour of any gentleman.'

'Aye and so was dame Alice Nutter,' Ralph interposed.

So the quarrel raged on to no useful purpose as is invariably the case when temper has replaced reason. Alice Hartley, working ceaselessly on the farmstead at Thieveley, had no idea that from now on her life depended upon the clash of personalities, the deliberations, and individual ambitions of the Justices in the Ribble Valley.

CHAPTER XXXII

Edward Talbot's Disgrace

When the disgruntled Receiver departed, saying that he was going to Read Hall to demand that Justice Nowell should arrest Alice Hartley before more harm was done, Roger Kenyon decided that, despite his poor condition, he had best make an early visit to the mine.

When, wearied almost to death by the arduous journey on horseback over the wild trackways and steep ascents, he arrived at Thieveley he was glad to find the immediate comfort of the farm kitchen, finding, as always, the well-conducted household and the welcome of a warm fireside, good food and solicitous attention. He thought to himself, 'This good woman is no witch, and I will do all in my power to have these scurrilous rumours quashed.'

Alice was only too pleased to give all her care to this gentleman, whom she never doubted was her friend, and whom she was shocked to find in such poor health since she had last seen him. Sensing her concern, and restored by the warmth and good cheer he was soon confiding in her the vicissitudes of his life since the onset of his distressing malady – finding solace and sympathy in her attentions; and she, in turn, told him of her fears during the time of the plague, and her fervent thanks to God that it had passed them by. Then, unable to suppress the hatred and resentment which she had harboured, in private, against Edward Talbot, she poured into Roger's ears her opinion of the state of affairs at the mine, brought about by that young man's neglect.

When Roger at last bestirred himself from the comfortable kitchen, and went out onto the bleak hillside he found only desultory work in progress in one groove, and water running through the dressing floor with no work in progress. Enquiring for the whereabouts of Ned Talbot, he was told, with suggestive smiles, that he would find him in the smelting house with Queen Jenet.

'Queen Jenet, who's she?'

'She be queen hereabouts, and rules over Ned Talbot wi' her petticoats.'

After a quick look round the area of the grooves, Roger then returned down to the farm where the smelt-house was situated on the farmlands at the top of Robert Hartley's small piece of ploughland.

He unhitched, and pushed open, the heavy door, and was just in time to see Edward jump up from an improvised couch within the gloomy interior. Blinded by the darkness after the brilliant daylight, he was spared the embarrassment of seeing Edward hastily adjusting his clothes, as Jenet moved diplomatically between them, her petticoat falling down naturally around her bare legs, so that she appeared instantly fully clothed. She recovered her composure immediately.

'Ah, it be Mr Kenyon,' she spoke, giving Edward time to recover himself.

'We be weighing, and a-checking of the ore. We be

expecting Mr Townley's gals to arrive for another load at any moment,' she continued adroitly.

Edward then came forward, and having recovered his composure, entered into conversation with Roger. But Roger was now fully alerted to the state of affairs at the mine, and insisted upon a complete tour of inspection – a tour which revealed all the discrepancies and dilapidations as described later in the Commissioners' end-of-term report.

Before the day was over Edward's disgrace was complete. Roger had even heard from the innkeeper's ready tongue of his grievous wounding, and the abduction of his greatest treasure, the industrious Meg. The whole panoply of Edward Talbot's high summer was revealed in a few brief hours; and worse was still to come with the final reckoning of the stockpile of ore. After deliberating over the situation for a few days at Parkhead, Roger returned to Holme Chapel; and, tracing Edward to the alehouse at Lightbirks, confronted him with his omissions, took possession of all the account books, and suspended him from pay and further employment.

There was nothing Edward could do except return to his father's home at Carr Hall, Wilpshire; and, true to the family's best traditions, he arrived home with a pregnant servant-girl riding pillion behind him. But, such are the merits of a good woman that, after the first recriminations, Meg became the most useful asset the Talbots were to receive from the King's ill-fated lead mine on Thieveley Hill. She quietly took over the domestic management of Carr Hall, and in addition, nursed John Talbot even to the day of his death.

After Edward Talbot's dismissal, Roger had a most disquieting report to make to the Commissioners, so much so that they dare not issue their end-of-summer report. They set to work with great vigour, and expense, to sort order out of chaos, and at the same time, save themselves from the Chancellor's displeasure. However, they dare not delay above a month, and despatched a diplomatically worded report, dated 3 December 1632.

The report excuses its lateness on account of the abnormally wet time, causing a collapse of the sough and a flooding of the mine. After allowing twenty days for its repair, they now find that twice that time will be required.

'Mr Townley has now built a smelting mill, complete with mill pond, headrace, and waterwheel, at considerable expense, and he is now ready to begin smelting, and has taken and paid for a greater part of the ore.' The Commissioners had advertised for miners in Derbyshire, Yorkshire and elsewhere: 'Diverse there were who came to see the workes and to understand the Orders upon what termes they were to worke, but most of them departed againe, refuseinge to medle with us, being so inured to Derbyshire Orders that they can relish no other.'

They also blame the conspiracy of Highley and Butler for giving the mine a name so that no new miners will start work.

The greater and final part of the report then explains their discovery of the failure of Edward Talbot and his neglect of the mine to such an extent that he had had to be dismissed. The charges against him were five in number. Firstly, he lacks the technical ability to manage the mine; secondly, that he is not industrious but 'dull, improvident and somewhat slothfull and few of the Myners more subtle than he are able to over-reach him'; thirdly, that he has not obeyed his instructions, particularly in inspecting weekly the orderly sinking of grooves and the adequate timbering of the shafts and drainage soughs; fourthly, that along with other workmen, he had rewashed ore which had already been in the fire, and paid for this as new ore at 12d per dish, sharing in the proceeds himself. Finally, the fifth and most serious charge 'which we conceave to be his Master-peece of ill-looking to, but wee rather feare plain deceipt' in that there is a grave discrepancy in the quantity of ore available for Mr Townley in the smelt-house. Suspecting this, the Commissioners ordered a check upon the weight and discovered that in place of the 28 tons recorded in Talbot's accounts, there are only 17 tons in actuality. Talbot tried to account for the 11 tons shortage by saying that it had laid so long that the weight had fallen by natural causes 'which wee thought impossible, rather suspecting that he had made his monthly accomptes for more Oare than indeede he receaved, and so receaved more money from us than he had Oare for'.

The Commissioners awaited the Chancellor's reply with some trepidation, but it would appear that he was so pleased with the prospects now that Richard Townley was buying the ore that there were no recriminations. However, the fate of Edward Talbot was not so promising as the Council endorsed his dismissal with the ominous instructions:

> The Commissioners are directed to examine upon oath the deceiptes and misdemeanors of the said Talbott ... and to

call him to account for the 11 tuns and 12 dishes of Oare wanting by his account uppon the admeausurement which the said Talbott is to make good, which if he shall fail to doe or then his wages yet unpaid hym, if anie be, to be respected and if upon examinacion the Commissioners finds just cause they are to bind hym over to appears in the Duchie Chamber at Westminster before the Chancellor and Court of the said Duchie in Easter or Trinity termes next.'

It could indeed be a grim outlook for Edward Talbot, his fate depending upon the mercy of the Comissioners, for if he were to fall into the clutches of the Duchy Court, there is little doubt but that he would be found guilty and imprisoned, or even sent to the West Indies sugar plantations as a slave.

CHAPTER XXXIII

1632-3 – The Winter of Discontent

With the dismissal of Edward Talbot, Roger Kenyon had the bleak prospect of having to undertake the day-to-day management of the mine himself; which, in his poor state of health, would have no doubt taxed his strength beyond endurance. However he was fortunate in that his wife was a cousin of the Townleys so that Christopher Townley volunteered his services. Among the accounts submitted to the Chancellor in December 1632 is an item 'Paid unto the workmen who are now employed in repaire of the Sough or Audit, which money for that purpose was delivered unto the handes of Christopher Townley, gent, who hath promised us for a tyme to looke to theire worke twice or thrice a weeke till other course be taken'.

During the winter of 1632-3, Christopher applied himself industriously to the repair of the neglected mine-workings, no doubt in hopes of a good supply of ore to keep his brother's smelt-mill in commission. There is little doubt that he found work in this task for his own employees for several new names appear: William Sumner, Sam Robinson, Thomas Humphrey, John Yellot, Thos.

Ossop and John Blackdene appear in the wages list of the Thieveley Mine.

But Christopher, too, soon ran into the difficulty of ready cash; and, as a younger son, being unable to pay the men out of his own pocket, sent an urgent plea to 'my very Loving Cosen Mrs. Jane Kenyon . . . to stoppe their clamorous mouthes . . . for els they can gett no tabling'.

Cousin Jane replied that she also could spare no money as her husband had gone to London, and the money he had left her had been loaned 'to a kind frend of myne'. The mystery is that these last words were in Roger Kenyon's handwriting, so it may be inferred that a little deceit was being practised.

It also seems probable that the Receiver had implemented his threat not to supply any more money while the witch Alice Hartley was at large, and that for his part Roger Kenyon had decided that enough was enough and that he was not going to provide any more from his own resources.

Christopher Townley replied on 8 March in a curt note to his 'very loving Cosen' that he himself would be away for a fortnight, and that the men must be content 'till eyther your husband, or I, come to the hill againe'. One wonders at the condition of the miners, and their families, without money or food during what can often be the most inclement month of the year, when nature has no bounty, on that exposed hillside during Britain's 'little Ice Age'.

Nevertheless, by March 1633, it was reported that the shafts and adit were repaired, and the mine ready to welcome more partnerships. But who was likely to come to such an ill-starred venture, where there was only hardship, poverty and conditions bordering on violence and anarchy?

It was to conditions such as these that the Chancellor sent a Mr Wright as bearer of a letter to Roger Kenyon directing that he 'is a partie that is recomended unto mee, to sucede Talbotte in his employment in the Leade Myne of Cliviger. Therefore I desire you to entertayne him upon the same allowance that Talbotte had, and to keep watchfull eye upon him.'

However it is not surprising that Mr Wright had no stomach for the task on the Thieveley hillside, for as soon as the 25th March Sir Ralph Assheton is writing to Sir Henry Agard, correspondent for the Thieveley Mine in the Duchie Council,

> This gent. Wright hath been here with us at the Lead Mynes, and seen and understood what his place, undertaking and entertayment should bee. Upon consideracion wherof it seemes hee hath no affection to the employment, nor in my owne conceipt do I thinke hee hath any reason to accept it, yt beinge fitter (or rather fit for none els) but a man that hath been reallie brought up a Myner or an overseer of Myne-workes, or a Berghmaister, such a one as hath speciall good Judgment in Lead oare, in the eyeing of the vaines and rakes in the earth, and can be able to direct the grooff workes for orderly working and tryall of the Myne, that will go downe into the workes twice or thrice a weeke, and oftener if neede bee, can judge what wages are set for the Kinge to give, and who are, or are not, expert and fit men to sett on worke, to pay ill wages, keepe a perfect Accompt, and indeed to bee able to do all things that belonges to a skillfull mynerall man.

And he concludes, 'desiring to heare from you so soon as may bee whether you please to send one over or noe (I will see the messenger paid), to th'end wee maie knowe what returne to make to Mr. Chancellor, eyther that wee are fitted from you or els his Lordship to seeke out some other elswhere'.

It will be seen that the Commissioners, after the disgrace of Edward Talbot, are determined that any new overseer shall be recommended by the Chancellor or some other member of the Duchy Council.

However it would appear that Sir Henry Agard, with the help of a mine-owner Mr Thomas Eyre of Snelston in Derbyshire, was successful in finding the right man for, in May, a certain William Harrison was engaged as overseer of the mine. From the way in which, aided by the optimism which is engendered by the arrival of springtime, he set about reorganizing the Thieveley Mine, it is obvious that he was the type of practical mining engineer whom the Commissioners had hoped for.

CHAPTER XXXIV

The Witchcraft Stakes of 1633

Ralph Assheton, the believer in witchcraft, was sorely put out by Roger Kenyon's forthright defence of Alice, and his refusal to take action against her. He directed his horse homewards past Portfield Bar, and along an ancient trackway following the run of the Little End of Pendle, until it was possible for him to cross over to the Clitheroe side of the hill through a mountain pass known locally as the Nick of Pendle. Once over the hill another track along the base of the Big End of Pendle took him directly to his desmesne of Downham Hall. Here even today the hall, the church and the Assheton Arms overlook the cottages and bridge of Downham, often claimed to be the most picturesque village in the North of England.

During his ride Ralph pondered long and earnestly upon the action which he should take both as a matter of personal conviction, and of his duty as the King's Receiver. Although this office gave him many privileges and much authority, the power of arrest was held by the county Sheriff, and his justices, who controlled the local constables. By a strange coincidence the present Sheriff of Lancashire was the hard-headed Commissioner Nicholas

Townley, and the local justice was Roger Nowell of Read Hall.

Unfortunately for Ralph, he was not on good terms with either of these men, for he had openly quarrelled with both; with Nicholas over the assessment of his rapidly developing estate, with its lime-working and coal mines; and with Roger Nowell in a private dispute over the boundaries of their estates. And both men considered themselves to be above a miserable tax-collector. It was a most humiliating position, and he soon decided that he could not go to them, cap in hand, for so controversial a request as the arrest of a respected yeoman's wife for the somewhat nebulous offence of witchcraft. Then he had the intriguing thought of going over their heads to Archbishop Laud, and his Court of the High Commission. For was not witchcraft, a contract with the Devil, possibly the greatest offence possible against the Mother Church?

Then he pictured the august gathering of churchmen, in their dreaded panoply of vestments and regalia, holding court to terrorize with threats of excommunication even the greatest peers, to whom such as his cousin Sir Ralph of Whalley, a mere Baronet, was but small fry. From these men they could extract large sums of money. For Ralph to ask such a body to examine a tenant farmer's wife would be an insult, fraught with danger to himself.

Before his journey reached its end, he had decided, like the Constable, to do nothing for the time being, until possibly the witch should hang herself. But he would teach that insolent fellow Roger Kenyon a lesson. There would be no more money for the mine from his coffers for the time being.

At Read Hall Roger Nowell, badly needing a successful coup to maintain his indispensability to the establishment, was carefully assessing the popularity of witch-hunts in the political stakes. In the times of James I in 1612 the commitment of the Lancashire witches to Lancaster Castle had brought him much fame, indeed, as it turned out, immortality, but it was now rumoured that James' son Charles did not share his father's whimsical beliefs or philosophical fantasies.

Roger Nowell realized that times were changing and that the persecution of a witch could bring more ridicule upon his head than approbation. It was upon such human traits, the determination of the ailing Roger Kenyon, the convictions of the hide-bound Ralph Assheton, and the vacillations of the ageing Roger Nowell, that the fate of Alice Hartley hung in the balance.

In a lower stratum of society the Constable was also busy pursuing his own ends, to extract the greatest possible personal satisfaction from his unpopular occupation. Exasperated by Alice Hartley's disdain, and being completely baffled in what manner to have his way with her, he at last made the direct accusation to her face that she was a witch. Rather than being overawed, Alice only laughed at his seriousness.

'Thee must be going soft in t'head ranting on about witches. I be'ant no witch, I do'ant ha the time for such nonsense, wi't'farm to run, and t'childer to look after.'

'That's as may be, but ther's mony as thinks different. 'Ow abeat neetime when tha flies o'er t'turf houses as a barn owl, and friskin' on t'common in t'early morn as a hare? And spiritin' t'ore from beneath t'picks o't'miners, an' turnin' their ale sour, an' stoppin' led fro' runnin' in t'smelthouse, an' worst on all settin' thi sen up as superior to t'menfolk, who God gave dominion over such as womenfolk and t'beasts o't'field, an' sendin' away t'plague wi' strange brews, an' bewitching thy betters, poor Edward Talbot, an' that silly old fool Roger Kenyon —'

'Stuff and nonsense,' Alice broke in. 'The's bin listening to t'whores and trollops i' theer mud ut's, wi' nowt better to do than slander decent folk.'

'Nay a's not. A's bin usin' mi own brains as God gave to menfolk and denied to wimen, and A knows what A'm on abeat.'

'Well get thee out o' my house, and doant bother to come back. A'll a nought o' thi insults, or thy nasty ways. Go on get thi ey'at to t'wimin in t'mud houses who'll no doubt gi' thy what tha't after.'

'Aye, I'm off alreet, to see Justice Nowell, and tha'll 'appen be a sorrier woman when A cums back.'

And this mouthing of the dread word Justice Nowell, who everyone knew had sent the women of Pendle Forest to their deaths, at last alerted Alice to the real danger of her situation.

When the door closed she stood, petrified, all the colour draining out of her face as the full impact of the Constable's words were assimilated. Then she dropped down onto her chair and burst into an uncontrollable fit of weeping.

Oh God, it's all the doing of this accursed mine, she thought, and Robert, Godfrey and Humphrey had had such high hopes of it in those happy carefree days, which now seemed so long away. What should she do, what could she do, against such sinister forces which seemed to be closing around her? Would it be best to give the man that which he was after, her marriage vows had already gone out of the door with Edward Talbot, and a certain cynicism had taken their place; what was one other man, more or less? But she was too proud to run after him. Perhaps if he came again, or was it too late? She would just have to endure in torment until they came for her.

Meanwhile Roger Nowell, after checking with Roger Kenyon, and being assured of Alice's worthy character, and use, to the men running the King's mine, decided that an arrest at this time would be impolitic. When the Constable arrived with his garbled story – 'Everyone on t'hill calls her Mrs Pym, never Hartley wife, what can that mean, Hartley wife is t'woman in t'house, but Mrs Pym is the witch that flits abroad' – he only smiled and did not bother to explain the allusion to a disgruntled Constable. And so the slender thread of Alice's freedom held firm upon the foibles of human relationships, and no order for her arrest was given. But it had been a very near thing; at the farmhouse, Alice was still in torment, and the rumours of her witchcraft, fanned by the Constable's enquiries, spread among the superstitious inhabitants of the Cliviger Gorge, whose notorious witch Old Loynd was even now being examined by the King in London.

CHAPTER XXXV

The Discontent
of the Commissioners

With all the summer of 1633 in front of him, William Harrison, started, with great vigour, to reorganize the mine workings. It was as though the early days of William Butler were here again. Streams of pack-ponies arrived with materials for a full trial of the mine by sinking two shafts to a great depth, where the profitable lodes of ore are usually found.

Edward Talbot had reported that Nicholas Birch went down at great speed; but he was always short of timber, so that the shafts were not safe and suffered continuously from the loose shale falling away. Finding a reluctance on the part of the Cliviger freeholders to part with their last stands of woodland, Harrison had to comb the whole area to find the much-needed timber. He had to go as far away as Scaitcliffe and the heights at Todmorden, before he could strike a bargain with the landowners, and he himself had to organize men, with axes, wedges and saws, to fell and split the timber into logs and boards. A smith, Christopher Baron, undertook the skilled work, unskilled labourers lifted and loaded, and the old army of packhorse men were re-engaged, carrying loads of timber over a rocky journey of over 5 miles through rough country in which there was not a single road fit for even a two-wheeled cart.

He soon had two or three smiths from Worsthorne, Mereclough, and Cliviger at work on the turntrees and bought many fathoms of rope from Rochdale, for lowering the men down the shafts, or hoisting out the spoil. The smiths were also re-equipping the washing floor with a new buddle, and various tubs and devices for jigging the ore. There was even a new bucker, a heavy square-faced hammer for crushing the ore into small pieces, before jigging and buddling, to separate out the heavy ore from the smithom or waste.

He built a new stone storehouse, with stout oak door, lock and key, and made storage bins for the different grades of ore. These bunkers were known as bings for storing binge, large pieces of ore which could go straight to the smelt-mill.

The trial shafts were soon down to a depth below the level of the drainage sough, without yet finding either the bottom or the main spring of ore. Once again men had to be employed during the night, bailing the water out of a sump into the drainage tunnel. To facilitate this, presumably to prevent the water running back into the shaft, calf and bullock skins were bought from a tanner at Dineley to form into a water-jacket. There is even an item in the accounts for oil, for dressing the skins to keep them supple and watertight. All this work left no doubt that William Harrison was practical, experienced, and thoroughly versed in mining practice.

And, just as Christopher Townley had brought his own

workmen, whose names now disappear from the accounts, a new set of names arrive with William Harrison. They are Wm. Wood, Ed. Guninne, and John Canumbye. These are listed as skilled miners from Derbyshire at a wage of 5s per week. Many of the old faithfuls remain as labourers dragging and winding the corves of spoil to the surface for tipping down the hillside.

The men sinking the shafts had instructions to ignore any side veins of ore; but always to continue downwards, in stages, with landings for the placement of the turntrees. Of course all ore found in the shaft was carefully separated and sent to the buddle for washing. Robert Hartley's original ditch still brought a constant stream of water from the Thieveley heights, and because Robert was deprived of the use of this water, and because the spring near his farmhouse had been contaminated, he was awarded a compensation of 4s a term.

Of course all this work required a ready supply of money, both for wages and materials, and there are frequent entries in the accounts of the Receiver's charge, at a fixed percentage, on each consignment, delivered to William Harrison on the hill. Ralph Assheton had received very firm instructions from the Chancellor that Harrison must have his full support, and presumably his forebodings of Alice Hartley's witchcraft had either been kept to himself or else overruled.

But despite all Harrison's efforts during 1633, and the summer of 1634, very little ore was coming forward from the mine to keep the Townley smelt-house running. Several men came to the mine with a view to taking meares of ground, but none were attracted by the prospect, so that there were still only two partnerships digging for ore.

Thomas Cockcroft with John Talbot still hoped for a lucky strike, Christopher Townley was financing George Casson's groove, and even Robert Hartley, searching desperately for a rich vein away from the mine, was having little success, so that the total amount of ore from the dressing floor to go into Harrison's new bingstead was pathetically small. The most consistent workers at the mine, from the day it opened until the day it closed, Nicholas and Jenet Birch do not at this time appear in Harrison's accounts for the reason that they were now employed, and paid, by the partnership of Cockcroft and Talbot, and surprisingly were joined at their work by the erstwhile overseer Edward Talbot, sent back to the hill by his father to work as a miner searching for ore in the grooves.

The Commissioners, showing that loyalty to their class which was to raise them to the supreme power in the land, had protected Edward from the wrath of the Chancellor. They explained that his shortcomings could be excused as a result of the cash shortage making it impossible for him to timber the shafts efficiently, that the ravages of the plague had demoralized the miners, and that these same shameless men had stolen the missing ore to reimburse themselves for their unpaid wages. In this way they saved Edward, from the vengeance of the Dutchy Court.

By the summer of 1633 two other factors had entered into the fortunes of the Thieveley Mine. One was the rapid deterioration in Roger Kenyon's health, and the second was the increasing desire of the other Commissioners to be rid of their task, fanned by a general discontent of the middle classes now prevalent throughout the length and breadth of England, and in less than ten years' time to lead to civil war.

Although, after the fateful year 1629 when the King decided to rule without a Parliament, the country had appeared to settle down to a period of peace and contentment with the majority of the people employed in agriculture and many others in a cloth trade which was recovering from James I's well-meaning but temporarily disastrous controls of the export trade, rumblings of discontent were spreading through the great middle class of country gentlemen.

By the year 1633, these men, performing their local government duties as tax-collectors, sheriffs, high constables, justices and magistrates, had become a coterie in close communication with each other, often meeting to organize local government, and on these occasions entertaining one another in their new stone-built halls.

They became a society dedicated both to public service and to their own survival, and the only power which could oppose them was a combination of the Crown and the Church. History shows how well they survived, through the Civil War, to rule England for the next 300 years.

To bring the matter nearer to the Thieveley Mine, all the Commissioners except Sir Ralph had been fined for not accepting a knighthood, and in addition all the encroachments of their estates upon the commons and wastes had been investigated, fines assessed and increased 'Lord's rental' imposed.

Having now obtained the appointment of an overseer, sent by the Chancellor, an attempt was made to opt out of the management of the mine, and to thrust the whole of the responsibility upon him. As a first move the Commissioners replaced their November 1633 report to the Chancellor, with one written and signed by William Harrison. However this seasoned official was too clever to fall for such a ploy, and quick to admonish them. He pointed out that Harrison's word could not take the place of their certified report. His letter is quite explicit.

The Chancellor to the Commissioners, 9 December 1633:

To the right worshipfull Sir Ralphe Aston, Barronett, Nicholas Townely, esqr., and Mr Roger Kennion, theis:

After my very hartie comendacions, I received your letter concerning the Lead workes by William Harrison the new overseer of them, to whome yow principally referred the relacion of the present estate of them, which haveing throughly examined, I cannot chuse but bee much astonished to finde that from soe great an apparance, even allmost an insurance, of prospering and perfeccion, they are now fallen to soe little hope, as onely to depend upon uncertaintie; for upon the last returne of the Comission from you, you certified that all things were fitted and readie to employe such store of miners as would bring a great proffit and advantage to the King, whereas it appeares by Harrisons relacion that there hath bin few workmen employed, and all this tyme spent in tryalls, to the Kings charge and expence onely.

But however in regard of the good report you give of this man's honesty and skill, and that the King hath bin so farr engaged in the Busines, I hold it fitt that it should goe on still till there maie bee an absolute tryall made of the Mines, which as Harrison enformes mee maye bee effected by Midsommer next, or sooner.

Now for his Accompte. I have referrde him backe to you that are the Commissioners because if it bee taken from his hands here it will not bee authenticall, and att the next Returne you shall make of thee busines, I shall expect from you an Accompte in particuler (since the last accompte) of all charges of worke and triall, of all the proffitt of lead oare gotten, and any benefitt that shall accrue to his Majestie, your opinions of the successe of the triall that shalbee made, and what maye bee expected from it hereafter. And I could wish there might bee soe many Mynors employed in getting of Oare in all places where any veine of Lead will serve for it, paying them by the dish the usuall price for what they shall gett, as maye by the benefitte that shall arise from theire worke satisfie or defraye all or the greatest part of the Charge which this further tryall now to bee made shall impose upon his Majestie.

As for himselfe, I desire hee maye be paid his due recompence for his employment, and bee allowed the reasonable Charges of his jorney, and soe overseene and encouraged by you that there maye bee noe miscarrysge in the busines by neglecte.

And soe not doubting of your Care for the true and Fayth-full carryage and agitation of this busines, I rest your verie loving freinde

Dutchie Howse, 9 December, 1633.   E. Newburgh.

And so by the beginning of 1634 we find a tripartite management structure at Thieveley, an enthusiastic and proficient overseer, in London a disgruntled Chancellor, and a Board made up of disillusioned Commissioners and a reluctant Receiver, while in the Cliviger valley, the Townley smelt-mill stands idle for want of ore and the only hope rests with the determined overseer and his remaining band of faithful workers.

CHAPTER XXXVI

The Beginning of the End

As explained earlier, lead ore is found within the infilling of a mineralized fault. These faults are expansion cracks caused by the upward folding of the earth's crust, and it is very rare indeed to find a truly vertical fault. They are all inclined at an angle, which was known to the early miners as 'the hade'. Also, as the faults are only in the upper layers of the earth's crust, they always disappear at some particular depth. This depth in the case of a mineralized fault is known as the bottom of the mine, below which there will be no ore.

By the sixteenth century it had become sound mining practice to, first of all, find the bottom of the mine, and then to extract the ore upwards. In this way, the valueless spoil could be disposed of downwards in the worked-out cavities, thus saving hours of human toil in winding it to the surface, and then having to dispose of it upon a hillock or spoil heap. It was also necessary to drive short galleries at right angles to the fault to discover both the width of the fault and the angle of the hade. These preliminary works were known as 'proving the mine'.

From his arrival in May 1633, William Harrison, as a sound mining engineer, pursued both these objects with a single-minded determination. But, unfortunately, very little ore was discovered in the main shafts, or in the offshoots, to pay for this very expensive exploratory work. Nor were the free miners, Cockcroft and Talbot, Townley and Casson, or Robert Hartley, having any greater success. In all, only a meagre twenty tons of ore were raised in 1633, worth some £63 against a total expenditure of £278. As Harrison had by now sunk well below the level of the sough, a constant charge of 30s per week appears in the accounts for the wages of six men employed in a no more useful task than bailing water out of the deep sumps and pouring it down the sough.

Just to demonstrate that little has changed in the principles of industrial economics since the building of the Great Pyramids, William Harrison had then to replace manpower by the latest advances in technology. This was achieved by installing two stages of chain pumps which would do the job with fewer men and in much less time. These ball and chain – or rag and chain – pumps worked on the principle of a chain running up through the centre of a bored-out tree trunk. At regular intervals on the chain were secured lead balls which were a running fit inside the tree trunk. The fit was generally improved by also using leather or worsted packing – hence the name 'rag and chain'.

There were chain-wheels top and bottom to wind the endless chain up the bore, the return length running back down the outside. The lower chain-wheel and the bottom of the tree trunk were immersed in the sump at the bottom of the mine, and by winding the handle on the upper chain-wheel, water was trapped in the bore by the lead balls, and lifted up to the top where it poured out of a slot and into a wooden trough running down into the sough. William Harrison's remarkable achievement is that he designed, procured all the parts, and installed not one, but two, stages of these pumps over 200 feet below ground in the narrow candle-lit water-groove of the Thieveley mine. The tree trunks were two 20-ft oak trees, purchased from Nicholas Townley. It would be a most difficult task today to bore a coaxial hole with a smooth bore right through the centre of a 20-ft tree trunk, but how this was achieved in the year 1634 in the Cliviger wilderness almost defeats understanding. Nevertheless, the evidence is there in the accounts, that two men, John Norris and John Duxbury were 'entertayned at the myne for three weeks at a cost of 15 shillings for their board' during which time they bored out the trunks at a price of 2s 6d per yard.

Forty-eight yards of chain were manufactured by a Padiham blacksmith, George Whitaker, at 2s per yard, and he also made the axle-shafts and chain-wheels. There is even an entry of '1s. for a corde to draw the chain through the pumps'.

A huge watertight cistern was installed on a landing within the darkest bowels of the earth, and the first stage pumped from the sump-hole at the bottom of the mine into this cistern, and the second stage pumped out of the cistern up to the entrance of the sough down which the water ran away into Dodbottom Wood. And so that not one drop of the lifted water would run back into the depths, specially waterproofed and softened sheepskin jackets caught the water at the top of the pumps to direct it into the cistern or the sough. Bottles of neatsfoot oil for waterproofing the skins are listed in the accounts. The incredible fact is that these huge pumps were designed, manufactured, and installed in a few short weeks of the dying summer of 1634. William Harrison could then report to the Commissioners that exploratory work at the lowest depths of the mine could continue throughout the winter of 1634/35.

Meanwhile, Roger Kenyon had become so worn out by his labours, and perhaps more so by his anxieties, that he was no longer able to visit the mine and had to leave the management to Harrison, and the provision of money to the Receiver. However, meetings of the Commissioners were held from time to time; and as the year 1634 advanced, the apparent poverty of the mine became so ominous that they had decided to end the venture as soon as they could justify such a course to the Chancellor without bringing a severe charge of neglect and incompetence upon their own heads.

Consequently, as the supply of ore for delivery to Richard Townley did not improve, they sent William Harrison down to London as bearer of their Midsummer report. It can be seen in retrospect that the purpose of this report was to soften up the Chancellor for an impending closure of the mine.

'Wee can send noe good newes therof to your Lordship. There is a great deale of mony spent and a smale quantity of Oare gotten, and not much more hopes of improvement for the future that wee dare perswade ourselves of.'

They then describe William Harrison's endeavours and write highly of his ability, and of the skilled men whom he had brought from Derbyshire, 'but neyther hee nor they can gett Oare unles the myne aford it'. They explain that the individual partnerships are working at a greater loss than the King, but struggle on in the hopes of covering these.

> Wee observe it to bee such a bewichinge hope that yt would draw men of the best Judgementes that way on to desperate experimentes and many tymes great losses, and as wee heare even in Derbyshire, the least dangerous place for faileinge, many men say, of the best Mynors themselves, have suncke and myned theire estates by followinge hopes and probabilities of this nature, for in any of them there is noe certainty further than the point of the picke.

They then stress the uneconomic cost of a venture in so lonely a place:

> The overseer hath beene forced for the most part to buy his tymber five myles from the mynes, most of it in Yorkshire and at extreame deare rate, but for carriage worst of all, being at 8d. for everie poore horseload carried on his backe, the rookie and mountinous waies not admittinge the passage of any carte in all these partes.

As the summer of 1634 advanced into autumn and Roger Kenyon was unable to follow the operation in person, the Commissioners called for a written report from William Harrison. As only small quantities of ore were now being produced there is no doubt that they intended to use this report, signed by Harrison, as a certificate in recommending the closure of the mine.

After the passage of nearly 400 years, Harrison's report, dated 28 October 1634, is an invaluable description of the proving of a mine, written in the handwriting of the man in charge.

At a depth of 33 fathoms (198 feet) they had driven sideways both north and south to determine the hade, but had found little ore. Then sinking a further 23 fathoms, they had driven southwards to the limit of the hading and discovered a reasonable amount of ore. But, also at this depth, they were drowned out by a 'shrode of water' which required the full-time work of all the miners to bail out. To eliminate the expense of all this labour, he had installed two sets of pumps to raise the water to the sough.

He recommends that, after taking all these measures, the trial should continue until Candlemass, but concludes 'what to thinke or how to deliver oppinnion absolutely, I cannot tell, the Oare which we meete withall lyinge so uncertainly'.

The Commissioners very cleverly endorsed this report with their approval and despatched it, over their signatures, to the Chancellor.

Meanwhile, they accepted Harrison's plans for the trial to continue, and provided him with sufficient cash to continue until the end of 1634 in a last-ditch hope of finding a profitable vein of ore.

CHAPTER XXXVII

The Commissioners' Last Report

The installation of the two sets of pumps in a wilderness without communications – and at a time when the only skills and services available were those of local carpenters, smiths, and wheelwrights – was a truly remarkable achievement by any yardstick. It was also William Harrison's swansong at the Thieveley mine.

The proving of the mine had now been driven to a depth of 53 fathoms, i.e. some 320 ft or 106 metres, but contrary to the usual expectations in lead mines in the limestone areas, the quantity of ore discovered was less at these depths than it had been near the surface. The reason probably was that, whereas in the rock the ore is concentrated in certain pockets in profitable veins, in the Thieveley shales it had been distributed in small deposits scattered at random over a large area. Consequently, its mining was totally uneconomic, as was proved when the mine was reopened in the lead-mining boom of the eighteenth century.

From 2 June to 20 December 1634, only 2 tons 16 cwt. of ore were mined for delivery to the Townley smelt-house. Having already come to the conclusion, on account of the poor results in 1633 and the early summer of 1634, the Commissioners had decided to close down the mine in October 1634. However, possibly in admiration of William Harrison's enthusiasm and ability, they had agreed to continue to the end of the year.

However, following upon the poor results revealed at the greater depths, the firm decision was taken to effect closure on 5 January 1635. Their reasons for this, and their method of transmitting the bad news to the Chancellor in Westminster Palace, are best given in their own words.

Right honorable, Our most humble duties to your Lordship remembred.

May it please you to receave this our last Certificate (as wee imagine) upon this occasion for the leadmyne workes in Cliviger in Com. Lancaster. Wee have gone on by all possible wayes and meanes wee could, aswell by our owne direccions (which wee trusted not much to) but cheiflie William Harison's, alwaies upon hopes to recover to his Majesty all or some part of his highnes expence. But still fyndinge little more than hopes which wee conceaved might drawe us on to an infinit charge and yett yeild nothinge but expectacion; in October last wee determined to dissolve the workes, and thereupon forebore to make any more Warrantes for supplies of mony, as holdinge it better to leave his Majesty with the losse then alreadie incurred (which workes of this nature many tymes bringe both upon the kinge and subject) rather than to contynue his Majesty at such a desperate charge without any certainetie of successe. Yett before wee would quite cast downe the whole workes which then stood in good plight for a further tryall wee writt to William Harrison to make a perfect remonstrance unto us in wrytinge of the true state of the

257

Myne and workes and of his oppinion and hopes or dispaire thereof, and his reasons for the same, who shortlie after returned us to answere in wrytinge accordingly, which for your Lordships better informacion wee have affixed to this our Certificat, upon perusall whereof (beinge also seconded by all the Workmen of skill, which wee imagined theire reall oppinions rather the contynuance of any great Wages they had, invited them unto). Wee then thought it not fitt to cast downe till even the last probabilitie might come to the hammeringe as wee should have done had the workes beene our owne. So they wrought on by the likliest waies (wee conceave) was possible for a finall tryall, and to gett Oare if the grounds did yeild it. But the more toyle and labour was bestowed and everie devise practised to have gained Oare and to have discovered the rakes and vaines if there were any worth the followinge; the more Mr. Harrison and the Workmen of Judgement (as they Certified us) were discouraged therein, beinge satisfied that the whole grounds do not afford eyther rocke, rake, or vaine of Oare of any value but here and there a short vaine at the first apparence very likly and hopefull, then presently fallinge off into sparkes not neare valuable to the charge of landinge the same, and so lesse and lesse to none at all. And so in generall by theire longe experience thereof and theire many (and many wayes contryved) assaies and practises they fynd the whole hill to bee. So that now, may it please your Lordship, wee purpose presently to give over the workes, haveinge putt the Oare and his Majestys goodes (such as they are) beinge (used in and about the Mynes) in safe keepinge.

Wee have herewith Certified unto your Lordship accordinge to our usuall maner and instruccions an Accompt of all Receiptes and paymentes since our last, together with William Harrison his Booke of the particulars. Wee expected Mr. Auditor Fanshawe his Deputie would have been prepared at the last Audit of Lancaster with all former Accomptes Certified by us to have taken and drawne upp on Accompt of all Receiptes, paymentes, Remainder of Oare, etc., and all other thinges wherein his Majesty ought to have an accompt from the first begininge till that tyme. But that faileinge, yf it may stand with your Lordships good pleasure wee purpose that Roger Kenion shall come upp the next Terme (or in Easter terme because wee suppose Mr. Auditor and his Clerkes wilbee busye in the Receavors Accomptes this next terme) to attend your Lordship and whoe you shall direct him unto for the finishinge of all Accomptes concerninge the said Mynes; as also William Harrison to bee then there to acquaint your Lordship with all things more fullie than wee can in a Certificate Expresse.

An Accompt of all the Monyes Receaved touchinge his Majesties Leadmyne-workes in Cliviger in the Countie of Lancaster since the last Certificat returned by the Commissioners appointed for that purpose into the honorable Court of the Duchie of Lancaster. As also of the Oare remaineinge in the Storehouse there, added since the last accompts, and of his Majesties goodes there remaineinge. Which Accompt is from the 21st day of June, Anno Decimo Caroli Regis 1634, untill the present daie, vizt., the Fifth day of January, then next following:

[Here follows a list of payments, etc.]

So in all humblenes wee take our leaves, restinge your Lordships in all dutie to bee comaunded.

Whalley the fifth of Januarie 1634(35).

Raphe Assheton.

Nic. Townley.

Rog. Kenyon.

CHAPTER XXXVIII

The Witch-hunt

As so often happens in the affairs of man once a firm and irrevocable decision has been taken, a contrariness of fate appears to decree otherwise. Even as the closing down date of 5 January 1635 approached, William Harrison believed he had at last found the rich vein that he was looking for. Mounting his horse he rode off, round the Big End of Pendle Hill to the home of Receiver Assheton at Downham, and, having wrung £10 out or him returned to make a last-gasp effort to save the mine. But almost immediately the rich vein petered out, and even William had to admit himself beaten. He bowed to the inevitable, and during the last two weeks of January employed his workmen in removing all the valuable equipment out of the mine, the windlasses, the tools, ropes and spare timber, and most of all his precious pumps. The lifting of the pumps had to be done non-stop, and in great haste, before they were irretrievably drowned. In all, eleven men, of whom seven were skilled craftsmen, the smiths, carpenters and masons who had worked on and off at the mine since its inception, and four of the last miners, all worked non-stop, at 8d per day, for two days and four nights. No increased hourly rate was paid, as is done today, for this continuous overtime and night work.

And the two workers who had clung to the mine through all its vicissitudes, Nicholas and Jenet Birch, both appeared on the last wage list of 31 January 1635, just as they had appeared in the first in 1629 – Nicholas still being paid the wages of 5s a week as a skilled miner, and Jenet the high wage, for a woman, of 3s 6d per week. The very last item in the accounts is the regular 4s paid to Robert Hartley as compensation for the contamination of his water supply.

William Harrison's bookkeeping ends with a detailed stocktaking of the assets of the mine even down to '50 yards of ould worne roapes, which are so fretted and gawled that they are little worth'.

Just as no extra wages were paid for overtime or night work, not one thought was given to the plight of the workers whose wages were to be cut off as with a knife. There was no such compensation as redundancy money or severance pay. In the early seventeenth century, England was not yet a wage-earning society, and so far as the common people were concerned it was still the subsistence society of the middle ages. It was assumed that every man had his toft, with its four acres of land and his rights of common to gather fuel and thatch and to graze his cow, his goose or his goats. It was believed that every man should feed, shelter, and clothe himself and his family without need of wages, and the only encumbrances upon the parish should be the sick, the disabled, and the old who were unfortunate enough to be left without a family to support them. Wage-earning was a new idea which enabled men, either to lift themselves into a higher class in the social hierarchy, or to drink themselves to death. Consequently the management of the mine conscientiously believed that they had no other duty than to inform the workers that the mine was closing down, and that there would be no more work for them to do. And, of course, it followed, there would be no more wages.

However, as so often happens when men have toiled together against great odds, a mutual respect had developed between those who by their very worth had remained to the end. When the last task, the recovery of the great pump barrels had been completed, William Harrison saw to it, at his own expense, that there was ale ready for the men. And so a spirit of great camaraderie was engendered amongst them as they took to the shelter of the old smelting house on this bitterly cold January day. The word spread to the women of the camp that free ale was being dispensed, and soon a considerable crowd was collected in and around the mine workings as for the last time, William Harrison saddled his horse and gathered together his personal belongings into his pannier bags for his journey back home to Derbyshire. Not one word was said against him, and everyone pressed forward to shake the hand of the man they had learned to follow, and to respect.

And when, at last, he was able to decently drag himself free, the little community gathered together upon the blunt end of Dean Scout to watch him ride away down the farm road, until man and horse disappeared over the edge of the steep incline down into Holme Chapel.

Then the miners, with the extra money which they had earned while working day and night to get up the pumps, invaded the farmhouse to buy every drop of ale, which Alice had in her small brewhouse, so that, as Dr Whitaker so truly said of these Anglo-Saxon people, 'every occasion must end in the alehouse'.

They needed the ale to hold something in their hands, to slake their dry throats, and to hide the maudlin sentiment which they had all experienced at Harrison's departure. At first their talk was all of him, and how, if the Commissioners had left him alone, he would have found the ore which would have made them all rich. Bit the Commissioners were men of another world, who only thought of their own estates and behind them in that great capital called London – with its mysterious Palace of Westminster – were great lords and churchmen who ruled with a sinister despotism. Here was power, the power of an establishment which they could not understand. And so they hated it; and, as the strong ale gave verbosity to them, they reviled the Commissioners for not supporting William Harrison, and the Chancellor and the Duchy Council for not supporting the Commissioners.

And all they could do about it was to drink more ale. As the men became more stupefied the women became more perceptive, until one woman cried out, 'If you ask me, it's nought to do wi' t'Commissioners it's the witch, Mrs Pym, as is at the bottom of it all.'

Suddenly everything became clear, and they clamoured amongst themselves of Alice Hartley's ill-doings, casting her spells over the menfolk, tying up the lead in the ore, so that, not even the Devil's fire would make it run,

flooding their grooves at night, and even spiriting away
the rich ore from beneath the very picks of the miners.

Why had she been allowed to do it when all the other
witches had been packed off to Lancaster Castle. Even
now four of them were in the Tower of London to be
examined by the King and his physicians. As the ale
disappeared the clamour against Alice Hartley increased,
until someone suggested:

'Let's duck the witch in t'furnace dam, and see if the
Devil will save her then.'

'Yes!' they all shouted, and mob hysteria and mob
violence took hold of them. They streamed down to the
farmhouse, straight in at the door, and dragged the
protesting housewife out. Robert Hartley came running
from one of the farm buildings, but one of the rough
women, with intuitive genius, gave him a fearful crack
over the head with a pick handle.

'Take that, you bastard. That'll teach thee a lesson.'

Robert fell to the ground, and was trampled underfoot as
the crowd half-dragged and half-carried Alice off down the
farm road. Nicholas and Jenet Birch hesitated a moment,
and then Jenet got hold of the Hartleys' terrified children.

'Now, run quick, down to Mester Whitaker's and tell
him to get as many men as he con and bring 'em to
t'Furnace Dam. Quick now – straight down t'hill and o'er
t'river to t'Holme.'

They watched the children run off, and then chased
after the mob who were half-walking, half-trotting down
the hill with Alice Hartley in their midst held by a dozen
eager hands. And among their number, fuddled with ale,
staggered a dirty and disreputable Edward Talbot.

In the valley bottom, at the junction of two streams, was the mill pond, held back by the dam, always called the Furnace Dam, thrown up by Richard Townley's workmen not two years previously.

It had stone facing in the water backed up by an earthen embankment, with a spillway at one end and a sluice gate feeding the mill race at the other. The mob streamed over the bridge of planks across the mill race to the centre of the dam from where the glassy surface of the pond stretched out to a grove of willows nestling beneath the great escarpment of Thieveley Scout. They clustered in the middle, and two men took a hold of Alice – one at her feet and one at her head – and began to swing her backwards and forwards with increasing rhythm.

'Now,' the mob shouted, 'let her go and see if the Devil will come for his own.'

Alice was hurled through the air to land with a great splash in the ice-cold water, and was immediately seen struggling on the surface as her voluminous clothes supported her. The crowd had gone completely silent, and then a lone voice spoke.

'She ain't gonna sink, t'Devil's hodding her up.'

So, in fury, they all ran to the river bed for stones with which to beat the Devil at his evil work. Nicholas and Jenet looked anxiously down the valley for any sign of a rescue party, but the country lay silent and deserted in its winter cloak. Then all at once they saw Edward Talbot leap into the water, and swim towards the struggling woman. He was probably the only person in the whole valley who could swim, an art he had learned as a boy in the deep pools of the Ribble and Hodder, which flowed through his family's estates of Salesbury, Dinckley and Bashall Eaves.

As the mob pelted him with stones from the embankment he reached Alice, and began to struggle with her to the far end of the pond, where it soon became shallow enough for him to touch bottom. When the mob could no longer reach him with their stones, and, perceiving his plan, they ran off either end of the dam and along the pond sides, but they soon found themselves held up by deep rush-covered bog, and thickets of willows from which the basket-makers cut their supplies. And when Edward had got Alice to her feet, and waded to the deep fastness of the thicket at the head of the pond, he found the infant Calder running on a stoney bed only about a yard wide, through the otherwise impenetrable willows.

'Come on, it's our only hope,' he said, and with the water streaming from their saturated clothing, they scrambled along the winding course of the little river – cut off from the world – yet hearing the frustrated shoutings of the mob on either side.

The thicket of willows ended at a vertical face of rock through which the stream, a raging torrent in times of bad weather, had cut a defile rising in a series of steps and waterfalls, interspersed with corries in which a little grass and many ferns had taken root, whilst even a few stunted rowans survived in the shelter of the surrounding walls, to the escarpment of Scarthe Rake 500 feet above. Hardly pausing for breath, Edward led Alice up tho rock climb, for the short January day would soon be at an end, and it was imperative to get out of this perilous chasm before the daylight failed.

They were both still young and active so that the long climb did not overtax their strength, and was actually a blessing in disguise by working the water out of their clothes and maintaining their body temperature. But when at last they emerged onto Heald Moor – the gently sloping plateau on the great ridge between Cliviger and Rossendale – there was no shelter to prevent the cruel wind from penetrating to their very bones.

'We must keep moving at all costs,' Edward gasped. 'We can find the Blackgate and follow it to your house down Dean Scout.'

'But we'll have to pass the miners' cotes – they'll have a great fire going and be drinking till midnight.'

'But there's nought else for it, we'll a t'get inside to t'fireside.'

'Well I'm noan goin' back to that mob – they'll be atter me agin in t'morning.'

'But we've got to go somewhere and quick,' and even as he spoke a great shivering shook his whole body as the warmth of the climb gave way to a deadly cold. And then Alice made her decision, and led off.

'Come on let's find t'road afore it's dark, and goa in t'opposite direction, to my father's farm, it's nobbut three or four miles from here – we can mek it in an hour.'

And so they hurried on, driven by the necessity to keep moving and encouraged by the thoughts of the roaring fire in her mother's kitchen, and the blessed haven which it offered, until the whole madness had died down, and Thieveley Farm was left once again to its lonely but peaceful existence.

Not long after darkness had fallen they burst open the

heavy oak door, staggered into the large farm kitchen, and with teeth chattering, almost crying and unable to speak, they fell down in front of the life-sustaining fire, while Alice's mother and father recovered from their astonishment, and brought towels with which to restore life to the newcomers' frozen limbs.

Epilogue

On the following day, a revitalized Edward Talbot returned to Thieveley to bring the good news to Robert and the children that Alice was in safe keeping at her father's farm. In his own mind, by rescuing Alice and bringing the good news home to the farm, he had assuaged his conscience and repaid a debt of honour. Nevertheless, after his return to Carr Hall the memory of Alice Hartley haunted the remainder of his days. In the following century, the Talbots of the Ribble and Hodder valleys died out, and were replaced through their female heirs by the equally prestigious Warrens.

The Hartleys prospered as a tenant farming family in Cliviger under the Whitakers and the Townleys. Robert was eventually given the tenancy of the Whitakers' best farm, then called Grimshaw 'the haunted grove'. Alice's potential was at last realized in her granddaughter, another Alice, who married Thomas Whitaker of the Holme, and so became the great-grandmother of the Rev. Thomas Dunham Whitaker, LL.D., the celebrated historian.

Roger Kenyon, after enduring the further ignominy of being examined by the Duchy Council for the unfortunate affair of the King's lead mine, and, broken in health, died in 1636. An interesting aside is that his daughter, Dorothy, had been married to Major General Charles Worsley of

Platt Hall, Manchester – Cromwell's most trusted lieutenant. It was Worsley who seized the mace upon Cromwell dissolving the Long Parliament, and who carried it off to Platt Hall, where it remained for two years before the summoning of the Little Parliament. This is the only occasion that the mace has ever been absent from the Palace of Westminster.

Charles Worsley became the first MP for Manchester, and his statue stands in front of the Town Hall. Unfortunately, he died at the early age of 35, and it is said that Cromwell and Dorothy stood together at his graveside with tears streaming down their cheeks. Dorothy's brother, Roger Kenyon junior, in a frenzy of jealousy at his brother-in-law's prestige, wrote in charcoal upon the gravestone: 'None worse lay here', but did not reveal the fact until after Cromwell's death. That implacable administrator had sworn punishment of death for the desecrator of his friend's grave.

That administrative ability often persists in families is demonstrated by a later Kenyon becoming Lord Chief Justice of England, and being created Baron Kenyon in 1788. The family continues in the person of the present Lord Kenyon.

The bawdy passages in the foregoing narrative are amply substantiated by an abstract from the Assheton Papers in the Manchester Record Office:

4th March 1636, Final order (judgment) made by William, Archbishop of Canterbury, the Lord's delegate, against Sir Ralph Assheton of Whalley bart., for incest and adultery with Alice Kenyon, Jane Whitacres, Elizabeth Holmes, and others, by the last named of whom he has had several

children whom he supports. Public penance committed to
a £300 fine for the upkeep of St Paul's London.

15th March 1636. Bond 1,000 marks to avoid the
company of nine named women.

The William, Archbishop of Canterbury, was the
infamous William Laud, who was later tried and executed
for his despotic disregard for English ethics of tolerance
and freedom. (His Church Courts were as unbridled as
the Spanish Inquisition and were one cause for the
outbreak of the Civil War.)

It is not surprising to find that Sir Ralph became a
prominent leader in the Parliamentary Forces in
Lancashire.

As with the Kenyons, the Asshetons have been active in
finance, industry and politics, perpetuating the name
Ralph, culminating in Ralph, MP for Blackburn West
from 1950-5, and created Baron Clitheroe in September
1955. The family still resides at Downham Hall.

The Townleys, remaining staunch Catholics, were
more prominent in science, art, and philosophy, but
unfortunately, the main line died out in the 1870s with the
death of the brothers Charles and John without a male
heir. Their huge estates were then divided by Act of
Parliament between their six daughters. Alice Mary, Lady
O'Hagan, finding that she could not support the
magnificence of Towneley Hall and Park on her sixth-
share, sold it to Burnley Corporation at the turn of the
present century. It is now the jewel in Burnley's crown.

The last of the direct line of the Whitakers of Holme,
Mrs Master-Whitaker died in 1912. After being occupied
by distant relatives, the hall and estate were sold by

auction in 1959. However, the American branch of the family, founded when Jabez settled in Virginia in 1618 – and now assured by the eleven children of James Walker Whitaker (1897-1925) – is in little danger of extinction.

Fortunately, the Holme, in its setting a gem of scenic perfection, as a listed building, is protected from desecration.